FAMILY NIGHT

FAMILY NIGHT

MARIA FLOOK

Pantheon Books   New York

Grateful acknowledgment is made to the following for
permission to reprint previously published material:

Dwarf Music: Excerpt from the song lyrics "Down Along the
Cove" by Bob Dylan. Copyright © 1968 by Dwarf Music. All
rights reserved. International copyright secured. Reprinted by
permission.

Irving Music, Inc.: Excerpt from the song lyrics "The Ballad of
Paladin," lyrics and music by Johnny Western, Richard Boone,
and Sam Rolfe. Copyright © 1958, 1986 by Irving Music, Inc.
(BMI). All rights reserved. International copyright secured.
Reprinted by permission.

Library of Congress Cataloging-in-Publication Data

Flook, Maria.
Family night / Maria Flook.
p.   cm.
I. Title.
PS3556.L583F3   1993
813'.54—dc20
ISBN 0-679-41647-1

Book Design by M. Kristen Bearse

Manufactured in the United States of America
First Edition

For Bill Bundesen

FAMILY NIGHT

n April, Tracy moved in with Margaret. It was the same week he joined Sex Anonymous. The rain shifted and drilled the apartment windows. Margaret watched Tracy unload cartons from a taxi, then walk through a froth of litter to pay the driver. He carried his belongings into the building, halting on the stoop to look up at her face, but she had stepped back from the sill.

Margaret cleared drawers and left them extended so he would see, right off, that she was ready. He crushed Margaret's dresses to one side of the closet and hooked his heavy coats over the rail. He gave her a bundle of knotted sleeves, but it was a severe cinch and she couldn't untangle it. She arranged his razor on the glass shelf over the tiny sink in the bathroom. The apartment windows were eye level with a billboard that had been left to fade since the national bicentennial two years before. It was the patriot Nathan Hale at the gallows. For months, Margaret had had to look at the doomed figure standing beside a large teardrop noose. If she turned away, she could still see the billboard in her vanity mirror. "A friendly reminder," Tracy said, and he told her to keep the blinds open.

"If we leave them open, people might see me get undressed."

"Do it for a condemned man, Margaret." She didn't know if he meant Nathan Hale or himself. She peeled her rayon blouse away from her shoulders and let it drift down her spine to the floor. Margaret was slender, high-waisted. Her hipbones presented opal knobs with corresponding hollows, left and right of her smooth belly. She stepped from her jeans, kicking the cuff free from her foot; the notch of her ankle was milk-white and delicate like the precise turning of Victorian balusters. She stood before Tracy. Her posture remained supple and expectant; she didn't feel self-conscious unless he tried to get her talking. He praised her, listing museum masterpieces. *The Story of Creation*," he said, referring to the stained-glass panel. He said she was "the penumbra surrounding every modern sculpture."

Her hips curved like "an antebellum staircase." She was everything, every lost world, she was "Dixie!" She smiled and shut her eyes. His talk held her in its spell for as long as he wanted. Then, Tracy took a basting ribbon from her sewing box. He tightened the tape around her blond crown, lifting her hair off her neck and letting it fall back to her shoulders. He snapped the ribbon free and fluttered it across her bare skin. Margaret felt the coarse weave of the fabric lisping over her nipples. He took the ribbon and worked it between her lips, sawing her tongue, until the corners of her mouth were burning.

Margaret's brother, Cam, rode up to New England to collect an antique wood stove for his mother, Elizabeth. On his way back to Wilmington, Cam stopped in Providence to see Margaret. It didn't surprise Margaret when Tracy seized her brother's obsession. For years, Cam had been trying to locate his estranged father, who was an ex-model for Arrow Collars. Tracy was always scouting, hoping to enrich his encyclopedic awareness of fixations. The Arrow Collar Man as missing patriarch was an appealing hybrid and Tracy recognized its element of glamour.

They still had some twilight, and Margaret and Tracy stood on the sidewalk beside her brother's pickup truck. Margaret admired the stove. Cam said, "I disconnected it from some asbestos pipe without the proper mask. I hope Elizabeth is happy with her antique because I breathed poisonous fibers." Tracy climbed into the back of the truck to help Cam arrange the heavy stove, which had slipped off-center. The two men tried to shove the solid block of iron. It wasn't coming. Tracy threw his weight against the stove, but its metal foot was snagged. Cam didn't like to give Tracy instructions. "Wait a second," Cam said. "Hold up."

Tracy kept pushing.

Cam said, "We're caught on something."

Tracy stood up straight.

"Shit. We scratched the bedliner. I knew it," Cam said.

Margaret liked to hear Cam complain about these things. The men switched sides until they had the right grip on it and carefully worked the stove against the back of the cab.

She invited Cam to stay for dinner, but he could come up to the apartment for only an hour. He unscrewed the solid brass finials from the stove and brought them upstairs so they wouldn't be stolen. They sat down in the small living room. Margaret cupped the heavy brass globes, letting their weight ache her wrists.

Tracy started right in on the Arrow Collar business. "Truth is like the mother of vinegar, it keeps producing—"

"The mother of vinegar?" Cam said.

"Insight. It's like madness at first—you think you can't contain it. It keeps developing, spilling over. You have to find out about your father. We all have to find out."

"We do?" Margaret said.

Cam rubbed the powdery stove black from his jeans.

He was making the stains worse. Margaret saw it smearing the settee. Her brother tried to follow what Tracy was saying. He was telling Cam that he had made a public commitment to always seek the truth, both his own and others'. He took a group oath. "This model of yours is a mesmerizing figure, don't you think?" Tracy said.

Her brother said, "You could say that."

Margaret said, "Mesmerism requires two equal parties."

"Since when do you tell everyone our family matters?" Cam said.

"I don't," she told him. "It's Tracy. He asks about our childhood."

Tracy said, "It was the Family Unit from Hell—"

"Will you shut up," she told Tracy.

Tracy said, "Snapping family portraits at your house was like squinting into a rifle scope in which the cross hairs never match up on a moving target."

"Do you shoot?" Cam said. "No? Never tried? Then you don't know what you're talking about."

Tracy said, "I'm not talking about guns. I'm saying that it's difficult to document a dysfunctional circle of kith and kin. It's impossible to see ancestral outlines. You've got a warped silhouette—the background keeps shifting."

Tracy knew what he was talking about. Margaret was the youngest in an awkward ensemble of stepbrothers and stepsisters, absent mothers and fathers, separate tribes coming together after the first territories were plundered. Cam's two older sisters were not interested in their real father, the model, and called him "a cad for all seasons." Cam didn't try to enlist them to his side. His mother, Elizabeth, gave him little explanation for his father's absence. It was a routine desertion, but his departure was tormenting in its methodical precision. He was like an equilibrist ascending a tightrope, dipping forward and back, pivoting, inching farther out. "I shut my eyes," Elizabeth said.

Margaret's own mother, Sandra, was deceased and Margaret was not related by blood to any sibling. She was indexed only to her father, Richard Rice. Even he seemed hesitant, perhaps unsure of his feelings because Margaret grew in the shade of a previous love. Cam reminded her that they shared a similar chronology: They both lost parents when they were just babies. What could she learn about her mother's death? Wasn't Margaret herself the first and last particle of evidence? She didn't share Cam's compulsion to keep backtracking.

They were reaching their thirties and were regularly employed. They had their recent divorces, or divorces-in-progress, and were still fighting over the children. Margaret said, "It's a crazy project to chase down a total stranger. Do we have that kind of time on our hands?"

"I guess not. That's the problem."

Tracy said, "No problem. Time is our medium. We can shape it. It stretches; it's whatever we want. It conforms *to us*."

Margaret watched Cam's eyes dilate slightly and contract.

"Maybe Tracy is right. I should just set aside the time—"

"Don't even dream about it," Margaret said. "Tracy always has these brainstorms, these bare-your-soul schemes; he wants everyone to choose the mystery door. I've seen people who go on TV after they locate their biological parents. It never works out."

Her brother wasn't listening to her.

Margaret said, "Tracy's been in a straitjacket, did you know that? In that jacket for days." Her voice was flat, like a clerk's.

"Is that the truth?" Cam said.

"I was a kid. Too much belladonna," Tracy said.

"A religious thing? The Madonna? My friend had some trouble like that. He had moles on the palms of his hands and on the insteps of his feet, like the stigmata. He decided to have the moles removed, but then he had the scars. It was a mistake; the scars were even more like the stigmata."

"No, nothing like that," Tracy said, "it was *bella*donna, you know, deadly nightshade. We used it to get high. We tried everything."

"Glue," Margaret said.

Cam looked at her. "You did glue?"

Tracy said, "That explains a lot, doesn't it?"

It was hard to watch Tracy and Cam shrugging their shoulders in synchronic timing. They looked like two fellows in an old monochrome movie scene, a Hollywood treatment of escalating male camaraderie. She tried to keep from laughing. Cam worked hard to maintain a blind, barreling-ahead naïveté; he was expert at whitewashing. Tracy envied the fact that what haunted Cam wasn't self-imposed, when he was certain that his own anxieties were fed by internal springs. "I'm a victim of my subconscious," Tracy complained.

Margaret said, "Don't listen to Tracy—he's intrigued by our family tragedy because it can't touch him. He doesn't have any claim. Tracy likes to rubberneck. He likes to watch condemned buildings being demolished, did you know this? He drives hours just so he can stand behind some yellow sawhorses."

"She's right, I'm a Blitz hound. First, they have to remove the gargoyles. Gargoyles are priceless. It takes hours and requires patience. Then, you're rewarded— the building starts to shiver and sink away. A perfect vertical descent. Detonators set in an exact chronology so that even the dust ascends in distinct levels. *There it goes; there goes the old Rialto.*"

Cam said, "I worked on a salvage crew once. We went through the building before another crew wired it up. I unscrewed all the EXIT signs, the doorknobs, the wall plates for scrap. You know how many EXIT signs in your average-size municipal building?"

Margaret saw it was getting off-track. "It's different when you have a human element," she said. "Your father is alive, living in his own free realm—"

"Retired in Rio somewhere. He's in his *GQ* golden years," Tracy said.

Cam smiled. Margaret knew that Cam held on to an image of the young model, the face in all the newspaper ads, a stunning double frozen-in-time. Cam's father, Lewis Goddard, was only sixteen when he became a model for Arrow Collars. He was the last to pose for the series painted by the illustrator J. C. Leyendecker.

Arrow made collars before they started making shirts with attached collars. Cam's father was one of Leyendecker's most popular models toward the end of that collar era, and since he was young to start, Cluett, Peabody & Company kept using him as a photographer's model in new shirt campaigns, starting with one they called "Versatility in White." Margaret had seen tear sheets of the Leyendecker drawings and the later ads from newspapers, the *Saturday Evening Post, Esquire*, and *Collier's*.

Leyendecker's images were crisp, almost too severe. He painted with a broad, deliberate stroke, which revealed a subject overwhelmed, almost harried by a masculine vigor beneath a polished, halting refinement. Lewis's face was perfectly balanced, yet it looked like a study in extremes. The eyes were electric, deep, accented with transparent cross-hatched shading. His nose was straight but not too narrow or snivelly, his hairline a firm black, angled in correct alignment to the conformation of the skull, sideburns trimmed level at the first crest of the ear. Margaret was most excited by Lewis's mouth; a tug of muscle made a central indentation from which the lips seemed to swell either side, full and yet seemingly reserved, blank. Waiting for an erotic imprint. Then, the cleft. His chin was so deeply notched, the left plane plunged into shadow before surfacing again on the right.

Cam shared some of his father's features, but the Arrow Collar ads were such pleasing grotesques, one couldn't be sure of their truth. Elizabeth said Lewis had the habit of wearing dark eye pencil even when he wasn't working. When he enlisted in the Second World War, they didn't send him overseas. It wasn't because he was a little older than the others, in his mid-thirties. He was simply too pretty. The sergeant in command placed Lewis in a kissing booth in Times Square, where he recruited one hundred WACs a day.

Elizabeth told Margaret and Cam about Lewis's silk and suede braces, his cashmere socks, his eighteen-karat-gold signet ring awarded him by another model. She resented these luxuries, yet she was forgiving of worse affronts, such as the time he borrowed her lip-liner and wrote another woman's name across his bosom.

Tracy came into the room with a bottle of beer for Cam. He handed the bottle to Cam and waited until he took a pull. "How do you like it? It's a longneck. I have to hunt for longneck bottles anymore. It's the end of the line for these," Tracy said. Tracy locked his eyes on Cam as he swallowed. Cam looked past Tracy and rested the bottle against his knee, marking circles on his jeans.

Tracy was testing it out. Maybe he could reach her brother with this shit, but Cam leaned back in his seat. He was putting it together. He was smiling.

"Okay," Tracy said, "we're all in favor of a manhunt? Organizing our posse, right? Cam takes the white horse, we ride the paints—"

"We can't do it," Margaret said. "We don't have the particulars. Anything could happen. Remember the innocent people who witnessed atomic tests without a proper explanation of the risks? The children held out their hands to catch the fallout, tiny white rosebuds of soot? That could happen to us."

Cam said, "What could happen? We could get nuked? You're being hysterical, Margaret. Anyway, I didn't say I was going to do anything about Lewis," Cam said.

"Thank goodness. It's Tracy's manifesto," she said.

"Yes, and I stand behind it. A man has to face his past," Tracy said.

"You're a shitload of chitty-chat," Cam said to Tracy. Cam looked at Margaret. She was smiling at her brother's conclusion, but she met Tracy's eyes. Tracy wasn't easily offended, and sometimes his resilience to remarks seemed almost threatening.

She looked at the two men. She had a sick feeling, as if all her smooth-muscle groups were tugging in counter directions. She sensed a shift from one sort of struggle to another; it was an unfamiliar hunger, a new evocative burden. She tried to think of her eight-year-old daughter.

Celeste was due back from a weekend at her father's. Celeste always suffered small injuries at her father's. Her teeth got chipped, her ankles twisted, her fingertips scalded. Margaret longed to take possession of her again and could never rest until her child was returned. Each time her ex-husband dropped off her daughter, Margaret had a habit of shutting the front door just as he started to say his last remarks.

Cam told Margaret he'd like to see his niece, but it was getting late. The roads might be icing. Cam stood up to leave. Then, he couldn't find the brass finials for the stove.

"They were right there on the coffee table."

"I don't see them," Tracy said.

They looked around the room and lifted the feather cushions from the settee. Margaret stooped over and looked under the chairs. Nothing. Cam knew something was funny. He let his head fall back on his shoulders and stared at the ceiling. Then he stared out the window.

"What the fuck is going on?" Margaret said.

"They just disappeared," Tracy said.

"They can't disappear! They must be worth a lot of money."

Tracy said, "It's like a paranormal event. Weird."

"What are you talking about?" Margaret said.

Cam walked into the kitchen, turned on the tap, and rinsed out his beer bottle. He was giving Margaret some room to take care of it.

Tracy said, "Don't look at me. I don't have those brass things. It's weirdsville, if you ask me. Maybe it's dematerialization or electrobiology. I've heard of these things happening at convents and monasteries. Loaves of bread fly out the window. Pebbles turn into grapes; the grapes turn into wine. Presto."

Margaret walked into the kitchen and back through the bedroom. "Tracy, my brother has to drive a long way. All the way back to Wilmington." She knew Tracy had the brass ornaments. For sex purposes or emotional ransom, for a practical joke. She didn't really want to know the reason.

"They could have rolled. Did you look everywhere?" Tracy said.

"Where is everywhere?"

"There—"

Margaret saw the finials behind the stereo speaker.

She nudged them out with her toe and handed them to Cam. They all walked outside to Cam's truck. The men were grinning, looking straight ahead, the way she'd seen boys grit their teeth after a successful hazing. Cam got into his truck. Margaret said good-bye, but Cam didn't answer. He gripped the side mirror, waggled it until it was adjusted right. Margaret told her brother that whatever he decided to do about his father would be his own doing.

2

racy spent a great deal of time with his Sex Anonymous sponsor. He was helpless against his lust for fresh emotional swells and depths of feeling, but Margaret was never certain if Tracy's private demons were a respectable threat or if perhaps they might be a sign of an extended, swooning adolescence. It might be an unwillingness to let rich feelings subside with age. She tried to contain her own disturbing impulses, but if she addressed a particular fear, it broke off into several splinter groups.

After her divorce, Margaret went to one meeting of Emotions Anonymous when her phobias increased and she couldn't ride the city buses. Each time the driver tugged a lever to check the hydraulic door, she hated the screak of the vinyl caulking. It was the same consideration that made her shy from elevators when the vertical seals squashed shut. Even public telephone booths used these rubber sweeps. She was told that she suffered panic reactions. Perhaps, after a bad marriage, a buildup of psychic toxins are released in a swarm. Emotions Anonymous was slow and gluey with saccharine phrases of encouragement. Tracy continued with Sex Anonymous.

"Just how many kinds of anonymous groups are there?"

Tracy said, "It's a fad. It's like clipping a deck of cards to the spokes of your bike. It's fifty-two different cards, but they're all clipped to one wheel turning the same way."

Margaret said, "Some people have real problems. You know, health risks and such. They don't require anonymity at the YMCA Stroke Club."

"You're talking about *support* groups. Look at the paper, there's a list of them. Here's one, 'Stuttering Support,' and 'Chronic Pain' meets at seven P.M. 'Single Again,' they're having a cookout—"

Tracy's therapist had recommended Tracy attend some Sex Anonymous meetings when he thought he had located Tracy's masochistic streak. The therapist said this streak was exacerbated by Tracy's rather flagrant, self-possessed androgyny. Tracy was married, divorced; he had several serious seasons with different women. Then there was a year when he was knighted in the piss halls, escorted by a moody entourage to the gay bars, the Venetian Room, the Boulevard Room, the Back Room. Margaret noticed the names of these bars sounded much more intimate than places he might take her. Their favorite spot, the Penalty Box, displayed photos of hockey players and boxers.

The therapist was certain that Tracy's splintered orientation came from surgery trauma.

"He says my operation gave me lifelong reverberations," Tracy told her.

"Your appendix?" she said. She knew he had his appendix out when he was seventeen. It was a routine operation which went awry when the cyclopropane tank malfunctioned, the gauge froze and stopped supplying the anesthetic. As the OR staff fumbled to administer a different drug, Tracy regained consciousness, waking to a sharp saucer of pain, rimmed and stinging. Then it was the sight of his belly clamped open, his penis taped against his thigh. It took a moment or two to sedate him again as he struggled to escape from the table. A nurse kept her palm cupped against the vent in his abdomen as he thrashed his legs. He saw her eyes above the green pleats of her mask; her eyes were pinched at the corners and looked quite merry. She couldn't suppress her bliss when the ho-hum operation turned into a Keystone Kops sort of thing.

During his weeks in the hospital, Tracy had dreams about the nurse in that mask. Sometimes the mask was not a mask but a bikini bottom pulled taut over his own mouth until he couldn't breathe.

"How does your therapist know?" Margaret said. "Do you tell him everything?"

"It's his job to identify something and label it. A shrink has to label everything. They once called it a 'sea change,' it happens," Tracy said.

The term "sea change" was a little too romantic for what it really was—a small clutch of gay lovers, each of them jealous of one another. It was just Tracy researching his own capacities. One evening, a fellow wielded a Swingline industrial staplegun and Tracy broke off from that circle. Margaret tried to imagine how Tracy had allowed someone to sink staples all over him. The scars were tiny yet deep, rows of parallel flecks across his chest and belly.

When she was fourteen years old and in love with a teen idol, she purchased magazines with centerfold posters of her favorite young singer. There were always staples interrupting the smooth shading of his skin, staples slashing his face, his hips. She liked to trace his sideburns, the planes and shadows of his lips and all the pores of his skin, the little squared dots of whisker coming in. Her stepmother was pleased that she loved something unreal. The radio called him an overnight sensation; Margaret believed it was just jealous ridicule on their part.

"Did you ever love a magazine idol?" she asked Tracy.

"Natalie Wood. Then and now."

Margaret looked at her feet as she ground the heel of her shoe back on. "Natalie Wood is really perfect for you," she told him, trying not to sound stung. "Natalie *looks* like you. You could be related." The actress made Margaret forget to ask Tracy about his sessions with the Swingline.

But Tracy wanted her to make further admissions. "Where's your centerfold now? He's a wormy pinup, thin as an onionskin in some landfill. He's a rotted cameo, a composted Adonis. He's getting lots of necro—"

"Okay," she said. She never knew what to do when he talked like this. She remained sitting at the kitchen table as he stood over her. He weaved slightly, side to side. He was weighted, off-balance, sinking into misery. This was exaggerated by the fact that he was physically lanky. A man with this kind of build, svelte and eager, looks twice as gloomy. His hair fell across his eyes in paralyzed curls. His brow crinkled and looked like a heavy filigree, an ornate fresco about to topple from the crown of a building. Then he stood before the little mirror in the hall and raked his hair with his hand. He picked up a protractor and with its sharp point he made a part down the middle of his scalp. He didn't wear a part in his hair. His hair was naturally wavy and lifted off his face, angling back in lovely drifts, but he had an odd habit of stopping now and then to part it. He tossed his head and the hair resumed its thickness.

Margaret had tried therapy off and on, but she knew it soon became something strange—a new arm of the illness from which she was seeking escape. She was not alarmed by Tracy's sexual history; maybe he was making too much of it. She listened to his confessions. "The flesh has a mind of its own," she said.

Tracy attended group meetings and went out for coffees at all hours. "Too much therapy can actually cause mental fatigue," she read from the newspaper. "Looking inward is strenuous."

Tracy said, "That's true. It's tiring." Then, Tracy saw a report of an airplane crash on the news. The plane went down because of something called "metal fatigue."

"The wings can just peel back, come off like chocolate coating from an ice cream stick," he told her. He liked the similarity of the terms *mental* fatigue and *metal* fatigue. These terms were reassuring; he no longer had to say he felt blue or he felt down.

In the beginning, Margaret asked the college girl upstairs to sit with Celeste, and she went along with Tracy to have coffee with members of Tracy's group. They found a booth in a diner somewhere, sometimes moving from one diner to another. Margaret listened to their talk. If they addressed Margaret, she smiled and said she was just auditing. "Audit means listen," she told them, making sure they understood she wasn't going to yap. They talked about how hard it was at first to admit to themselves that they weren't in control.

"When I got out of the driver's seat, it was the happiest day of my life," a man said.

Another fellow said, "Whenever I get *back* in the driver's seat, I fuck it up, man, it's the end. I can't be in the driver's seat. Never again!" Tracy discussed spiritual signposts, the lyric versus the clinical voice of the *I Ching* as Margaret watched her doughnut decay on a saucer. Its white glaze turned clear in just an hour; in two hours the grease and sugar had merged with sodden granules of cake, making a circle of clotted amber.

After that evening, she stayed at home with her daughter. Tracy would return to her, no matter the hour. On bad nights, he rubbed his face with his hands as if trying to remove a gummy substance, his sadness jelled over his sharp features. She saw enough disturbed people, real madmen, at her job teaching grammar at the Adult Correctional Institution in Cranston. She handed out pencils and collected them at the end of each lesson. "A pencil can gouge out someone's eye," her supervisor said. Even the soap was shaved so they couldn't put a heavy bar in a sock and swing it over their heads. Yet she recognized that Tracy's sometimes arrogant, stylized remorse was more compelling, more miserable in its heightened forms than the cut-and-dried maniacal fits of the worst psychotic inmates.

II

Margaret first met Tracy at a Shriners' Parade. When her divorce went through, she waffled back and forth between a feeling of stunned relief and several new and higher forms of anxiety. Cam often telephoned long distance; he was ending his marriage with Darcy, and they tried to cheer one another. He said these were the dog days for them both. "Horse latitudes," he said. She thought this was a silly idea, but she remembered how sailors looked for signs of land—the floating kelp, driftwood, the birds increasing.

To kill time one evening, she took her child to watch the Shriners' Parade. Celeste was excited by the clowns, but it was Margaret herself who wished to be distracted. She was recovering from a bout of threadworms, a condition that her daughter had contracted at the school and then passed on to Margaret. It wasn't a serious illness, but its symptoms were nightmarish. While lying in her bed, she believed she felt the worms churning through her lower bowel seeking their breeding place. She took medication with her daughter, but for weeks she imagined the worms coiled through her. She hardly ate and could not sleep.

Celeste was too small to see over people's heads, and Margaret tried to lift her up once and again. A man was standing nearby. It was Tracy. He recognized something about Margaret. Her flickering smile, her clean slate. Then he talked to Margaret, shouting at her over the racket. It was a strange, appealing way to meet a man, to have him shout small talk, his voice booming. Now and again, he was forced to pause, to grin at her for long moments when the drums or cymbals were too loud. Soon Celeste was riding his shoulders.

Majorettes hurled batons into the twilight, the silver sticks froze high in the air before falling back. As the girls marched out of sight, Margaret studied their fringed white boots, the way the leather tassels shivered. Then, the floats arrived, towing crippled children and children recovering from hideous burns. The crowd applauded the children. Margaret smiled at Tracy; she turned back to watch the parade at measured intervals. She didn't want to appear anxious or hungry, but already she was feeling renewed; she thought of the tribes of worms inside her and doubted their existence. The sight of the maimed children seemed appallingly reassuring. Margaret looked at Tracy, who steadied Celeste at a comfortable height above the street. After the parade, Tracy called her. She was surprised to hear his full name; it was the same name as someone who wrote for the local newspaper.

"Yes," he told her, "I wrote that feature on plastic flowers. It was an entire warehouse of flowers, a synthetic Amazon jungle."

Margaret said, "I've read your column, but I didn't recognize you from the sketch next to your by-line—"

"That's a mystery sketch. It's yanked from the files. Who knows who *he* is."

"It's a sketch of someone else? Isn't that crazy?"

"You read the column? That's the important thing. My editor tones it down. It's too bland. If I slam politicians, it's usually just a bad haircut or a loud sport jacket. You know, Mayor Cianci wears those navy shirts and the white ties—"

"I like your writing."

"You do? It's nothing. I have this facility. I can't stop myself. They print it, then I wad it up in a ball. It's cleansing. In just twenty-four hours I write it and throw it away in the trash. Last night I went to seven discos to write my Energy Crisis report for '78. I'm behind Carter on this. They've got colored lights under the glass block floors in these places. A strobe takes more energy than a *constant-on.*"

"I didn't know that."

"It's just one of these details. Don't give it a second thought. Did you see my story 'Satin Connection'? About those lingerie emporiums on Thayer Street? After the story ran, they sent me some free camisoles, mostly Big Girl sizes they couldn't unload. Interested?"

Without the marching band in the background, his voice was even and gentle. He waited for her to form her opinions, to answer his friendly proposals. She heard him take a breath and hold it, a silky tug against the receiver.

Cam learned about her lover, and he tried not to ask her any questions. "Just tell me one thing, Margaret, where does this leave *me*? You have your divorce, now I'm getting my divorce. You said it yourself, it was a tandem kind of thing. We were going to keep an eye out for one another. Cool our heels. Now you're joining up with someone all over again?"

"Into the frying pan, I know," Margaret said. "I'm crazy for punishment, I guess. I should have waited."

"That was what we talked about," Cam said.

"Tracy's just like a friend, really. He's nice to Celeste," she told Cam. "I mean, isn't that lucky?"

Tracy was good with Celeste because he pined for his own daughter, who lived four hundred miles away. Sometimes he took Celeste aside and made plans without

Margaret's approval. One day during the winter, Tracy drove Celeste and Margaret into the country. It started snowing again, dusting the grey drifts with new white, and it was hard to see the shoulder of the road. Tracy stopped the car at a small amusement park, closed for the winter.

"I remember this place," Celeste said as she jumped from the car and her legs disappeared through a crust of snow.

Margaret pulled her collar together and looked back over her shoulder at the car. "We can't just leave the car there, can we?"

"Leave it," Celeste said. "Isn't this great? Everything's buried."

"There ought to be something in here," Tracy said.

"It's closed," Margaret said.

"Not really," he said.

"Aren't we trespassing?" Margaret said, but she followed Tracy and Celeste through the big gate and into the center of the park. In one of the pavilions, bumper cars had been left in awkward arrangements when the power was shut off at the end of the season.

Celeste was amused by her echo in the high arcade. Tracy put Celeste in one of the cars and Margaret climbed into another. Margaret didn't expect anything to happen, but Celeste sat alert in her seat, her hands gripping the wheel. Tracy pushed Margaret's car forward until it rammed her daughter's. Next, he went behind the girl's car and she steered it at Margaret. They crashed. Celeste was laughing. For ten minutes Tracy shoved the cars; his hair was drenched.

Margaret watched his face become an exhausted mask, strained by some interior effort rather than by his physical exertion. She told him to stop but he edged her around and threw her car into the low wall. He rushed Celeste's car into her. The collision caused Margaret to tumble onto the oily floor, but Celeste was unharmed. They walked back to the car. The sweat in Tracy's hair started to ice and peel away from his temples.

Celeste's father came to get her on Friday evenings to take her for the weekend. Tracy listened for the buzzer. When it rang, he held the girl's coat by its collar, positioning the parka behind her back, guiding the sleeves on, tugging the tight elastic cuffs over her wrists. He looped the long muffler four times around her collar.

"She takes all that stuff off once she gets in the car," Margaret told him.

"No, she won't."

Margaret's ex-husband took Celeste, saying he had to hurry home to a queerly suburban activity, such as smoking two-inch pork chops in his new backyard contraption.

"It's just a year-round barbecue at your place?" Tracy said.

"A smoker doesn't grill, it *cures* meat. Any time of the year," Celeste's father told Tracy.

Margaret watched Tracy's eyes narrowing in wariness. "Don't worry about her," she told Tracy when her ex-husband had gone.

"The influences she gets there, shit," Tracy said.

"It's just that suburban stuff, it's harmless. Unless Celeste really grows to like it," Margaret said. "We influence her, too, you know. Maybe we should think about that."

"What can we do to her, make her too human?" Tracy said.

"Yes, I think someone can be too human, too unhappy that way. You, of all people, should know that."

He didn't look pleased with her remark, so she poked him. She said she was referring to his work as a journalist. "I mean you write about the human condition for the paper, don't you?"

"I write *against* the human condition. It's a subtle distinction, maybe you have been missing the point?"

She didn't argue.

Margaret came home from work one Monday and found Tracy scratching notes for a story. On his knee, she saw the little ball peen hammer they sometimes used to crack shellfish.

"What's with the hammer?" she said.

"Oh Christ," he said, "I hate to tell you this."

"Tell me what? What do you hate to tell me?"

He stood up and walked over to her writing desk. He pointed to her favorite trinket, a smooth piece of petrified wood her father had given her. "I was just tapping it," he told her.

"What do you mean?" she said, but it was too late, the paperweight was halved; its small violet center glistened on the green blotter. She examined the stone, she tried to see that it might not be ruined, it might be more interesting now that it rested in two separate chunks.

"It was an accident," he said. He looked at her for a sign.

She shrugged. "I see. You just had to hit something with a hammer?"

He made a florid gesture, fanning his hands open, palms up, feigning contrition, but his face was dark.

She stood very still. Perhaps they would laugh. Tracy could make her laugh, that deep, utterly unselfconscious laughter from low in the diaphragm. If she felt a little threat, it was small, hard to discern, like a thin layer of ice that forms on a pond before it melts off in the sun.

Then it was the bedroom. Lying beside Tracy, Margaret could still see the high end of the gallows through the bedroom window. She didn't consider it. Margaret followed her primary instinct, which was her greed for him, for his form and weight. She loved the feel of his breath, its rich, humid phrasings against her skin. She listened for the slight congestion building in his lungs as he fucked her, the way he cleared his throat. Her sheets, scented from cheap bluing, kept riding up at their corners.

This was when Tracy's daylong despair seemed to charge him; it condensed in a helpless eroticism. Tracy seemed to suggest that sex had no meaning beyond its one meaning, its physical manifestation, its act. This blank assurance excited her. If his attention shifted, focused on a remote particular, he was just showing the concentration and reserve of a jaded technician. She was impressed by his fatalism and mistook it for a level-headed calm.

"Don't talk. Don't think so much, Margaret," he said. "We want total omniscience." She didn't believe Tracy was any different from other people. Sex was a transgression any way you looked at it. Everyone has some first terror that describes his role. Tracy's orientation probably had nothing to do with "surgery trauma." Margaret's first erotic treasure was a book cover from a dime novel. On the cover, a girl is tethered to a post. The coarse yellow cord winds under her arms and crosses again at her hips, her bare feet are tangled in kindling briar where a rosy cloud has started. Her smock is torn at one shoulder, exposing part of her breast and half the nipple's small medallion. The fire—the girl's sex buzzing, snapping with the twigs' ignition, the tiny filaments of ash stirred upward. The picture had a familiarity that common sense couldn't explain; Margaret recognized a connection. She read about these trances later on in junior college. It was an idea that a person might have lived a previous life, perhaps as an Egyptian king or Joan of Arc. Somebody's life. The dime novel gave her this notion and the martyred figure became Margaret's first erotic vision.

She tried not to think of her young daughter during sex, but she heard sneezing or the little cricket chirp of a bedspring. Celeste flickered on and off in the background like a strip of wavering neon. Years before, when Margaret had slept beside her husband, Celeste always fell from bed. Every night the child's weight shook the ceiling. The light fixture rattled, a dusty moth's wing drifted down. The fall was not steep and Celeste was never injured, but it was a harsh event for Margaret. Each muffled thud loosened plaster chips behind the wallpaper and Margaret heard these sifting specks, the house crumbling.

With Tracy, Margaret managed their carnal struggle with the same free rein she gave to her maternal instinct. These impulses should remain in opposition, but more often they seemed inscrutably linked. Her daughter no longer fell in the night. Margaret was tucked against Tracy, trying to sleep. Yet, she got out of bed and went into the other room. Celeste was dreaming; she lifted the girl's wrist and massaged her fingertips.

C
am was in the worst period of his divorce: before court proceedings, far enough into it to have lost all the minor comforts of his previous life without gaining any new advantages. After Easter, Cam moved out of his house. His last chore for his wife, Darcy, was to take the spoiled colored eggs out to the trash. He didn't place the eggs in the can. He hurled them one by one into the street, where they rolled under the parked cars.

He was living in his office at the Bringhurst Apartments, where he managed the units, cleaned the swimming pool, and kept the parking spaces reserved for the tenants. Margaret knew he had other duties, but Cam didn't like to mention plunging the toilets, running a snake down the drains, or spraying chlordane to kill the cockroaches. He told her that his boss gave him extra jobs, "personal errands," such as taking suits to the cleaners or picking up liquor for parties Cam wasn't invited to. Cam kept asking her to visit. He called her every day, and when the telephone rang, Margaret lifted it off the hook before Tracy could get to it.

"I don't have anyone. Why don't you come back to Wilmington?"

"Is it my fault you still live in Wilmington?" she told him.

"It's our hometown," Cam said.

"I'm never going back there. Don't you understand?" Her voice shifted to a high level, her throat closing tight on her words. She hung up the telephone.

Tracy was standing behind her. "Listen to yourself, the hysteria in your voice—"

"Cam makes me crazy with these ideas!" Margaret said.

Tracy said he wouldn't mind a change. "The Delmarva area. That's okay. Anywhere above the Mason-Dixon is fine with me. I could try to get a job writing for the *Philadelphia Inquirer*."

"Shut up," she told him.

"Wilmington has a lot of growth going on."

"Out of the question. Who cares if it's growing?"

Wilmington, the Chemical Capital of the World. She recalled Du Pont's billboards, BETTER LIVING THROUGH CHEMISTRY. Then, during the fuss about napalm and chemical weapons, the motto was changed to BETTER THINGS FOR BETTER LIVING. Tracy said he could probably get a job writing copy just like that for Du Pont brochures, label instructions, manuals, for more money than he made at the paper. She just looked at him.

Cam once took a part-time position at Du Pont, afternoons after high school. His job was in a basement film library where Du Pont's educational and sales films were sorted and rewound, sometimes spliced, before going back out. Only a few of the films addressed ethical questions: *Man in the Twentieth Century* and *Chemicals— For or Against Mankind?* Cam brought Margaret back to the tiny office. It was a small, hot room with projectors and stacks of empty film cans. She stood next to Cam in the dim light as the celluloid accelerated, lisped, and fluttered on the reels.

It seemed like everyone in Wilmington worked for the company, and Margaret was always pleased her father had his own business. Cam reminded Margaret that Richard was just as dependent, since he distributed industrial equipment to all the Du Pont plant sites.

Margaret disagreed. "He sells everywhere. He sells to Atlas and Hercules too, he sells to Doeskin Paper," she said. She liked the mural on the side of the Doeskin Paper plant, a baby deer, his tail lifted like the large, oversized puff that came with her Avon Bath Powder.

Cam shook his head. He said she was ignorant. She didn't understand these big monopolies. They could call

it the chemical industry, but it was a *dynasty*. To prove
it, he drove Margaret up the Brandywine Valley to see
Grenogue, the Du Pont family's seventy-room mansion,
French style, which overlooked the Brandywine River.
The house crowned a great hill; steep pastures spiraled
down in shades of deepening green until the fields
touched the river. Several stone silos dotted the pastures
and reminded Margaret of Rapunzel's tower. Driving
past on the county road, Margaret looked up at the
castle. She counted eight chimneys, and in the middle
of the slate roof a giant cupola, big as a walk-through
gazebo. At the very bottom of the hill were the servants'
bungalows. Right there, eye level, laundrywomen were
hanging sheets on fresh plastic wires. The contrast
excited her.

Cam was letting the car idle, gunning the engine at
the entrance to the private drive. The drive was complex,
winding through many switchbacks bordered by rose
hedges. Margaret thought of the winter and all the rock
salt it would take.

"Industrial pimps!" he was saying, as they looked up
at the mansion.

"Sssh," she told him.

"It's like the story of Rumpelstiltskin."

"You mean Rapunzel," Margaret told him. "Rapunzel's tower."

"No, the other one. You know, it's where they spin
the nylon into *gold*."

A woman came out of a servant's cottage. The woman
wore a starched uniform with a Peter Pan collar, which
looked unnaturally brilliant against her deep skin. Cam

pushed Margaret out. She stood holding the car door, but he locked it. Margaret turned around and looked at the woman in the white uniform. She smiled back at Margaret, a gentle smile showing small teeth with neat spaces between them.

Cam rolled his window down. "Ask her if Rumpelstiltskin is home."

The woman stared at Margaret and Cam, shrugged, and pointed to her lips, her ears.

"Me-no-spicka-no-English?" Cam said, drumming his fingers on the steering wheel. The woman recognized this phrase and her eyes narrowed.

Margaret reached in and unlocked her door, then she got in next to Cam. He drove the car away. "You asshole," she told him.

Margaret explained the story to Tracy. "You see? That's what the Du Ponts can do, they bring out the worst in somebody. I never heard Cam say such a mean thing. You wouldn't want to work for the company," she told Tracy.

Tracy said he might look into it. "Mansions don't scare me," he said. He told her the good thing about being a writer was that he could write anything. "Somebody is always looking to explain something, convince somebody. Sell, sell, sell."

Margaret was working full-time at the prison. If she didn't want to visit Cam, she could say her job kept her. All summer, she had followed Cam's troubles, but she refused his invitations. In August, she decided to go

down and see him. "I guess I have to nudge him all the
way through to his final decree," she told Tracy. Tracy
believed that Margaret and Cam's love couldn't be just
familial. There was no true blood boundary between
them.

"He's my brother," Margaret said. "Why don't you
worry about the milkman?"

"The milkman is extinct. That's not a good example."

"All right," she said, but she didn't give him a better
one. Tracy was finishing two stories for the paper, two
big, puffy features that would keep him occupied. Every
morning for a week he went exploring at the new indoor
mall in Warwick. He liked walking from one end to the
other, talking with the heart patients who exercised
there. He named the heart patients' routine "Mall
Medicine." The other article was about the 20th Century
Diner in Pawtucket, so she knew he would be eating out
there a few times. The diner had some good specials.

Tracy started giving her advice the day before she
left. If she found herself in a difficult discussion with
Cam and her folks, if she was cornered, she should look
out the window and say, "Look at that bird! I didn't
know you had bluebirds here."

Margaret told him he was crazy. "Bluebirds?" she
said.

"It doesn't have to be bluebirds, it could be some
kind of woodpecker, or even a dog, but make sure it's
a *white* dog, a whippet or a greyhound, something exotic,
something to transform the moment."

"Is this what they teach you in therapy? To lie?"

"It's not lying, it's when you have to change the

subject, dispel a bad mood. A little fib can be alluring, it can heighten the moment just when you're bottoming out."

"Look, let's not talk about it. I hate to go there anyway, and you're making me a nervous wreck. I just want to see my brother."

"He'll live. Everyone has to be divorced at least once. It's a rite of passage."

"He's different, he takes it personally," she said. They laughed, then they tried to stop laughing.

Celeste was going on a small trip with her father. He took her for a week every summer to his parents' house on the Chesapeake Bay. It was a peculiar life, Margaret thought, to always pack suitcases for her child. Each time it was difficult to let go of Celeste. She folded the little T-shirts, rolled the socks, shook out the ruffled bathing suit to see it, a velvety hot pink. Her daughter looked lovely in it, sweet, like ribbon candy. She packed the suitcase with Celeste's favorite things—her velour beach towel, her sockmonkey doll, and two new girl-detective mystery books that Celeste had asked for.

Tracy needed the car to drive back and forth between the mall and the 20th Century Diner, so Margaret was taking the train to Wilmington. The morning of her trip she woke to find the kitchen floor covered with grit. The windows were open a few inches and ash from the nearby power plant had collected on the sill, sifting out across the floor. It was soot from the stack at Narragansett Electric, much worse since the plant had switched back to coal during the oil crisis. The soot crackled when she walked over it, bursting into dark blots on the linoleum. She couldn't just leave it there. She wet a dish towel at the sink. She pushed the cloth over the floor, but it left dark smears.

"I need this filth. I really need it!" she told Tracy when he came through. He walked over to her with a broom. Tracy swept the broom over Margaret's hips, pushing her skirt high. He pulled the broom down her thighs, and returned to her waist. He toed her firmly with his shoe, tipped her off-balance until she lay curved on her side against the linoleum. He kept his foot weighted on her hip and stroked the broom over her.

"Will you stop this?" she said.

"I can't," Tracy said.

"You can. You can if you want. Do you want to stop?"

Tracy was sweeping her underwear down. He was kneeling behind her. He pressed the heel of his hand against her spine and fucked her. She began to doubt if she had lived a previous life. The girl at the stake was probably just a commercial artist's rendition of a popular theme: a girl's innocence going up in smoke.

"Let me go. I'll miss the train," she told him.

"Just don't think of it. Jesus, don't think of it now."

"I'm late—" Her voice sounded small, out of range. In a moment, he let her stand up. She tugged her panties up over her knees, adjusted the waistband of her skirt, and smoothed her hips. Her clothes were spotted with soot. "Shit, Tracy."

Tracy said, "I'll be in Wilmington tomorrow."

"Oh no, you don't. Cam needs to talk," she told him.

"Talk all you want. Give it a big chew. You have twenty-four hours, that's plenty of time. Isn't that plenty of time?"

She couldn't answer him. Her words would be deflected no matter what she said. "It doesn't matter," she told him. She took her case and went down to the street. He trailed her out of the building.

"You and Cam talk all you want," he said. "Just rest assured, Margaret, I'll be cutting in on your bull session."

II

When the train reached New Jersey, she decided that Tracy's behavior that morning was just childish jealousy. She was approaching her home turf and, feeling its threat, she missed Tracy's company. Then her tailbone hurt from sitting so long and she left her seat to walk through the cars. She straddled the aisle and welcomed the effort of concentration, the little box step she performed in order to keep balanced when the train rocked over a crossing. She made small talk with a woman as she swayed beside her seat.

"Wilmington," she said when the woman asked where she would get off the train. Did the word sound as evocative, as chilling to the woman as it did to Margaret?

"My brother lives there," she told the woman, "and my folks." She shrugged, a tiny, uncontrolled spasm.

The train followed the Delaware River and she looked down at the impermeable lead-colored water. She saw the stacks at Edgemoor, the razor-wire partitions at the plant where they made toxic white pigments, and across the river, the mysterious Chambersworks. The

Delaware Bridge is not something to admire; it rises above the sulfurous mist and sinks into it once more. Yet the bridge was the logo on her father's Econoline vans. The trucks showed a bright cartoon drawing of the bridge with the words RICE INDUSTRIAL SUPPLY COMPANY printed in a grand arch. To advertise, he had ordered hundreds of Zippo lighters decorated with a map of Delaware, the bridge, and a minuscule rhinestone to signify the Diamond State. Ballpoints and pocketknives displayed the company's name, her name, and a picture of the bridge. She liked best the decks of cards with the bridge superimposed upon the suits and, on the back side of each card, a variety of industrial products: winches, hoists, heat-shrinkable tubing, hydraulic jacks, carbide drill bits, belt sanders, compressors, pulleys, nylon fan belts, and links of chain.

Margaret would get off at Claymont Station. It was the same platform where she had been reunited with her sister Jane, after Jane had been missing for two years.

Jane disappeared when Margaret was in high school and Cam was on tour in Korea. Cam was only sixteen, but he had a letter from Wilmington Family Court and the signatures of both parents. It was several years after the war, but the American forces were doing the policing and some cleanup.

Jane had returned from the family doctor and was holding a prescription behind her back that said the words *Marbles, three times a day*. She had been crying; Margaret could see it right off because Jane had the kind of eyelashes that kept the tears in place long after there was any cause. Even so, Jane could always smile, an odd, drifting line. Margaret was waiting for the explanation, but it didn't look like it was coming soon, and she said, "That's three times a day, isn't that right?"

"That's right," her stepmother, Elizabeth, said.

"Well, three times a day isn't too bad," Margaret said, but this was just more of her prying.

"If you have to know," Elizabeth said, "your sister has flat feet. She has to pick up the marbles with her toes."

"I see," Margaret said. She tried not to laugh. She had a bad record with that; it was worse with Cam being in the service, since she felt she had to hold up his end. She had to laugh twice as often, twice as dry.

Jane practiced with a tin wastebasket. Jane picked up some marbles with her toes and dropped them in the can. Margaret could hear this throughout the house; they could hear it out on the sidewalk, a sad *plink, plink, plink*. One day Jane took an ink pad and she made some footprints on a paper bag. They were flat as ever. Margaret couldn't keep out of it, and her own high arch left only a thin crescent on the brown paper.

Margaret wrote to Cam about it; she told him half the marbles had rolled into the furnace grate—she heard them bouncing down the duct. Then Jane disappeared.

The newspaper ran a photograph of Jane with the word *Runaway* beneath it, and they put a question mark after the word. The story said she could be dead or alive. A police officer wanted a list of Jane's boyfriends. "Jane didn't have any," Elizabeth said.

"Are we sure?" Richard said.

"If she did have a boyfriend, Richard, why was she so gloomy all the time?"

"Love is strange," the officer said.

Cam was home on leave, watching a detective show with Margaret. On the screen they showed the chalk outline of a body. Margaret said, "Look, it's Jane." Cam liked the joke, but he elbowed her, jabbing her ribs until she felt a stitch.

Almost two years without word, then Margaret was drunk on wine in a car full of people the night Jane called home. The next morning she drove with Richard to the train station to meet her sister. They parked the car right before the track. Their breath made a mist on the windshield, and her father took his cuff over the heel of his hand to wipe a circle for himself and one for Margaret.

"Don't be nervous," she told him. It was a bold thing for her to say to her father.

"I don't know what it is," he said.

"It's everything," she said, "everything from then until now."

He studied her face for a moment, as if he could not remember when she was small and speechless. From that minute on, he never again looked directly into her eyes. He was always wary. Jane stepped off the train and kissed her stepfather on his cheek; you could see she had suffered in the planning of it. Jane showed Margaret her smile. It was the same mysterious line.

4

The cars kicked back as she stepped off the train and she landed hard on the platform. The soles of her feet were stinging. At the same instant, a rush of cicadas started their shrill ascension, a papery swell through the trees overhead. She saw Cam waving from his car in the small parking lot. He pressed the car horn, a bright snarled note that hushed the insects in the trees.

Cam stood up on the driver's side of the car, his arms outstretched over the roof. Greetings unnerved him, and he drummed the hot metal. He was making an effort not to lunge for her, but she would have been happy to accept his embrace.

"It's absolutely steamy here," she told him. She tugged Cam's waist, then touched his back in the hollow between his shoulder blades. His muscles felt tight under his blue Oxford. His studied repose seemed comprised of agonizing adjustments in thought and motion. She pushed her fingertip up his spine an inch or two. It was like touching the insulation around an electrical conduit in which a great current pulsed. Then it was his shyness that kept him from offering her the usual help men provided, opening doors and lifting the suitcases. Her case was made out of the same fabric as a parachute. "Don't bother," she said when she saw him staring at her bag. "I can get it." She threw her case in the backseat.

"Is that all you have?" He looked as if he hoped she had some trunks, lampshades, or mooseheads.

"No, this is it."

"Tracy didn't come?"

"He might be down later. He's writing a story for the paper."

"I wish you hadn't moved off," Cam told her.

"Moved off? *Moved off* sounds so awful," she said.

"You know what I mean. I could use you around here."

"I'm here, I'll get behind the yoke now," she said. She wondered what she was saying, what was the offer she'd made?

He looked at her and smiled. He rubbed his mouth,

ashamed of the rush of gratitude that tugged his features. Margaret said, "How's Laurence? Did he lose any
of his baby teeth?" But she could see this was the wrong
thing to ask—it was touchy.

"How's your job at the prison?" he asked her.

"It's good. I had to get bonded, can you imagine?"

"They didn't find your record?"

"My record? That was a juvie record. Besides, they
bond anybody unless you're an active criminal."

"I wonder what they did with our JV records?" Cam
said.

"Oh, in the shredder, I guess. It was ordinary teenage
shit."

"We pinched your typical four-door and totaled it
graciously."

"Please," she said.

"Remember the half-wit cop writing the report? He
says, 'Any identifying marks?' " Cam looked at her to
see if she recalled.

Margaret said, "You were all crashed up, twenty
stitches, and the guy asks you, 'Any scars?' "

"Just a birthmark on my ass shaped like Italy."

"That little boot," Margaret said.

"He takes another look, 'Kid, you've got scars now.' "

"Finally, he noticed," Margaret said.

"They're stupid. Cops and postal workers, equally
vacant," Cam said.

"What does it take to sort some postcards into a sack?"
Margaret said.

"Two mailmen. Two mailmen and what? I don't know
that one. What's the punch line?"

Margaret laughed. "I wasn't telling a joke! That was just a rhetorical question."

"Shit."

She pressed her hand against her teeth and tried to keep her lips from tingling. She didn't want to laugh at the wrong times with Cam. Cam liked to bring up these episodes when they were in trouble together. They had reached a certain level of intimacy, standing shoulder to shoulder before the family court, and they might never again achieve that sense of partnership.

They drove over to the Bringhurst Apartments, where Cam managed the units for Town and Country Realty. Cam told her he had to clean the pool and add some chemicals to the water. He was stalling. That was fine with her, she didn't want to rush home to her parents.

"Do you have everything you need in your apartment?" she asked him.

"It's not even an apartment. It's the office. It's got a Castro, I do fine."

"That's ridiculous, you need a real place," she told him.

"It's fine," he told her.

"You don't have a stove to make yourself some eggs?"

"Look, drop it," he said, "okay?"

She was happy to get out of the car and walk along the edge of the pool with Cam. He dipped a large square net into the water and skimmed some poplar leaves. No one was swimming in the water or sunbathing in the lounge chairs, and they continued their talk. Cam told her Darcy wanted custody of Laurence, but he wanted to keep his son.

"I didn't have any of this trouble with Phil. It was uncontested. Celeste gets to visit the robot, she's with the robot now," Margaret said.

"You're lucky, I wish I had it so easy. They don't give the kids to the men."

"It's changing."

"Wait, you're forgetting. I screwed up. Her lawyer says I've got an incapacity. An incapacity. Is that something you would say about me?" He jerked the white net through the water trying to get a drifting rubber loop, a hair tie.

"If he means that time in the apartment, well, that's a long time ago. You were just making a statement, a dramatic gesture, it wasn't as if—"

"Look, it was nuts. Holding a gun to my head, saying I was going to pull the trigger? Shit, I'd say that was a little more than a dramatic gesture. I didn't think then I was going to live to this day to worry about it."

"So that's Darcy's idea of evidence? A moment's instability? She thinks that's going to wrap things up? An ancient suicide threat years before Laurence was even born?" Margaret said.

"God, will you not use that word! I was just trying to get my point across," he told her.

"I know, I know," she told him.

"My lawyer says it's impossible for me to get more than joint custody."

"Could you live with that?"

"Are you serious? If I don't get physical possession

that means Darcy can go anywhere with Laurence. Florida! She talks about going to Fort Lauderdale, can you imagine? She went there on a vacation during spring break in high school, almost fifteen years ago, and she thinks it's like heaven. I would have to chase after her to see Laurence. It's a tactic. Some women move around until the fathers give up."

"She's bluffing. She won't move out of town. Get another lawyer." Margaret picked up a poplar leaf from the tiled gutter. She didn't know what to tell him.

Cam said, "I don't mind cleaning the pool. We could hire someone else to do it, there's lots of pool-maintenance companies, but it saves them money and it calms me to come here. It clears my head," he told her.

"Let me try it," she said. She dragged the net through the water. The net was heavy, awkward, even when she collected nothing. "Sometimes I wash the dishes twice just to have some time to think, or I iron something, you know, *ironing my thoughts*," she told Cam. She pressed Tracy's handkerchiefs. She liked the heat radiating upward, the fibers scented arid, lemony, near scorching.

Margaret said, "You waited too long to break things off. You were an optimist or a masochist, which?"

"Whatever you want."

She was sorry to see her brother in trouble. She liked to think of him still single, riding his motorcycles and bringing his friends to the house. She always moped around and tried to sit with them for a few minutes before she was shoved out of the den. She was banished and they took control of the big Zenith stereo console, a polished wedge-shaped piece of furniture with a hinged lid housing a springy turntable. The boys came with a new forty-five still in its paper sleeve, and sometimes she was invited to listen before she was told to leave them alone. The memory was very old, she realized, the records were proof—a Buddy Holly tune, brand-new, with a skip in it. Her brother and his friends discussed the bubble in the record as if it were the end of the world, but Margaret made them play it through anyway. It sounded absurd; Holly's ordinary hiccoughing style was increased, exaggerated by an imperfection in the recording. She was included in their rounds of laughter and Margaret returned to the room with her own records. "My Baby Must Be a Magician" by the Marvelettes, but Cam's friends didn't like these black singers, and she wasn't allowed to play them.

When he was alone, Cam invited her into the den to play her records for him. Margaret liked what was called the Philadelphia Wall of Sound. She lip-synced to Ronnie Spector records, lifting her arms over her head in a shaky backstroke, imitating the way she saw it done on dance shows like "Bandstand" and "Summertime at the Pier." She raised her arm, pointed to the left and right, turned her hip out, and sidestepped forward and back. She liked dancing in front of Cam. He was embarrassed but settled back; he started to smile at her. He looked at her face, looked her right in the eyes and never let his gaze drift over her body. She knew she was testing him somehow; it was a pleasant sensation. She liked her momentary height over him, her control. They understood it, the exchange. When it became too great, Margaret stopped dancing, stopped the record, and turned around. She closed the lid of the Zenith and sat down on it to face him.

II

Cam finished high school when he was just sixteen. Margaret had two years more. Cam spent half a year skulking around. After wrecking a car, he went to Fort Dix with a letter from family court explaining his young age and his need for productive rehabilitation through his participation in war games and three-day marches. From Fort Dix he was sent to Korea. The army was sweeping up after Korea while the next war in Asia was just starting. Already, the topographers were drawing up some preliminary blueprints of the Vietnamese jungles. Cam had a rare blood type, AB Negative, and this mix, according to the army physicians, was a hematological find. Part of his routine was to give pints for operations and emergencies in the refugee camps. The army was supposed to feed him some extra beef, but Elizabeth sent over some desiccated liver and tins of chocolate kisses to make up for the foul-tasting supplement.

Margaret wrote to him using the blue Crane stationery, and he sent her postcards that showed near-naked Oriental girls or a city's narrow streets crowded with surreys and bicycles. Margaret imagined Cam in a rich landscape with bamboo thickets and white egrets, but he wrote and told her it was wet and freezing cold. She wrote to Cam, and his cards came back sometimes three at a time. The cards were delayed in the government mail pouch, her father would tell her. "No soldier has time to write three cards in one day." Margaret didn't know whether her father seemed uncertain of Cam's commitment to the service or if he was jealous of Cam's commitment to her. She shrugged. She excused her father, figuring that his mistrust of people was a trait that developed when he was orphaned at the age of five. At that age, someone's trust is like a custard; it either firms up in its proper mold, it sets, or it turns out thin and hard to predict.

Cam sent her a jewelry box. The cardboard package showed Oriental lettering; it must have said *Fragile* in that strange ladder of signs. The jewelry box was glossy with horses galloping over the lid. The horses floated over the landscape of black enamel, legs extended, eyes white, nostrils flared open like lotus petals.

After she received the jewelry box, Margaret wrote to Cam and asked him what it was like to give blood all the time, to give it to the Koreans. She told him she knew that he didn't mind not giving it to white people, but did it make him tired? Was he eating the desiccated liver, she asked him, because it looked disgusting.

He wrote back and told her that he put the liver in gelatin capsules and swallowed it that way, but he didn't do it often. She should tell Elizabeth not to send any more. He said he was sick for the last week with fever sores all over his lips because they weren't waiting enough time before taking more of his blood, and he was still doing the regular work there without any more rest than the others. He was getting pretty sick of being a volunteer donor.

She wrote back and told him to put his foot down. She said she hated getting fever blisters; they looked like leprosy. Cam told her that all the grunts had fever blisters, rashes, funguses, anything that takes hold of the flesh overnight after drilling all day or working too hard. It was better to be in Korea giving a pint now and then than to be leaking it yourself somewhere in a war. He was satisfied to be where he was, and he wasn't about to complain over his fever sores or his collapsed vein. They had been using the same vein until it got too bruised; now they were sticking him somewhere else. At least his arm wasn't sore from junk; some of the fellows were developing addictions, but he wasn't. He told her that some troops were sent to Vietnam to retrieve equipment for the French and two men were killed. Margaret wondered when the army would decide that Cam's blood was more useful circulating in his own veins, circling like a target.

It turned out otherwise. Cam contracted hepatitis. After two weeks in an infirmary in Manila, he was discharged with honors. He served eighteen months and was freed. They didn't wait for him to get better and he came back to Wilmington looking yellow as butterscotch. He landed at Dover, Delaware, where they often send U.S. casualties. The place was empty. Cam told Margaret if he was lucky only once in his life, this was it.

Cam slept for two days because of jet lag and because his condition left him weak. Margaret put a pitcher of ice water beside his bed in case he woke up and was thirsty. It was the old blue pitcher, its shiny glaze crackled with dark veins. She set the ice water down and stared at the pitcher as Cam slept; its round shape mimicked an eight ball. She stared at the pitcher until it started to sweat.

Elizabeth didn't give Cam more than a couple of weeks before starting a family discussion about his working at Rice Industrial Supply. Cam wasn't interested. "Think of the benefits," Elizabeth said. "You can be a partner one day, then who knows, when Richard retires, you can be king!"

"King of material-handling equipment? King of the double nylon fan belts, of planetary winches? King of worm-drive hose clamps—"

"Why won't you work with your father?" Elizabeth asked him.

"I would, I would work for *my* father," he said. "Tell me, what was his line? Modeling? Do I have the profile for that? Or what was it, Prince Valiant Escorts? An escort service of some kind, if I recall, for women of all shapes and sizes. Isn't that right?"

Elizabeth touched her hair. She plucked an auburn wave and let it bounce to her cheek again. She lifted her necklace, running her thumb under the chain. She tugged the amethyst left and right, then let the pendant fall against her blouse. She walked out of the room.

Cam refused to work in the family company and moved out of the house into an apartment. Margaret helped him arrange his things in boxes; she took two thick towels and the pin-striped sheets from the closet and stuffed them in his duffel. There was an ID tag on the duffel that said *Cameron Goddard* instead of Cameron Rice.

"You really did this, you changed your name?"

"I didn't change it, that *is* my real name."

"I know. But you never even knew your father, you never even met the guy."

"I don't have to meet him. It's just a matter of genes, lineage."

"What have genes got to do with it? You can't see genes, you can't feel the difference," she said.

"It's a matter of knowing. Just knowing what you're made of," he said.

"How can you know?"

"I know what I'm not. I'm not half Richard. Half of me is a kind of mystery, but I'm not going to let just anyone claim it. I thought you, Margaret, would get it. You aren't too tight with Elizabeth, are you?"

"Of course I am. I love Elizabeth—" Just because Cam had turned against her father, she wasn't going to dump Elizabeth, her stepmother. Elizabeth was all she knew. Margaret couldn't really remember her own mother, Sandra, whom she saw only a few times at the Granville Sanatorium. She could picture only a final visit there, a scene she wasn't sure was real. Her recollection was perhaps just a story her father had told again and again. There had been so many embellishments, details were often mercurial until the story itself began to bubble with its own yeast.

She was three years old. She wore black patent-leather shoes in which her face was reflected. Her own face, its one off-center dimple, and lips too red from always licking them in winter. The sanatorium was unattractive; everything looked down-to-business. The halls, disinfected with pine detergent, scented the cavernous rooms. It didn't smell clean like the scrub pines on the sand dunes at Lake Michigan; it was pine cleaner masking an odor of rancid cooking oil worked into old, porous linoleum and woodwork.

Margaret's mother was waiting in the solarium where patients received visitors; the room was crowded, everyone coughing. Her mother held a handkerchief in her lap, a small triangle of linen, which she discreetly put against her mouth when she needed to expectorate a red smear of phlegm, then folded it carefully away from sight. Although the nurse warned her, Margaret's mother took her daughter on her lap. Had Margaret perhaps only imagined, then put to memory, the embrace? It was clutching, but it loosened now and then, letting her fidget. Her mother's voice was low, her words like plunks of rain on dust. The woman's intensity made Margaret fearful, and she couldn't sit still. Finally, she wriggled off her mother's lap and stood just out of Sandra's reach. How long did Sandra lean forward, her arms extended, before she sat back in her chair, dabbing her lips with the balled-up hankie?

Her father always told her the same words, "The last time you saw your mother you wouldn't sit still." He followed this by saying, "And there was nothing they could do for her. It wasn't just TB; it was lung cancer." After all, they had expected her to live with just the tuberculosis; the physicians said it was improving. Sandra was at the Granville Sanatorium resting, taking steam, then sunning. She had been sick throughout her pregnancy. Margaret was born early, terribly scrawny. They said she looked like a beef tongue lying in the cradle. They gave her rice formula, then soy, and she responded. But Sandra never improved; she coughed until the cough itself weakened. It sounded small, closed off, then the red drifted up to her lips and she touched the hankie to her mouth.

When Sandra was hospitalized, it was just Margaret and her father. Instead of hiring a nurse, he brought her down to the plant and she played in the cinders outside an office trailer. One of the secretaries watched Margaret from the window as she lotioned her hands to clean off the blue carbon before she started in on another one.

"A little girl needs a mother," her father said to her. "These tragedies shouldn't happen."

"But did she have a will to live?" Margaret wanted to ask him. Whose fault was it if she didn't have a will to live?

"I *do* get it," Margaret said to Cam. "It's kind of a free-for-all, isn't it? I guess it's par for the course that you take your rightful name. Just for the record, I do feel a kind of love for Elizabeth."

"That's your problem," he said.

"Well, I do, and you can't do anything about it. We

had good times. Elizabeth and I used to iron clothes and listen to Pegeen Fitzgerald on talk radio. You know, on WOR? She used to talk about her cats."

"You're getting it mixed up, Margaret. You're remembering your good times with *Pegeen*," Cam said.

Cam signed up to work for a contractor, and on weekends he began riding bikes again, competing. Her bond with Cam seemed strong as ever. Cam didn't like Margaret's clothes. Margaret wore black turtlenecks pulled up to her chin, and she carried a fringed bag that always had a little sheaf of incense sticks and an eyedropper bottle of patchouli oil. She scrawled political slogans on poster board. Her favorite hitchhiking sign said ANYWHERE, WORLD. Cam wore a dirty nail apron and his jeans were straight-legged at a time when everyone's pants ballooned and swirled around the ankles.

He started to win an assortment of glossy Motocross trophies, which he displayed on the back windshield of his truck until they obstructed his rear vision and a policeman gave him a warning citation. He tried to get Margaret to appreciate his bike's conformation, the rise of the handlebars, the elongated globe of the tank, solid chrome with yellow stencils, the rich, throaty tones of the engine. He raced the same Triumph Trophy Trail for years, and she teased him, saying it was his bride. He didn't like a Japanese bike, complaining that the engine sounded like a can of bees. His racing career left him with pipe burns and injuries; he took the reverberations through his feet, ankles, into his knees and hips. Riding the street, he lost a footpad at fifty miles an hour and he put the bike down; the skid burned through his boot and shaved his anklebone against the asphalt.

Cam's most interesting accident happened when he was working on a clutch in the driveway. As he was lying underneath his bike, a metal shaving chipped off from the head of a screw and implanted itself in the iris of his eye. He had to keep from blinking until he reached the hospital. Margaret was fascinated by his willpower. Cam stalked through the house, his face tilted, head angled forward, his posture frozen, rigid like Frankenstein, as he kept his eye with the metal shard, wide open.

One day Margaret came home from the high school for lunch and Cam was there, in the kitchen, with a girl. Margaret noticed the girl's hair was blond like hers. Margaret's hair sifted in loose gold snarls to her shoulders, but the new girl kept hers woven beneath a tortoiseshell clasp like a sensuous puzzle. Cam was kissing her at the kitchen sink, keeping his hand flat against her buttocks. She was wearing a tight tweed skirt, which Margaret saw as secretarial garb, and Cam was squashing the fabric. He didn't stop for Margaret. He pressed his face closer, deeper into the kiss, hiding from his sister. The girl was pinned against the stainless-steel counter, but she still could have waved hello to Margaret. Margaret left the room without any acknowledgment.

Cam married Darcy on Kentucky Derby Day. Darcy

thought she was pregnant, and when it turned out not to be so, the arrangements had already been set in motion. The TV was going at Darcy's house during the reception. All the men gathered to look at the race. Margaret edged in to see the screen. She watched how they broke from the gate, calling out the silks for her brother, who was across the room with his new bride. Margaret kept looking over her shoulder at Cam to tell him who was moving up, who got bumped, which horses broke down and missed their opportunities. He looked back at her, frowning, as if telling her to stop acting so stupid. Darcy stared at Margaret without blinking, enforcing Cam, who, without her warnings, might have given in to his sister. Margaret felt betrayed, unhappy in her sudden estrangement. She turned back to the race but the horses were finished, the jockeys lifted in their saddles, and the men around her became officious as they divided up the kitty.

Perhaps it was coincidence or a queer snag of fate, but Margaret was at the horse races at Delaware Park, to watch Kelso's last race, the day Cam threatened to shoot himself. The sky was arid and glassy as if there were a great magnifying hoop held over the Earth. The sun intensified, taking clear aim at them. Elizabeth was complaining even before they parked the car. She would perish unless they could go up into the clubhouse restaurant. She quieted down once she was seated in the stands with a collapsible aluminum drinking cup as Richard poured gin from a flask. Margaret bought a *Baltimore Sun* from a machine and sat making hats for her parents and one for herself. She could make paper hats or paper boats.

Elizabeth refused to try hers. "I won't wear it," she said. "It's silly and it will ink my hair."

She was right to be cautious. Her hair was so porous from color treatments, its hollow red strands would have soaked up the print. The sun wobbled overhead, its heat radiating in parallel lines that jelled over the horizon, wavy, until it looked as if the field were tearing up in places.

After the fifth race, before Kelso made his farewell appearance, her father's name was announced over the loudspeaker. He was called to the offices and put on the telephone. It was Father Cullen, Elizabeth's priest. Cam was in his apartment with a gun. Darcy had told him she was leaving and he countered this news by pointing a gun to his head and releasing the safety. For eight hours after, Richard, the priest, and several others took turns sitting beside Cam on the sofa, but he never pulled the gun away from his temple except to rotate its chamber once or twice, begging for Darcy. She wouldn't appear. At last, when she did come forth, it was at the request of her own parents. They might have preferred to leave it up to Cam, but they told Darcy, if anything happened, it was a mark on the family. Darcy told Cam she'd stay with him a while longer and just see.

After the suicide threat, Cam sometimes came over to the house. He must have been lonely in his own place, but he never again let on he was at a low point. He picked up a screwdriver from the kitchen drawer and tightened the metal plates over the wall switches, or he went outside and lifted the heavy whitewashed stones along the driveway and set them back straight.

He began to take Margaret out to eat.

"She's not even cooking?" Margaret asked him.

"Poison."

"Are you kidding me?"

"I can't sit across from her. She gives me these poison looks. Besides, it's always macaroni and cheese from the freezer."

"I like that stuff," Margaret said.

Cam told her, "Do you want to go over there and eat macaroni? Go over there right now."

She didn't want to side with Darcy. "I just said, I like macaroni sometimes. I don't want it now."

As his marriage deteriorated, Cam tried to get Darcy involved in some recreational activities. She never learned to balance on the scooter he bought for her, so he purchased a speedboat and rented a space at a marina in Ocean City. One time Cam invited Margaret to go out in the boat with Darcy. Margaret wanted to see exactly what was happening with the two of them and she agreed to come along. Darcy sat in the back, stretched out on the padded boat cushions at the stern. She kept looking up at the sun from under the little awning of her hand as she dotted herself with Sea and Ski, smoothing the cream over her tight belly, over the ledge of her hip, dodging the taut nylon triangle and continuing down her legs. Cam watched Darcy stroke her legs, a few brief swipes. When she noticed him watching, she slowly fingered the instep of her foot with a last drop of lotion. Darcy wasn't talking. Margaret sat in a swivel chair next to Cam, who stood at the helm, his hand on the throttle.

The boat was very fast; its bow rose slightly, then

leveled as they accelerated over the water. The hull
knocked against the troughs until they sailed too fast to
feel the dips and gullies of the waves. At top speed, the
surf became a solid, aggressive surface. They criss-
crossed and slammed through their own wakes. The
sun fell upon her shoulders; it touched her scalp where
her hair was parted. Because of the heat, they anchored
for a swim in the deep water, and still the sun reached
them. She stayed beneath the surface and looked up.
The green notches of current created a wall of glass
blocks, mortared with foam. She pulled her brother
underwater. She gestured toward the surface—did he
see this strange roof? It was beautiful, wasn't it? He
misunderstood her, grabbed her wrist, and pulled her
up. He climbed back into the boat and turned to help
her.

"Can't we stay longer?" she asked him. She swam a
few feet away from the boat and started treading water.

"Come on," Cam said. "It's time to go. Why do you
give me this shit, Margaret? Why are you always being
contrary? Always making a contrast?"

Why was it *she* who was making a contrast? Wasn't it
Darcy? Cam looked back and forth between the two
schemers. He wasn't in the mood for it. Margaret
climbed back into the boat; she stood there dripping.
Darcy was wrapped in a terry robe; the broad brim of
a straw hat fluttered under her hand. Her silence was
razor-y.

"We're all getting too much sun," Cam said.

"We're having too much *fun*?" Margaret said. Yet,
Cam was right. Her skin had burned, and after swim-

ming she felt exhausted, dizzy. She sat down near Darcy. The small wedge of cushion wasn't enough.

That night, in her bed, she could still feel the movement of the boat. She felt the waves slap the hull and send her back. It was a biological phenomenon having to do with the inner ear, common after sailing small craft in choppy water, but she couldn't sleep upon those uneven swells. She thought of Darcy, who had not spoken all afternoon. Was she lying beside her brother, Cam, right now, in the same sickening echo of the sea?

Margaret never advised Cam about Darcy; she never offered sympathy because sympathy infuriated Cam. She listened, letting her eyebrows rise up and down, and this alone, her face shifting through several stages of comprehension, seemed to comfort him. Then, when Margaret became serious about a man, five years her senior, who ran a marijuana trading post, Cam couldn't keep out of it. He forced her to accompany him to the Penny Hill Police Station. She was impatient with his interference, since she was beginning to see for herself that something was funny. The drug trafficking didn't alarm her, but she was disturbed when her boyfriend started calling his dick Winston. Her boyfriend had read a book somewhere, perhaps long before his fancy for her, which discussed how men should go about introducing the phallus to virgins. The book said that sometimes it was comforting to the young initiate if the man gave a name to the penis, a tender nickname of some kind. The names suggested in the book were Poky, Slim, Duke, and other Western cattle-punching tags. Her boyfriend named his cock Winston, sometimes reciting the cigarette slogan, "Winston tastes good like a . . . ," inserting the other word. Of course, she laughed. The book said laughter was good, but hysterical laughter was to be avoided; it only caused the hymen to clench. She started to realize that he must have been calling his penis Winston for years before she met him.

She was getting the picture. Cam didn't have to butt in. They stood at a desk in a private office at the precinct station where an officer arranged a sheaf of documents. The officer told her that these papers were preliminary reports concerning her friend.

"Where should we begin?" The policeman smiled.

She didn't say anything.

"Honey, it's going to happen soon. We don't want you involved."

Cam said, "Be practical, Margaret."

Practical. Nothing to do with desire and longing is practical. So, her boyfriend was a selfish jerk on his way to the slammer, but what could she do about it? She tried to imagine someone else, other pet names. She couldn't see anyone but Cam, who stood to one side, his hands in his back pockets. He was pissing her off. He stood on the wrong side of the desk, abreast of the policeman. He was letting the policeman assume his authority, but he wasn't giving up his hold on Margaret. She looked at him; his full mouth looked unnaturally blank as he tried to remain neutral. He should know. It's hard enough without having to deal with the cops.

"Look," she said, "I don't know what you're talking about."

When they left the police station, she told Cam, "It's

my business what I do. Besides, this guy's not the last person I fuck. I'm going to fuck a thousand more, and you better keep your nose out of it."

"Just use your common sense," Cam said. He didn't seem to believe she was going to fuck all those people, and this made her angry.

She shadowed him all the way to the car and waited by the passenger door. He stood across from her, smiling.

"Oh shut up and let me in the car," she told him. A cruiser pulled out onto the street. Its siren and light pulsed once, hesitated, and started up for real.

"They're probably going to get your boyfriend right now," Cam said, as he opened the car door and she slouched down in the seat beside him.

"I'm not destroyed," she said. "I'll live. I'll be living the good life while you go around snitching. You should be on the payroll. They take good care of their own in the golden years."

Cam roared out of the parking lot and tagged up with the cruiser at the light. "Everyone's going to the party," he said.

"I doubt it. These fellows are heading out for some doughnuts."

Cam smiled at her. "Are you saying you're hungry? Do you want to get a half dozen, Margaret?"

She wasn't going to accept sweets from him. "Maybe Darcy wants some doughnuts," she said.

III

Margaret watched Cam shake a box of chlorine crystals into the pool, tapping the bottom of the box so it wouldn't come too fast. "This stuff will turn your hair green, but the kids are always pissing in the water."

"Don't tell me you never did when you were a kid?"

"Look, I've seen everything in Asia. Piss in a swimming pool is a minor infraction," he said. He didn't always mention his time in the service. He felt funny about his luck. He could have seen action in Vietnam at any time, but he was sent home. He was too "yellow." Literally. They laughed about this.

Again, he asked Margaret how she handled her divorce. Wasn't there any question about custody of Celeste? She told him that she requested physical possession of Celeste and her request wasn't challenged.

"Maybe because Phil trusted you would share her," Cam said.

"I don't share her! I permit her to *visit* him, I kind of relinquish her, temporarily. It's very separate. It's not something we share, it never was."

This kind of talk wasn't helping Cam.

He said, "Phil gets her on Christmas, right?"

"Yeah, I give in. His family has this really big, traditional Christmas with all the uncles and aunts; it's disgustingly merry. It's better than what I can do."

"You never have her for Christmas?"

"Come to think of it, it was Christmas when I decided to jump ship."

"Holidays do that," Cam said. "Murders, marriage proposals, desertions—all those sudden decisions people make when the world is busy following some kind of mindless ritual," Cam said.

"That's right," she said, smiling at Cam. Margaret liked seeing Cam's harder side.

The last weeks she spent with her husband were right before the New Year. She agreed to visit his big family, thinking in secret that she would never have to do it again. Her in-laws had always treated her with a distilled interest; they showed polite tolerance, but it was always a bit too formal. When Margaret stayed with them, she felt as if she were visiting an embassy of a country she couldn't imagine existed outside its official residence and gardens.

She couldn't bear the festivities and she left her seat beside the fireplace to avoid having to sit for long periods beside her husband. She walked into the kitchen. On the Formica counter, stationed near the breadbox, someone had set a mouse trap with a square of cheese placed carefully at center. Attached to the metal bar was a taut wire leading to a big Nikon fastened to a tripod. The shiny components reflected the twinkle lights from the next room. Margaret looked at the trap, the tripod, the cheese.

She took a wooden spoon from a drawer and tripped the wire. The bar snapped through the soft cheese, the flash went off, the shutter clicked, all in the same breath. The engineering of it seemed impressive. She knew that her husband would come in and reset it and they would get their photograph no matter how she might try to interfere.

Later that afternoon, when she was upstairs with her husband, dressing for dinner, she found a louse. It was gripping the lace edge of her panties and she had trouble picking it off.

She told Cam, "My last holiday with Phil and he gives me crabs."

"There's a first time for everyone," Cam said.

She remembered feeling very calm, the way someone relaxes on a jetliner that's ascended and leveled off at a certain height in its flight pattern. She liked the sensation, as if everything were holding still while she alone plunged forward. "I told Phil to get something to kill the bugs or I wouldn't come down to dinner. He drove off and came back with two bottles. One for me. One for him. He admitted that he might be a source of the problem."

"Nice," Cam said.

"Oh, well. At that stage blame was unimportant. It's wasteful to feel blame. It steals your power. You should remember that yourself.

"Jesus, I could smell the roast beef and Yorkshire pudding while I lathered with that noxious gel. It was like something used to clean carburetors," she told Cam.

Cam said, "Yes, I've once or twice had the pleasure."

"You too?"

Cam was smiling. "So, that was that? Parasites that broke the camel's back?"

"I told Phil I would always remember our last Christmas. Christmas lice." In fact, she had started to forget everything, minute by minute. She took her razor and shaved the small, dark triangle. Her skin was stinging from the harsh soap, but she no longer thought of her marriage, its first young sentiment. She hurled open the glass door and adjusted the showerhead to a tight needle spray.

5

C am finished with the net, and he put it away in a shed outside the pool's enclosure. They got back in the car. The road into the old neighborhood was a sun-baked straight-away that ran a mile alongside the B & O railroad and parallel to the old Willie Du Pont estate. At the end of the straightaway the road plunged down a steep hill into the woods. Her stepmother, Elizabeth, had al-ways played a game when driving along this stretch. She put the car in neutral, turned the motor off, and let it coast.

Everything was quiet but for a slight tearing noise of tires over the asphalt. They coasted down the steep hill, their bodies hunched to increase forward propulsion. The little car bolted, sank, reeled around the curve at its greatest velocity. Then, almost immediately, as if at the sight of home, it slowed, dropped out of the race, died. They were left there, thirty feet from the driveway. They had to start the ignition. It was cruel that Elizabeth always put them through this test. Then Margaret saw that Elizabeth, too, was agitated; she had been exercising faith, and it never met the standard.

Cam drove her down that same stretch, past the old estate. Something was different. There was a tangle of yellow construction vehicles moving back and forth, backhoes and other earth-moving equipment. Cam told her, "They're putting an industrial park here."

"An industrial park? You're kidding."

"Why are you taking it so personally? You said you never want to live here again, anyway."

She shrugged. The neighborhood still looked good, the trees heavier, the lawns obscured by large blankets of ivy and low juniper. The landscaping had matured, reaching full cycle; some homes showed replanting. They turned into the driveway; the old yucca at the entrance was giant, like a colossal sea urchin, an explosion of sharp tongues. "That's my favorite," she told Cam.

"That figures," he said.

They pulled in behind Elizabeth's car. Margaret saw the bumper stickers, which always annoyed her. She went into the house first, ahead of Cam, to find Elizabeth. "I'm here," she called out as she went through the sun porch; its cork floor gleamed with little blue streaks flickering from the full-length windows. In the dining room she stopped to look at a bowl of fresh flowers, newly arranged at the center of the table.

Elizabeth liked to cut the stems and float the flowers in ice water, letting each rootless bloom drift on the surface of its immediate perfection. The flowers' colors were enhanced by the shock of decapitation. The effect was thrilling, although the flowers might not last as long this way. Margaret called through the house for her stepmother; then she saw a strange sight. A clipping was clothespinned to the chandelier over the dining table—a glossy photograph from a magazine. It was a familiar image and caption: BABY JOE OR BABY DOE? The photograph showed a twelve-week embryo, eyes hooded and bulging, little hands, its fingers webbed and stiff like rooster combs.

"Jesus Christ," she said.

Cam came in. "Oh. She's back on her campaign."

"I can't believe this."

"She's always raging about this, since Jane's abortion," Cam said.

"It's not Jane, someone must have told her about *me*." She didn't look at Cam.

"God, is this something to do with you? I think it's just Jane. It's Jane she's always talking about."

"Look, Jane must have told her about me," Margaret said.

"You didn't say anything about this."

"Why should I? I don't even want to think about it.

It was March. I don't have to tell everyone—" Margaret said.

"You told Jane?"

Margaret didn't say anything.

Cam said, "This happened last spring? With Tracy?"

"Of course it was Tracy, what do you think? I can't believe this shit. On the fucking chandelier—"

"Okay, just be calm. You don't have to put up with this. Don't give her a reaction."

Don't have a reaction? Margaret remembered Newton's Third Law in Physics: "For every action there's an equal reaction." A stationary object is struck and incorporates the offensive motion, even if it results in its own destruction. "The Conservation of Momentum." In its neutrality, its passivity, it shatters, thus it *moves*. Sometimes, under a barrage of gunfire, a person is lifted off the ground, suspended, flung.

"I was sort of looking forward to seeing Elizabeth, really." Margaret cleared her throat. She worried she was becoming tearful.

"Come on, it's okay," Cam told her. "It's just the same horseshit. She gets the bumper stickers at the church bazaar."

"What's that smell? God, she's making ratatouille. She knows I love it." The air was rich with the fragrance of olive oil and eggplant. And rising through that heavy scent, Margaret could detect a familiar breath of Estée Lauder. "She's making that dish for me," she told Cam. "Christ. These mixed messages."

"Just because she's stewing some eggplant, don't go soft on her."

They heard Elizabeth coming down the hall; the light click of her pumps on the terrazzo tiles was unmistakable.

"Have you finally decided to arrive?" Elizabeth called. She appeared in the archway between the living room and the dining room. She stood there, centered, her hair gleaming in great cinnabar waves. "Margaret," she said. "I was certain you stayed on the train and went to Florida."

"I'm sorry, we've been playing hooky. Cam had to clean the pool at the apartments."

"Did you see the industrial park?" Elizabeth asked her.

"It's terrible," Margaret said.

"I hear the bulldozers all day; they make a constant *beep, beep, beep* when they back up. It's torture."

"Those are warnings. Saves lives," Cam said.

"Oh really? Well, it saves some lives and ruins others," Elizabeth said.

"Is that ratatouille?" Margaret said.

"Fresh eggplants. You should see them, tiny as thumbs."

"Thumbs struck by hammers," Cam said.

Elizabeth said, "He's in one of his moods." Margaret nodded.

They stood around the big mahogany table. The magazine scrap twirled slowly in the air, its jellied skull, its rooster-comb hands extended in a frozen greeting.

II

Cam said he had to be back at the Bringhurst Apartments to show a two-bedroom at four o'clock. He would get Laurence from Darcy and come back for dinner. Margaret walked him to his car.

"Sorry about that embryo," Cam said.

"I used to hang things from the ceiling for Celeste, rabbits and stars; the stars absorbed the daylight and glowed in the dark."

"Sure, I know."

"I took those things down when I read a baby was strangled in his own mobile."

"How often can that happen?"

"It happens."

Cam backed his car out of the driveway, and then he was gone behind the hemlocks.

Margaret went back into the house to get freshened up, and she saw that her old bedroom had been claimed by her father. His big desk looked wild; every drawer was fully extended until she believed the whole piece would topple if not for a heavy canister of pennies he kept on a top ledge. On the floor, his ledgers and tomes were stacked in waist-high, tilting towers. She lifted a tall spindle, leafy with receipts, and found an old storybook. Its spine was cracked and the book fell open in the middle. Once, she had tried to read a favorite passage to Cam, but he wasn't impressed. He was pitching a sock into the air and catching it on his pointer finger. He was trying to distract her when she was feeling bookish. Then, some hormonal message caused the capillaries in her nostril to rupture. A sudden, red spill forced Cam to look down at the page. He was mesmerized by the frothy circle. "Get me a Kleenex!" she yelled, and she slapped the book shut. When she turned back to that page, there it was, a winged blot.

Margaret went down the hall to find her stepmother. She asked about her father. "I thought he was supposed to be retired?"

"He's down there straightening out something for the new owners. They have to learn the inventory."

"That's not easy, let me see—reversible ratchets, speeder handles, dock bumpers, augers, portable sandblasting kits, grease guns, exit signs." Margaret enjoyed reciting that litany.

"You can remember all of that?" Elizabeth said.

"Of course I do. I helped with the spot inventories."

Elizabeth set out the glasses and lifted the heavy double-sized bottle of scotch. Perhaps she found Margaret's gift of memory intrusive. "What about Celeste?" Elizabeth said.

"Phil is bringing her here on Sunday, and we'll take the train back."

"Back to your friend Tracy?"

"Of course," Margaret said.

"When will I see Celeste?" Elizabeth said.

"Don't worry, you'll see her," Margaret said. "She's taller. She's grown since—"

"I'm certain she's a perfect young lady now," Elizabeth said.

"She's just eight, you know, don't expect miracles,"

Margaret said. "I see a change coming, but it hasn't happened yet."

Margaret helped Elizabeth unfold the big padded mats that protected the dining room table. Then she put the linen cloth down and tugged the hem at each end until it was even. Margaret avoided knocking into the glossy magazine scrap as she smoothed the cloth.

At five o'clock Margaret started watching the clock. The clock's white face was rubbed silver from years of friction. The hands were bent and could never be corrected no matter how often they tried it. Margaret said it wasn't the hands that were crooked, it was the *face*, the face of the clock was warped.

Cam arrived with Laurence. Cam's eyes looked different, veiled. He must have had a scene with Darcy. Margaret watched to see if her nephew saw the picture on the chandelier, but he was waist-high and didn't seem to notice. Laurence had his father's looks, the chin's deep shaded hollow. She pushed the palm of her hand over the top of his head, combing his hair through her fingers. The boy liked her attention and kept his fists in his pockets as she tugged his cowlick left and right, trying to get it flat. "It's hopeless," she told him.

"No, try it," he said. "Please try more."

Margaret curled her index finger and lifted his chin with her knuckle. "That's it for now," she told him.

She went over to the sink, and she made Laurence a grenadine and seltzer so he could be part of the group, but he didn't like the flavor.

"Well, it's *pretty*, isn't it?" Elizabeth scolded the little boy.

When her father walked into the room, Margaret embraced him. She never knew what to say except to mention how green the place looked. She praised the shrubs, the ivy, the old Atlas cedar woven through the power lines. "Is that giant yucca still mine?" she asked him. He liked her teasing.

"It's yours," Richard told her.

They took their drinks out onto the flagstone terrace, and Margaret slipped out of her shoes to feel the warm, uneven slate. She lifted her glass and toasted Richard. "To your premature golden years."

"That's right. I'm through with industrial supply. The End. I would have stayed with U.S. Steel until they forced me out. You know, all the way—until I got rickety. That's a different story. I used to *make* steel, not *sell* it."

Richard missed the steel industry, which he had left, unwillingly, in order to move out of town to marry Elizabeth. He never wanted to go into selling. Throughout her childhood, Margaret listened to his complex step-by-step narrations about open-hearths melting practices. She was the only student in her grammar school who knew that steel wasn't mined. It was man-made. She learned both the matter-of-fact and the gothic thrill of metallurgy. She understood semi-killed steel and dead-killed steel. Richard told her about slag viscosity, about ingot molds and the Theory of Solidification. He used to get her to see the difference between big-end-down versus inverted-hot-top molds. She knew about the open-hearth furnace, its stacks, flues, and checkers.

"It was dangerous work," Richard said, "I might not be here today—"

Elizabeth groaned. "Don't start. Not the one about rescuing Mr. Trojanowski."

"I like that story," Margaret said.

"Trojanowski was snagged on a ladder just as a ladle was ready to pour," Richard said. "Now, I have to figure—I can get to him by going up to the second tier and coming down the other side, but the shortest route to get to Trojanowski is to run beneath the ladle of molten steel. I can run right over there, but the nozzle is ready to tip. There's Trojanowski. Twenty feet as the crow flies. What am I deciding? In a second it's going to tip." Richard was grinning at Margaret.

Margaret knew the story; she liked its drama.

Elizabeth said, "It's stupid to run beneath molten steel." Elizabeth fidgeted, scratched her elbows, touched her hair all over. Richard often ruined her cocktail hour in this manner. Cam didn't like it either.

"So, you saved the Polish guy," Cam said.

"For the time being," Richard said. "He had a bad accident the next year."

"See?" Elizabeth said. "It was pointless to go out of your way."

"It's a good story," Margaret said. She didn't want Elizabeth to shush him, and she said to her father, "So, tell me again—you can condition an ingot mold with an aluminum wash, or in a tar tank, then there's graphite—"

"Graphite has a poor splash repulsion," Richard said.

"Oh, I forgot. Well, there's molasses, it covers well but you say that creates a lot of burnt carbon. Carbon causes scabs and blisters."

"That's correct. And you don't want to use brine; brine makes fumes; the men can't stand it and it damages the electric wiring on the cranes—"

Elizabeth said, "Will you both please stop it!"

Richard gave Margaret a much too technical explanation just so she would be inclined to keep asking. He would have gone on as long as she wanted.

Cam said he might go down to Ocean City to see a boat that was for sale. Maybe if Margaret came along they could take the ferry over to Cape May to see Jane.

"Do you really need a new boat, son?" Richard said.

"Another Donzi. It's secondhand, but it's a deep-vee Classic with a 350 King Cobra."

Margaret said, "It's a good time to look at boats. Midsummer, prices come down, don't you think? Everyone worries they'll be stuck at the end of the season."

"The divorce," Richard said. "It might seem frivolous at this point in time to purchase a speedboat."

"Life goes on, doesn't it?" Margaret told her father. She turned to Cam. "I loved your old boat."

Cam shifted in his chair: crossed his ankle over one knee, then crossed his legs the other way. He let Margaret defend him, and soon the matter was settled. She would drive with him to see the speedboat and they would visit Jane afterward. Elizabeth went into the house to fire up the Jenn-Air and Richard took Laurence around to the garden to look for cucumbers the right size for the salad. When Margaret was alone with Cam, she asked him, "What happened tonight with Darcy?"

"She didn't want Laurence coming over here."

Margaret dropped her shoulders, rested her elbows on her knees. "Do you have any lovers?" she asked Cam. It was a surprise question. She didn't even understand what made her say it.

"That's not how it happened," Cam told her. "It wasn't a third party."

"No, I wasn't saying that. I just thought it might help you to have someone else. It would help you to see things clearly."

"How can that help? I'd just have another thing to worry about."

"There's no one?" Margaret said.

"A girl at the courthouse. A social worker trying to help me keep Laurence. She's interesting. She has some interesting cases."

"Are you her case?" Margaret was laughing.

"She gives me background on the legal stuff. The lawyer charges too much per hour to do my tutoring."

"I see, this girl is *tutoring* you? A social worker?"

"What's wrong with that?"

"Maybe Darcy is making it hard because she doesn't really want the divorce."

"You're wrong. She wants it. We all want it."

III

Delaware summers are heavy; moisture builds in vapor tiers. At evening, these wet curtains intersect and sink over the lawn. Laurence had wet grass clippings up to his knees, and his bare feet were black from exploring the rich garden. "I'll hose him down," Margaret said, and she pulled Laurence by the elbow. She twisted open the tap and they followed the hose to its end at the driveway. She let the child drink from its rusty nozzle and she liked the scent of its ferrous splash on the hot asphalt. When Laurence was rinsed, she sent him into the kitchen. She was hosing her bare feet when a Diamond cab pulled into the drive; its headlights illuminated the spray as she rotated her ankle. She tried to see who was getting out. It was Tracy.

He stood beside the cab and put a stack of papers on the roof as he paid the driver. He was making good on his promise to canvas the local papers. Tracy couldn't walk down a street without inserting quarters in those corner stands that pull open like oven doors.

She dropped the hose and watched it shudder left and right before it fell. "You're absolutely too early," she said, but she walked up to embrace him. Tracy gripped her and didn't let go even when she wanted to take her weight back on her own legs.

"I took the train after your train," he said.

"You must have," she said.

"Aren't you glad to see me? Bitch?" He was smiling. "Miss Irresistible. Spicedrop. Little Red Hot," he said.

Her eyes were large, shiny with a glycerin of tears. "Sure. I'm glad." She couldn't look at him.

She heard the back door and she turned around. Cam was standing in the darkness of the garage, giving her time to sort it out on her own. And yet, there was something about his slumped posture; it looked too wistful or insulted. She couldn't think of that now. She told Tracy about the picture. "It's like a piece of flypaper. It just dangles from the chandelier."

He studied her face as if it might show him, reveal to him, what her words meant. She often spoke in non sequiturs when she was disturbed, but this time he couldn't decipher it. He looked away from her face.

"Cameron. My man," Tracy said, walking over to her brother, who leaned against the trunk of Elizabeth's Mustang. They shook hands.

Cam said, "Just in time for chow. They're slopping the trough."

"This monkey house needs another monkey," Tracy said.

"Why the hell not?" Cam said.

"Coolsville," Tracy said.

Margaret cringed at their exchange and went inside to explain Tracy's arrival. Her legs were trembling and she leaned back against the GE. She told Elizabeth, "I guess Tracy missed me. He's been working hard. He needed a break." She didn't sound convinced by her explanation.

Her father came in. "Tracy's here for some R&R, is that right?"

Margaret said, "He can have my lambchop."

Her father put another setting on the table. His face looked very still. He was avoiding the little banner on the chandelier.

"Can't we take this down for dinner?" She addressed her father.

"Your mother wants it there. She knows what she's doing," he said.

"I can't believe it. You're going to let her keep this thing here?" She looked at her father.

"It's your mother's desire."

"But it's disgusting. You know it's ridiculous."

"It's not ridiculous. A religious belief is a serious thing," he told her.

Elizabeth walked through. "What's the matter, Margaret, why does it upset *you* so much?"

Margaret stared at the chandelier; its dusty prisms and glass beads refracted the light. She let her eyes lose focus until the rainbow aura swelled, the lamps wobbled. Then a timer went off in the kitchen and she went to get it, letting the buzzer rage until, at last, she clicked it off.

Tracy was seated at one end of the table, Richard across from him at the head. The others had to pass plates up and down while Richard and Tracy could remain kingly. Tracy was effervescent at the slightest sign of tension in a room. He could handle relatives, huffy landlords, employers who have reached a plateau of disbelief and who might be ready to lower the boom. He displayed an elegance of feeling the same way children can; he mastered an innocent inflection despite whatever unseemly dialogue might occur. Margaret was relieved when he took over the dinner conversation. He was talking to Elizabeth, explaining his views on the American shopping mall. He was going to title his article "The Malling of America." There was too much land being gouged, *mauled*. Then, he admitted, he *loved* malls; there couldn't be enough of them as far as he was concerned. This befuddled Elizabeth. Wasn't this a contrast of feeling? she asked him.

Margaret passed a bowl of cucumber salad to her left. The bowl was beautiful, washed-out Canton, and the paper-thin discs of green against the blue dish were soothing. "Oh, what about the eggplant?" she asked Elizabeth. She didn't see it on the table.

"That's for the freezer. I'm freezing that for the winter," Elizabeth said.

"I see," Margaret said. The talk was losing its boundaries.

Tracy was saying, "I write about pop culture. Real pop culture, not the Andy Warhol thing. I mean Mom and Pop Culture. Shopping malls, diners, bowl-o-ramas."

Margaret thought that her father bristled at the mention of Andy Warhol. Margaret used to watch Warhol's group on the old Merv Griffin show. She ate dinner by herself and wheeled the portable TV right up to the kitchen table. Elizabeth would say, "You take such small portions." Margaret would say, "It's nothing against you." Griffin invited drunks and drug addicts from Manhattan: The drunks were always talking about Sardi's, and the young models and rockers were joking about "snow" and "horse." Ultra Violet, Viva, Edie Sedgwick—these women had intrigued her. Gnatty Warhol actors mingled with enigmas like Monty Rock the Third, Selma Diamond, Toti Fields, and Arthur Treacher, who lurched forward in his seat as if suffering horrible cramps. Then, Twiggy sits down, pinching the hem of her miniskirt, and Merv says, "Fashions change. The world is changing."

"So, this is new?" Toti Fields asks. "I've seen everything." She leaned forward and looked straight into the camera. "Nothing comes down the pike that surprises me."

Margaret welcomed the memory. She had loved the way these lost souls gathered and began acting too familiar, like maiden aunts and cousins.

Tracy was interested in going to see the boat with Cam. He asked if they could test-drive it.

"You don't drive a boat, you sail it," Elizabeth said.

"A speedboat. Does it use gas? Does it have a steering wheel?" Tracy asked.

"It doesn't actually have a sail." Margaret sided with Tracy.

"I surrender," Elizabeth said, "but if you're going to see your sister, you can take her one of these." She went over to the sideboard and freed a sheet of paper from under the silver service. She gave it to Margaret. It was a form of some kind.

"What's this?" Margaret said.

"It's an affidavit. We need two signatures from our children. Just to prove we've informed the family. Cam won't do it."

"They want to leave their bodies to science," Cam said.

"When we pass away, we want to give our remains to an institution," her father said.

"Really?"

"One final selfish gesture," Cam told Margaret.

Elizabeth said, "It's the opposite. Even Father Cullen told me it was generous."

"Sure, what does he care? You're already excommunicated. You aren't with the flock. You don't take the sacraments," Cam said.

"Church rules," Elizabeth said, "like City Hall."

Tracy said, "Why don't you just go up there, go up the aisle with the rest and take Communion, regardless?"

Cam stared at Tracy. Then he said, "A proper burial, a monument somewhere. That would be the right thing to do. If they go that donor route, we'll have no way to pay our respects."

Richard began, "Respect is something—"

"You're too cheap to buy plots. What are you pocketing? Four or five thousand?"

"A piece," Tracy said. "The land is one thing. Then, caskets are pricey, it's all that taffeta. If you go with bronze or brushed stainless, it skyrockets. Did you know that in the United States, cemeteries are the third most popular place for joggers? It must be thunderous."

Margaret tried to hush him. Elizabeth and Richard were gracious but annoyed; they forgot that it was Cam who had stung them. Cam was smiling and staring at his plate.

"I'll sign the paper," Margaret said. The last thing

she wanted to imagine was visiting graves. "It's Johns Hopkins?" she asked. She once knew a medical student who told her what a mess they make. Scavenger hunts through cadavers, messages scrawled with a scalpel, even love notes sewn into hearts, a clitoris removed and placed in a jar like an olive.

"It's a very generous thing you're doing," Margaret told Elizabeth. "We'll get Jane to sign the paper and then you'll be all set, okay?"

"Wonderful," Elizabeth said.

"What's the difference?" Margaret said to Cam.

Cam turned in his seat to face her squarely. "Follow this," he said. "The facts are, your mother's dead, my father is on the lam, and now Elizabeth and Richard are off to the bone factory by their own free will. It's a horror show."

"You can't stop it anyway. These papers are just formalities, like RSVPs. We don't need you," Elizabeth said.

Tracy went with Cam to drive Laurence back to Darcy's house. Elizabeth and Richard had a bridge party and Margaret was left alone in the kitchen. She was glad to wash the dishes and she took her time.

She heard a car pull into the driveway, and Cam walked into the kitchen with Tracy. The men were quiet. "What's going on with you?" she asked.

Tracy said, "We've been talking about the Arrow Collar Man."

"Cam's father?"

"We've been discussing the options," Tracy said.

"The options?" she said. "Which options?"

Tracy said, "Cam should look him up. Locate the Arrow Collar. Seek and ye shall find."

Cam went to the liquor cabinet. He unscrewed the top of the Old Crow. "Tracy's right. He's a hundred percent on target."

Tracy liked this. "I'm straight as an arrow. An arrow in pursuit of an arrow; an interesting concept, right, Margaret?"

She was wiping a cast-iron pan with a dish towel. The towel came away smeared black. It was always this way. She cleaned the pan, but its blackness remained, a constant; it thrived. She didn't mind the smudge. These recurring stains were comforting, like a wisp of menstrual blood on her sheet, a scallop of cloudy chlorophyll on the knees of her blue jeans.

Margaret told Cam, "So you've decided to locate your natural father like any stupid asshole on those talk shows?" She felt her hair tingle at the roots, her widow's peak sting. She was breaking new ground. She had always sidestepped the issue.

Cam ground out his cigarette in a saucer that he cupped in the palm of his hand. "Did anyone ever tell you that you have a smart mouth?"

"Look," she told him, "this guy must be a real prize, a total shit to begin with." She shrugged her shoulders and waited to drop them back. Cam towered over her. He was tall. Too big to jump out of a plane when he was on tour in Korea. She always doubted that story. She wanted to ask him, "Were you really too tall to jump from a plane? What has height got to do with falling through the sky?" but he was walking away. He went into the living room. She heard him strike a match but she could not hear it flare. Then he was back.

"Did you ever see these?" He handed her a folder of yellowed clippings. She recognized the illustrations by J. C. Leyendecker, pictures of Cam's father. The man's mouth was clearly Cam's mouth, a tiny, emotional knot at the center of the upper lip above a full amber ridge. His jawline was carved, his chin sharply defined by a dark gully. It was his cleft chin that set off the shirts in the advertisements. Her gaze halted at the starched collar.

"The Arrow Collar ads? I've seen them. They're great."

"I look at these every day. It's like I'm looking at *me*."

"You do look a lot alike," she told him.

"That's not my point. I look at these pictures. It makes me crazy."

Margaret walked past Cam and saw the old clock, its worn numerals. She opened the glass, tapping the ornate minute hand with her fingertip.

"I feel crazy," Cam said, turning to Tracy. Margaret couldn't watch her brother. He was falling apart. She went down the hall and waited in Elizabeth's bathroom. She turned on the faucets so she wouldn't hear the men talking. Margaret twisted her hands beneath the flow, but the water was too silky and quiet. Against the hushing vowel sound of the tap, she heard Tracy's voice. He was painting a picture with broad strokes, outlining a plan for Cam.

"The thing is, we are borne by the mother but without the father," Tracy said.

Cam said nothing.

"In utero, you have no introduction to the father, no heartbeat, no paternal body heat, no placental message or exchange. Nothing for nine months. The father never fits into the *Structure of the Unconscious*. You're alone in a *Maternal Abyss*. Then the day arrives, you're pitched into a Lucite bassinet. If the father doesn't step forward, that's that. Usually, the mother creates a myth: 'Your daddy died in a war.' 'Your daddy is an angel in heaven.' Elizabeth was uncooperative, don't you think? I mean, up until now, what did you have? Some newspaper clippings? These Arrow Collar ads aren't holding up. It's probably acid paper, you know; it's disintegrating even as we stand here yapping."

"Who's yapping? It's you running off at the mouth," Cam said.

"So—listen to me, then. You're in that Maternal Abyss until you do something about it. Don't you see the opportunity here?" Tracy said. "You have your sister in Wilmington, just like you want. She's ready, if you say the word. We'll get in the car, find Lewis, and complete our survey. It's up to you to make the countdown."

"Margaret won't like it."

"We can work on her. There's time, we have a big forty-eight-hour window."

Margaret waited until she heard her brother's car. She looked out to the street and saw the taillights flicker when he caught the speed bump too hard. Then the car was gone. She went into the kitchen, but she didn't find Tracy. The house was too quiet. She turned back to the kitchen sink and dotted the stainless with Comet. The broom closet door creaked lightly, falling open. Tracy stepped out of the dark. Margaret took a breath. "Are you trying to give me a heart attack?"

"You disappoint me, Margaret," Tracy said. "Cam was *reaching out*, and you disappeared."

"Cam didn't want me to see him fall apart like that. Besides, I heard you telling him something crazy. What are you trying to pull off?"

Tracy had his back against a door frame, scratching his shoulders against the molding. "It's a bore, really. Cam's thing. It's always the same note, your basic middle C on the piano: *bong, bong, bong*, but the tune never happens—"

"What are you talking about? Are you talking about music?"

She rinsed the sink and wondered what to do next. The big cast-iron pan showed a ring of rust where she hadn't finished drying it. She told Tracy she was going out to take a walk. He came over and tucked her wrist behind her back. "Me too. I'm taking a walk in Wilmington, with you."

"I want to go by myself," she said.

"You can't go out there alone. It's the old neighborhood."

She twisted against him, trying to escape a streak of pain. "All right," she told him. "You're invited."

On the street, she showed him the houses and told

him the names of the families. "They're all engineers for Du Pont," she said.

"I could write about their chemical compounds, pigments, plastics, whatever it is, just as well as the next fellow."

"Richard was saying that the new thing is stain-release fibers," she said. She was relieved to talk about this. The night had a peculiar density; the surfaces looked furred by the odd moonlight. The shrubs seemed waffled and grotesque, and she wanted to turn around and go back.

They entered a park with a small amphitheater, several old magnolias, and a mammoth apple tree in the middle of the sloping lawn. The tree had an incredible circumference; the branches opened out and turned down at the edges, making a scalloped canopy, like the dark awnings at funeral sites. They stooped low and crawled under the foliage until they could stand erect inside, encircled by the branches. Tracy jumped into the roomy hollow where the tree forked. He pulled Margaret up beside him.

Margaret said, "I ran away from home and hid in this tree. I waited until dark so Elizabeth would worry."

"You were seeking the proper effects even back then? The world was a prop for you."

"What do you mean?"

"You had to utilize these great abstract powers like day and night to call attention to yourself."

"Jesus, did I do that?"

"You and your brother. Sleepwalking through Siberia. Absolutely no self-awareness."

She looked at Tracy; she was unwilling to argue about it.

A white tomcat moved toward them. Its coat looked thick and mirrory in the moonlight, like suds. They watched it walk to the trunk of the tree, tail lifted; then it jumped up to the first gnarl and used its claws to go higher. It kept climbing above them until they could no longer see it.

"It must be his hangout," Tracy said, and he pulled Margaret down from her perch. The ground was damp, littered with tiny green knobs, misshapen fruit that had fallen before ripening. Tracy's body was familiar, its angles, its nervous zones. He held her and then he pushed her off. She looked at the dirt. She saw a white scrap, a piece of paper with someone's gas mileage written on it. The figures were followed by question marks and exclamation points. Tracy stepped up to her again, rubbed the heel of his hand against her eye socket, a slight pressure that made her see dots and flashes. This pleased her. His hand smelled of tree bark and chlorophyll.

She heard the white cat crying, making his inquiries from a great height. "It's gone up too high," Margaret said. "It wants to get down."

Tracy didn't answer. Margaret circled the tree trunk and turned around. She saw the apple branches waving open and snapping closed again. Tracy was gone. She called his name. Nothing. She fingered the papery leaves and found her way outside the dense switches. She couldn't see Tracy anywhere on the big lawn. The giant magnolias had a leathery severity in the night. Without illumination, the colorless ruled, the deep encircled the pale. She walked toward home, stopping once or twice to turn around and shout Tracy's name. She knew he was going to jump out from behind something. It was just a matter of *when* it would happen. She studied the shaggy hemlocks, the long bulwarks of forsythia where Tracy could be crouching. Her tri-octave, full-diaphragmatic scream was what he was after. He wanted her throat to tear with one harsh syllable. He once told her, "All fear is self-inflicted. We carry it around, concealed on our persons, like a little shiv. We use it against ourselves. We have only ourselves to blame."

Panic loosened her gait and she walked down the street in a loose zigzag like a drunken woman. Then she broke into a run. There he was, standing in the center of the black asphalt. Tracy was holding the tomcat in the crook of his arm, but the animal's hind legs were pumping, its ears were flattened back. She stumbled into her lover and lost her ability to stand up. She felt her words form and stray from her lips; she was whimpering. Even as the cat struggled, she rested her face against its white fur. She heard something—a taut snarl evolving from its gut and surfacing at full volume, as if one central cry escaped from all three of them.

6

They were sitting three abreast in the front seat of the car. It was a first-edition powder-blue Plymouth Duster. "This is a magazine specimen. It's mint," Cam was telling Tracy. Cam had bought the car years ago for Darcy's birthday. It was the maiden Duster 340, the high-performance model. He was telling them everything. "A two-door—it's more aerodynamic. It's a V8 with four-barrel carburetion, high-flow cylinder heads." He brushed his hand around the three-spoked steering wheel, the chrome horn ring, thin as a wrist bangle. "Today it's horn *pads*; they don't make chrome horn rings like this anymore," Cam said.

"That's probably true." Tracy looked pretty tickled. Margaret worried that Tracy might start to laugh or make remarks. Cam's enthusiasm could have a peculiar effect on Tracy.

"Mags with chrome nuts. Wire wheel covers, fourteen-inchers. Check them out when we stop."

"Oh, sure," Margaret said.

Cam said, "No kidding, Margaret, this Duster is more than just a souped-up Valiant; it's a little hot. Don't you think it's hot?"

"It's a real piece of Americana," Tracy said.

Margaret liked the car. It had a split-back bench seat with a folding center armrest. She could sit high on the little knob of the armrest or push the armrest in between the seats and ride the usual way. She liked sitting high on that cushioned perch, her arms resting across each seat. She could pluck at Cam's collar tab, or finger Tracy's hair at the back of his neck. Cam drove into the parking lot of a big Kentucky Fried Chicken.

"Watch this," he said.

"I don't see anything," Margaret said.

"Just wait a minute," Cam said.

They circled the restaurant and came out on the other side of the building. The far side had a metallicized plate-glass window, like a bronzed mirror, and she saw them reflected, the Duster a dreamy golden image. Margaret watched the smooth lines of the car, its swept-back roof and ventless windows. Its powder-blue aura like cue chalk.

"What a great idea," Tracy said, "people buying buckets of chicken just so they can see their cars on that fantasy screen. Go through again."

Cam steered around the restaurant once more.

"Ultra neon," Tracy said, as they cruised past the window.

"It's really nice," Margaret said. "I like the decal on the fender, that little cyclone."

"It's a tumbleweed," Tracy said. "We're tumbling tumbleweeds."

"No, that's a cyclone, isn't it?" Margaret said.

"Dust devil," Cam said.

Cam drove onto the highway. The car had power, a steady acceleration, a lilting forward propulsion. Tracy said, "Great car. People think it's a nice middle-of-the-road vehicle; that's its secret. It looks benign, but it's peopled by love-starved maniacs!"

Margaret didn't disagree with this, but she looked at Cam to see if he allowed himself to be included. He was smiling. Maybe just happy to be in the Duster. She liked the surroundings—the vinyl seats glazed and plumped, the dashboard that gleamed with chrome inlays. Margaret punched the radio buttons.

"Oh Christ, it's WMAR," Tracy said.

"WMAR?" Cam was asking. "Never heard of it."

"It's Radio Margaret, we're sunk if she's at the controls."

"You each get one veto, that's all." She turned up the volume when she found something.

They stopped for ice and she spilled it over the asphalt as they filled the cooler. An ice cube on the asphalt is a beautiful sight, Margaret thought. It floated on a river of its own making and quickly flattened, disappeared into that speckled dark. Cam arranged cans in the ice and tapped the lid until it fit.

"Do you have to drink beer to buy a speedboat?" Tracy asked. "I'm going to try to get us a Nehi."

"A Nehi soda?" Margaret said. "Are you crazy?"

"I thought this was a nostalgia cruise, a little side trip to jog the memory. These roadside stands have everything—"

"We're not going on any psycho side trips. We're here to look at a boat," Margaret said. Tracy went into the Quick Stop and came out with three Philadelphia Phillies sun visors.

"It's going to scorch us," he said to Cam, who didn't want to wear the visor. "Okay, suit yourself. Doctors will start shaving little bumps from your face. Old salts always end up like that."

Margaret took her visor and let it slip down over her nose. "It's too big."

"Too big? I've never heard you complain," Tracy said.

"Tracy is always making references to his dick."

"I'd hate to be trapped in your mind," Cam told Tracy.

"It's cramped, but it's rent controlled. Give me the hat," Tracy said. He worked to tighten the plastic band.

Then they were driving. Margaret watched the road for a moment and shut her eyes, letting the feeling swell, increase, that pleasure of sitting between two men. She knew there was a bit of something, a swirl of vanity and greed, which she had to monitor. She couldn't be dreaming these things. She looked at her brother. He was very appealing to look at, and she studied him without feeling self-conscious; perhaps because their intimacy was tested over years, it was proved. She knew his profile, its crooked jog when it met the cleft of his chin. His eyes were hazel with gold flecks, the color of light tea, almost translucent, but the pupils were always oversized, making him look on the edge of alarm. His eyelashes weren't unnaturally long, but they grew dense at their roots and shaded a thin line along his lids as if they had been penciled. It was odd for a man to have such accentuated eyes. Tracy was looking at *her* looking at Cam, so she knew she was dreaming too long.

When she and Cam were teenagers and the home situation became stiff or itchy, they drove down to the shore. The roads were flat, running straight through the tomato fields. Cam pressed the gas pedal to the floor and let go of the steering wheel. He locked his hands behind his head and shut his eyes until Margaret screamed at him. The landscape was lush, groomed and parted. Rows of beans and lopes. There were truck stands at every crossroad, melons stacked high in pyramids like shiny bomblets. Cam drove like a practiced madman. They would be ripping at eighty and ninety. It was a cleansing forward motion. A first refreshment before the refreshment of the sea. There might be someone standing beside the road, a farmer or a kid with a ball. They blistered past and dust ballooned over the road. When Margaret looked back she couldn't see the figure. They might have killed somebody. When they reached Rehoboth or Ocean City, they fell into the water. It was a fixation, brown and sudsy, clouds of sand churning in the breakers, the swells and suction of the sea that rinsed them of their little pains, anxieties. Rinsed them of home.

Tracy kept studying her.

"I was daydreaming," she told him. "Shit. It will be good to see the boats. I haven't been on a speedboat since you had the *Lucifer*," she told Cam.

"*Lucifer?*" Tracy looked across at Cam. "You named your boat *Lucifer?* Did you have one of those novelty plates that say BORN TO RAISE HELL?"

"It was better than naming a boat after your wife," Cam said.

"Yeah, there's too many of those cruisers with the wife's nickname: Dottie, Evie, you just have to go along the docks and count them," Margaret said.

Cam said, "I saw a boat once—it was called *Miss Take*. I liked that."

Tracy said, "I need a little poetry in a ship's name, like in Newport—that old sloop, *The Black Pearl*. Then there's the one called *Soulsearcher*. You could go down with a ship if the name was right."

"Sailboats always have those romantic tags, Latin ones even. A speedboat has to have a real jock name," Margaret said.

"If I buy this one we're going to see today," Cam said, "Laurence gets the final say. It's really going to be for him."

"Then he should be coming along," Tracy said.

"Look," Cam said, "there's no question he'll be coming

with me every time." The fields blurred as Cam's foot moved down on the accelerator.

"Shit, slow down. This is scarier than I remember," Margaret told him.

"Schoolteacher," Cam said.

"Well, I've got a kid now. You've got Laurence."

Tracy told them, "Make that three sprouts." Cam was disgusted. He toed the accelerator, but it was a brief protest and he slowed the car. They didn't talk for a moment, reined in by the thought of their children.

Cam started to tell them about Darcy. She was reluctant to trade cars for the day. "She knew what kind of fun we could have in the Duster," Cam said.

"Jealous," Tracy said.

Cam shook his head. "Not even that, just mean. I left mine there and took this one."

Margaret told Cam he was asking for trouble.

"I just switched cars for the day. I left her the Bronco."

"You might find a bucket of fish guts dumped on your front seat when you come back. I saw that once in Providence. You don't think fish are so bloody, they seem so pure, straight *agua* pumping through their veins. Then you see some mackerel guts sinking into the upholstery," Tracy said.

"Look, I gave her this car in the first place."

"That makes it a pretty self-conscious gesture. You're making your point with the Duster."

"Can you translate?" Cam asked Margaret. "No, don't bother."

Tracy said, "What's the problem? What is it? English as a second language?"

Margaret pulled her chin in tight and let them shoot it back and forth.

"Go ahead," Tracy said to Margaret, "be interpreter for us like you do for those poor souls in the joint."

"No, thanks," she said.

"Evaluate," Tracy said.

"Is that what you do?" Cam said.

"I write reports. I write down the subjective, the objective, the assessment, and then the plan. The S.O.A.P."

"The S.O.A.P.? You mean it's that head-shrinking stuff?"

"It's my job. We make assessments and then we make plans."

Tracy said, "You know, it's all that Behavior Mod, and then the moral lesson."

Cam said, "That's how you make a living?"

"You clean swimming pools, isn't that right? Well, I've had jobs," Margaret said. "Every kind of clerk. Then I was a chambermaid. Don't get me started on that."

Cam pressed his thumb down on her kneecap and lifted it off.

Let's forget our work, he might be trying to say.

She would tell him, *Okay. Let's ride the Duster out of the realm of toil and monetary needs.*

Tracy might say, *We'll roll into the lowland of the senses.* Down to the seaside. When it was quiet for a minute, these dreams overwhelmed her.

. . .

Before she started working in the prison, she had a
housekeeping job at the River Lodge. Even after she
left the motel job, the idea of the *single hair* stayed with
her. She told Cam, "I didn't mind making the beds,
tearing the dirty sheets loose and wadding them down
into a hamper that was nailed to a trolley. The televisions
were going in the rooms, soap operas, and the women told me who was cheating on who, but I couldn't
keep up.

"Then I had to hunt down these private hairs. One
kinky hair left unattended would get my supervisor all
worked up."

"Just one hair?" Cam said.

"One of them. Maybe in the tub, or back in a corner,
curled around the ceramic doorstop. She'd always find
it."

Tracy plucked a glossy hair from his belly and twirled
it against Margaret's cheek. "Will you stop?" she told
him. He laid the hair against her bare knee. She brushed
it away. "I wasn't supposed to use water to clean the tub
or sink. Water leaves spots. Washing hairs down the
drain creates a clog, you know?"

"The implication being—that water itself, like the
corkscrew hairs, is yet another kind of filth?" Tracy
said.

"That's right. So I quit," Margaret said.

She had not yet met Tracy. When her savings ran
out, she developed a new sense of reality. It all had to
do with having no money. Cam said it must have been
hard to scrub bathrooms after she had been used to a
comfortable lifestyle with her husband.

"That breadstick? I'll take my job at the prison," she told Cam.

"Why can't you teach regular school or do Avon?"

"Mary Kay," Tracy said. "Mary Kay gives you a company car, a pink Caddie when you sell ten thousand powder puffs."

Margaret said, "I don't like to sell. I work for the state. The state isn't run like a business and I don't have someone breathing down my neck about making a profit.

"All I had to do was take the civil service examination at the state employment office. Next, I went for an interview for the position of corrections officer 'with a possible emphasis in tutorial work as an English instructor.' I showed them I could spell multisyllable words and they hired me."

Tracy said, "I told her she didn't have to go work in a prison. I make almost enough at the newspaper—"

"Almost enough? Almost enough isn't *enough*," Cam said.

Tracy turned in his seat. "We do fine. I host some high school dances with the disc jockey from WPRO. The kids like my column. I'm a fucking celebrity—"

"With the Cranston pubescent scene," Margaret said.

"I get a couple hundred a week for these disco horror shows, but what does Miss Do-Gooder want? She wants to walk into a maximum-security setting and conjugate verbs with the foreign exchange students. Colombian, Cuban, Puerto Rican, Hmong Chinese. She teaches them how to say 'please' and 'thank you.' They get back on the street and do you think they remember Miss Manners? You should have seen Margaret the first day on the job—"

"What do you mean?" Margaret said. "I looked fine." She told Cam, "I had a plain tan skirt and a white blouse with a Peter Pan collar. Two-inch heels—"

"She looked like an airline stewardess," Tracy told Cam. "What will it be, coffee, tea, or hootch? 'What's hootch?' she asks me."

Cam said, "There's a lot to learn about law enforcement." He was smiling at Margaret. "You need a dictionary of slang. What's a screw?"

Margaret said, "For your information, a screw is a guard. The word comes from the idea of turning a key in a lock. Not what you're thinking. Hootch is homemade brew; sometimes it's made from raisins or even potatoes. They can make it in a wastebasket and hide it in a dropped ceiling. Do I pass?"

"Go straight to jail," Tracy said.

She said, "If I *knew* what hootch was, that would say something about me, wouldn't it?"

"Isn't she pure? Like Ivory soap. She floats."

Cam said, "It's just a matter of time."

"That's right. She's a hostage profile," Tracy said.

"Oh really? This is a modern prison. All kinds of professionals work inside. What George Raft movie have you been watching?" She looked to see if her comment was shooting them down any, but she should have thought up a different actor.

"A movie?" Tracy said. "Baby, life is a movie. Your cunt is a little roll of celluloid, twenty-four frames a second, a sixteen-millimeter fuck show. Just remember that."

"Shit, Tracy. Aren't you glad I'm getting the money?" she said. The state had arranged to place her paycheck directly into her bank account. She wouldn't have to wait in line for the teller.

Margaret's first weeks in the prison, she worked in a small icy room in the tower. The tiny suite was called Master Control. A wall of video monitors showed the hallways, the intersections, and the external gates. The room was flanked by cabinets of gleaming weaponry: rifles, pistols, sawed-offs, stun guns, tear-gas grenades, hand and ankle cuffs, belly chains, flares and prodders. The air conditioning was up so high, she had to ask her training supervisor for his jacket. She knew this was a dangerous request, he might mistake it for flirtation or for physical weakness typical of the female. He told her the place was cold to keep the ammunition dry, and the cold would keep her on her toes.

Margaret wondered when she would be allowed to teach composition as she sat on a swivel chair before the large boards of blinking lights and video screens that controlled the system of electronic doors throughout the prison complex. Each doorway was comprised of two electronically operated glass panels, only one of which could be opened at a time. Margaret had to learn to work the electronic levers that operated the doors, maneuvering the first door closed before the next door could be opened.

Once or twice, Margaret accidentally closed the door on someone. She jostled a prominent psychiatrist, brushing his shoulder with one door, and by the next door she was out of synchrony and she struck the doctor

again as he angled out of the compartment. Tracy
enjoyed hearing this story. "You squashed a shrink? It
could have been anyone—the vending machine person,
the laundry people. I love it. You're incredible! You got
the Mind Control guy without even trying."

She started to have dreams about the prison. Her
daughter was trapped inside the glass stall. Tracy told
her she was starting to act funny in her sleep, her body
jerking, sometimes rising up to a sitting position. "It
must be a terrible job," he said, but she disagreed, she
told him she was managing. "I'll be teaching composition
soon," she said.

Margaret started sleepwalking. She left her bed and
went to the window. She threw up the sash and leaned
out over the sidewalk two stories below until the cool,
sooty air revived her. She sank back inside, terrified,
suffering a vertigo intensified by her dream condition.
A therapist told Tracy that it was not uncommon for
people to sleepwalk during the first months of an
employment situation that required hours of confine-
ment. In a prison, or on submarines, on deep-sea oil
rig platforms, there was a high incidence of somnam-
bulism.

She began to tutor the men in the prison, and
Margaret was pleased when an inmate showed her some
song lyrics or a poem he had written. She felt more like
a substitute teacher or a guidance counselor than a
corrections officer. Some of the inmates called her
"Teech," and she liked the nickname. Others started to
call her "Sidewinder," because, no matter how hard she
tried to adjust her gait, she couldn't keep from moving

her hips when she walked down the halls. One kid showed her an apple tattooed on the inside of his wrist, a smudgy blue sphere. His name was MacIntosh. He told her, "Teech, I'd give you this apple, but you wouldn't want it. It's got worms."

"Worms don't scare me," she said. This was how she talked to them. It impressed some, but she could never convince everyone.

II

Cam was the only one in the family who had an interest in boats. Yet, Margaret remembered seeing an old photograph of Elizabeth sitting in the prow of a sailboat. Elizabeth looked beautiful, dressed in white slacks with the cuffs rolled up. She wore a tight sailor's shirt, a tiny anchor print. The blouse was showcased in *Vogue* magazine, Elizabeth told her. The boat was small, a "catboat," with an old-fashioned, spoon-shaped hull.

"Who took this picture of you?" Margaret asked.

"My first husband," Elizabeth said.

"The Arrow Collar Man?"

"Who else? It's Lake Michigan. In the winter the waves freeze on the shore. Big chunks, giant saucers, like broken crockery."

"What?" Margaret didn't think she heard correctly.

"The waves freeze on the shore." Elizabeth walked out of the room. Margaret passed the snapshot beneath the lamp; its hot cone fell on her wrists as she cradled the photo. Margaret was puzzled by Elizabeth's non sequitur, "The waves freeze on the shore." At other times, Elizabeth might speak in depth, describing her struggles with Lewis Goddard. Margaret believed she had learned more about him than Cam and his sisters ever had. Perhaps, because Margaret wasn't her real daughter, Elizabeth was able to confide in her. Richard was different; he kept his cards close to his chest, and she learned about his private life from what he left out. These holes in the narrative explained a great deal.

Margaret looked at the picture of her stepmother in the little catboat and she understood that, in order for Cam to have been abandoned by his father, Elizabeth herself must first have been deserted. This was the term used in Elizabeth's divorce: "mindful neglect, desertion." Lewis went off after a few years of marriage, leaving Elizabeth with two daughters, Tina and Jane. She was forced to leave New York and move back in with her parents, who lived on the South Side of Chicago, a leafy neighborhood fading from its turn-of-the-century glory. The house had a small yard with a cherry tree, which inked the children's play clothes ruby red. "It was the bane of my existence—everything stained," Elizabeth said.

Lewis came back when he couldn't get modeling work. He returned for an item of clothing or a loan of money and, as a second thought, he claimed he'd seen a priest who forgave his sins, why couldn't she? He borrowed the money, swiped her silver brush and comb set to see what he could get for it. She never turned him out, letting him sleep through the afternoon. Then he was gone all night and half the next day. He returned rumpled, his clothes marred, imprinted with the vermilion lip rouge and fleshy face powders of outsiders. His final intrusion was a first Saturday in May.

He waited until Elizabeth's parents went shopping, pulling the aluminum-mesh grocery cart behind them. He came into the house, passed by his girls playing with china saucers, and found her.

Elizabeth told Margaret, "He was there under an hour, just enough time for me to give in. He ripped the tiny hook and eye on my skirt, he tugged it down over my hips. A hook and eye doesn't offer much protection."

"Today, they say that's rape," Margaret said.

"They do? How would they know? It's not rape if the woman is still conscious."

"You mean you can't have a technical knockout in sex?" Margaret said.

"I don't know what you're talking about. Anyway, he's making love to me and he takes my change purse from the bureau and removes the bills. He's got it *in* me and he's counting the tens and singles. Then he picks up my pen and is writing an IOU. He's writing! He puts the pen down and gets back to business. He tells me: 'It's not that I don't love you. It's not that I don't love *this*.' "

"This?" Margaret blinked.

"That's right. *This*," Elizabeth said. "It was everything to him."

Margaret always had a hard time not picturing Cam when Elizabeth talked about Lewis Goddard. She imagined Cam tugging someone's skirt down. But that would be Tracy. Tracy might or might not take the cash.

Elizabeth had told Margaret, "It must have been God's wishes. I gave in."

God's wishes? What kind of summary is that? From that, what could she make of God? Then she was pregnant with Cam. Elizabeth couldn't bring herself to pat her swollen belly or to think of a name for it. Later, when Cam asked questions, his sisters shrugged. No one knew anything. Cam told Margaret he used to imagine his father was like Jesse James, someone with a bad side, a mean streak, but wasn't that the kernel of all great adventures? Weren't heroes always tempted, weakened, didn't they fall before they returned to prove themselves?

Lewis lost most of his modeling jobs soon after leaving Elizabeth. His drinking caused some blood vessels to rise on his cheeks; his eyes became rimmed and puffy. Even so, he was incredibly striking, and his girlfriends and acquaintances still called him "The Model." During the war, the army reluctantly agreed to evaluate him and concluded that his acute vanity verged on the autoerotic. He would be useless in action. For a few months, until the end of the war, he did double shifts in a kissing booth for the Women's Army Corps. That's when they assigned him to Times Square, where he waited in a plywood shack, complaining to his sergeant that the kissing booth was freezing, until they installed a portable heater. He touched his lips with a camphor stick to prevent catching head colds from the ladies who filled out forms and queued up to receive a kiss. He was ordering out for spiked coffees and hot gravy sandwiches, but he was doing so well, recruiting hundreds of women, plain and fancy, they allowed him these privileges.

Margaret's father had also tried to enlist, but they wouldn't allow him to leave the steel mill. They told him he was worth a thousand soldiers if he would just stay where he was and run the open hearth. He wanted to go over, because years after a war it's not so attractive to say you stayed home, even if you were running a steel mill. Margaret's mother, Sandra, was pleased he was staying put. It was hard enough worrying about those pouring ladles; sometimes the nozzle gets a crack and, instead of pouring a clean jet, it sprays molten froth everywhere, men running in all directions. When Richard heard about Lewis's kissing booth, he wondered what kind of man kisses women all day long while others were getting imprinted with shrapnel, lead slivers the size of mint leaves, a bloody filigree.

During her years on the South Side after the war, Elizabeth often left her children with their grandparents and went dancing. She went to the Palmer House, to the old Aragon Ballroom in North Chicago, or to the Trianon on the South Side, where they heard Wayne King or it was Frankie Laine. Elizabeth's girlfriends arranged blind dates, or she came alone and suffered the usual sots and dandies; even the married men were pestering one another for a turn with her. Elizabeth, having been acquainted with Margaret's mother during her one semester at De Paul, was invited to sit at a table with Sandra and Richard. Because Elizabeth was there

without a husband, Richard felt he should look after
her, keep her glass refilled, check on her coat when it
was time to leave. Even then, Sandra was having trouble
breathing. She cleared her throat too often, tapping her
breastbone with her small fist, rubbing her knuckles
against her collarbone. By the end of these evenings,
she was coughing. The following summer she was in
Granville Sanatorium.

Elizabeth's parents said it was unseemly for her to
start dating a fellow whose wife was so ill. Shouldn't he
be at his wife's bedside, not at the Aragon? Didn't he
have a tiny baby at home? Wasn't it sickly, a premie?

"That baby is fine now. And you can't sit with Sandra
all night in a hospital," Elizabeth told them. "They kick
you out. They wash under the beds."

Soon after that, Richard brought Margaret to play
with Elizabeth's three children. Elizabeth and Richard
told Margaret the story with similar emphasis. They said
it was their "turning point." They met at the lake. The
older sisters walked in front, kicking tufts of sand that
blew backward, into the babies' faces. Cam was three
years old, one year older than Margaret, and both were
young enough to tire from plodding through the uneven
wells and drifts of the beach; they had to be herded
forward. Richard liked the parade. If anyone watched,
they might assume this was his tribe, his offspring
marching in a pleasing gradation. Then, Elizabeth
looked out at the water and saw a sailboat. The wind
caught the sail until the craft surged and tilted, revealing
its small crew, a man and woman. The mysterious couple
faced the shore and waved.

"It's him," she said. "Isn't that Lewis with some bimbo?"

"I don't think you're right," Richard said.

"It *is* him. I should recognize Lewis, don't you think?"

"You're wrong, honey," he told her.

"I know that boat!"

Richard told her, "They rent several of those catboats."

"No, it's him. He's rubbing my face in something."

They watched the little sailboat lift and settle on the chop. "You really can't tell who it is," Richard told her.

"If we're going to get married. Let's get married now."

He halted on the beach; suddenly his shoes were weighted with sand and he pulled them off to tip them. He touched her shoulder for balance as he lifted one foot, then the other.

"If we *are* getting married, when exactly?" Elizabeth said.

"I wanted to have an opportunity—" He struggled to say something. He wanted to say, "Couldn't we wait until Sandra is dead?" His wife's name would have cast a spell and he didn't mention her.

Elizabeth told him, "You can get a divorce. Arkansas lets you take a divorce in ninety days. You can go there, get the divorce, and come back and get me."

"What about the war?" This had been the nation's line of defense when faced with domestic situations, food shortages, problems with transportation.

"What do you mean, the war? The war's over!" she told him.

He turned around and looked at the city, its familiar skyline smudged with mist from the lake. He couldn't look at the water and think straight. "I can't leave the plant. We're making adjustments, some changes in production. It's chaos, and they're laying people off since—"

"Since the war?"

"What am I supposed to do in Arkansas? How do I make a living?"

Elizabeth said, "I read the ad in the *Tribune*. Men getting divorced are selling aluminum storm windows and floor tiles. Home improvements, that sort of thing. They're making a killing in Little Rock."

Richard imagined divorcing his wife, who was dying. Dying alone. Alone now at that terrible threshold, then alone forever. But it was true, it could take months. He recalled the one psalm he had put to memory as a child. It was the twenty-third. He envisioned its tiny inch of text; it offered him nothing, no remonstration, no comfort. The light sifted over them, that resistant, pouty April sunlight, not enough to heat the air. Didn't he remember a warm lake glow? When was it like that? The small ration of sun had triggered the first bloom of plankton in the lake, and the scent was drifting in. He pictured divorcing his wife, but he couldn't see quitting his place at South Works. Even without the war effort to consider, he couldn't imagine walking away from Open Hearth Number Four to start selling aluminum storms and floor tile in Arkansas.

"Look at the children," Elizabeth said. "A nice large family. A boy. Men dream of it."

III

Cam drove into Ocean City and found the Talbot Street Pier. He parked the car before a network of horseshoe gangways where boats were docked. A few beat-up cabin cruisers rested out of the water, centered on shipways or makeshift perches where a man worked patching a hull with grey fiberglass compound. Cam told them to wait in the car and he went to find the man who had advertised the Donzi. Margaret watched him go along the pier and turn down one of the gangplanks to a long, floating dock. He was reading the names of the boats and looking at the berth numbers. A speedboat went past and she watched its wake roll the floating pier with Cam on it. He looked different, a hundred miles away, rising and sinking there all by himself.

Margaret tried to share the weight of the big Coleman cooler with Tracy, but it kept bumping against her leg when she took one of the handles, leaving a wet smear of rust on her skin. Cam waited beside the Donzi, tipping his fist against his lips and pretending to chug-a-lug. Tracy's face looked still; his mouth kept an even line. It must be the idea of going out on the water, Margaret thought. He was usually skittish when confined to a small space. The tiny deck of the speedboat would be a test. He was telling her it would be a personal challenge.

"I can't locate the owner," Cam told them when they arrived. Margaret looked down at the boat.

Cam saw her taking it in and said, "The Donzi deep-vee, remember?"

It was a glossy red-and-white with a low deck line, 9but not too sneering. Everything was sleek; the chromed grab rails and hatch hinges gleamed with little pricks of light.

"It's just like the old one," Margaret said.

"That's why it's called the Classic, it's almost exactly the same year to year. Look at this rub rail," Cam said, "every Phillips head is turned in the same direction. That's one of Donzi's trademarks."

"Pretty anal," Tracy said.

"Excuse me?"

"Anal compulsive," Tracy said. "Amazing example."

"It's detail," Cam said. "There's a difference."

The boat could seat two at the helm and three on the back bench if you had to take a whole party, but three was the perfect number of people. The boat wasn't something for maiden aunts or grandmothers. It was for erotic mix-and-matches, slave duos, race-minded marrieds, any pair of intimates, maybe a love triangle.

"Look at the upholstery, the graphics. These aren't decals, they're gel-coated right into the vinyl," Cam said. He waited for Tracy's opinion.

Tracy said, "I see."

Cam waited.

Tracy said, "I think it works. It works for me."

"I told you. It's the Classic deep-vee. Not too sterile or Miami. It's the original, and fast. It pulls out clean without too much bow lift," Cam said. He followed the lines of the boat, he was grinning. Margaret liked seeing him forget himself.

"I'm sure it's fine unless there's glitch in the Cobra, but I can't tell a thing standing here."

"Let's just take it out, otherwise the man might lose the sale. You look ready to buy," Tracy said.

"We can't take it out without a key. You're thinking of a rowboat."

"A rowboat. There must be a secret to a rowboat. When I try to row, I go in circles," Tracy said.

"Oh, Cam can teach you how to row. Can't you, Cam? You could show Tracy how to keep from digging with the oars," Margaret said.

The men looked at opposite specks in the distance. The idea had upset them both.

"It can't hurt sitting here for a while," Cam said, and he stepped down into the boat. He sat down on the bench, taking a beer from the cooler. Tracy landed too hard and the boat shivered, rocked for a second, then lofted back to its trough on the water. The marina was pretty quiet; most of the slips were empty, it was a perfect afternoon to be out sailing. A man walked heel to toe along the side of his yacht. He was using a squeegee to clean grey lichens of crystallized salt from the windscreen. Then, on one of the big cabin cruisers, a woman in a string bikini was splashing a hose over the gunwales. Margaret noticed Cam avoiding that sight, although, looking in the other direction, he faced the sun. He looked at his shoes; then he took out his wallet to count his money. Tracy watched the woman hosing the boat; he followed her in and out of the galley and back up to the bow, where she emptied a Coke can into the water. Her skin was deep from the sun and flushed from her activity. The cruiser was called *The Mermaid*.

Tracy said that she must be Ethel Mermaid. "There's no business like show business," he told Cam in a flat voice. Cam kept his face angled down. He wanted another look, but the woman had gone around to the other side.

"There's no head on this boat?" Margaret asked.

"No, it's too small, where's it going to go?" Cam said.

"Where is *she* going to go—," Tracy was saying.

"King of Korn," she told Tracy, but she wasn't smiling about it. She jumped back onto the dock and told them she wanted to go find a bathroom. She walked back to the parking lot, where there were some little shops. The Hot Dog Nook. She could smell the malt vinegar people spilled on their French fries. As she headed that way, she passed a small sailboat that was painted black. The amateur brush strokes were coarse and blistered on the mast. She followed the mast to the top and saw the old pirate's flag, the Jolly Roger, a white skull and crossbones on a black background. The flag snapped open and closed in the wind, an ugly tearing noise overhead. The sight alarmed her; it made her recall the black-and-white scrap on the chandelier at home. How similar these things seemed, although she didn't know why she felt it so strongly. It was a common logo—she had seen it used on the back labels of household cleaners. Even so, there was something too evocative about the skull, its frontal stare. It made her feel what she always worked to evade—that deep unfinished silhouette rising to the surface. She wanted to suppress it, especially this day when she was keeping in the present tense. Keeping steady with the men.

After she went to the toilet, she purchased a large

brown paper sack of fries and poured vinegar over them. She walked back to the men. As she passed the black yacht, she recognized the snapping of the skull flag, but she didn't look up. She kept digging in the bag and lifting the wet, fragrant potatoes to her lips. She sat back down in the Donzi and shared the potatoes. Tracy was sawing a Budweiser flip top through the boat's fiberglass finish. A deep gouge and its glossy shavings marred the surface.

"What is he doing?" Cam asked her. "What the hell is that for?"

"I don't know," Margaret said. "Tracy stop it! What are you trying to do? Destroy property?" She knocked Tracy's hand and the aluminum snip flew into the water.

"Carving your initials? Is that it?" Cam was trying to understand. Maybe it was wild sentiment that made Tracy so reckless.

"It's just so fucking cherry," Tracy said, "it makes me crazy."

They looked at him. Once again, the woman on the cabin cruiser was back outside, splashing her legs and ankles with the hose, but they kept their eyes on Tracy.

"That's it." Cam stood up. "We're finished here."

"Your owner's not coming?" Margaret said.

"He's not going to show," Cam said.

Cam snatched the soaking bag of fries from the seat and got out of the boat. Margaret followed. They looked back at Tracy. He was rubbing the heel of his hand over his nipple, looking thoughtful. He was doing his pouting-queen imitation. His eyelids fluttered: No One Loves Me Enough. Margaret looked past him. His bluff was short-lived and he followed them back to the car. Perhaps it was Cam. Cam moved in a linear way, plowed through, and bumped Tracy into a new juxtaposition with the world, with Margaret. Margaret watched Tracy regain control over it, his bad will, the seed of his imagination. It must be as exhausting for Tracy as it was for them.

They rode the upper deck of the Cape May ferry on their way to visit Jane. Laughing gulls collected like harpies, keeping steady with the big ship and diving after French fries and hamburger buns people hurled into the air. Margaret cringed when a bird hovered too near her, clutching something starchy thrown into the sky. She stretched out on one of the sunny benches and put her arm over her eyes. Occasionally, she felt the slight roll of the hull, which some people found nauseating. She worried about seeing Jane. There wasn't much to say. Jane had a new daughter with her boyfriend, a two-year-old, and that would be something they could discuss. The subject of children can neutralize the conversation if it becomes too acid. Margaret could never describe the years when Jane lived at home. It was as if Jane's childhood with Margaret had been sucked into a vacuum the day Jane got into some man's flashy car. Jane displayed a strange self-imposed amnesia, which Margaret found threatening to her own pristine recollections. Margaret tried to say, "Remember that Christmas when the tree crashed into the piano? Remember the dog Trixie? What about that spastic boy, the one who had to wear a helmet?" Jane would shrug.

She told Margaret she couldn't recall a minute of it.

"What about the time I caught my ankle in the porch glider? You pulled it out—"

"Take it easy," she told Margaret. "I don't *want* to remember that house." But it must be better for Jane now. She had a good setup. Her boyfriend was sweet, always quiet, maybe just dog-tired because he worked nights delivering fuel oil.

Cam and Tracy avoided one another. Cam left Margaret on the deck and went down the ladders to check the Duster. She saw him kick the wooden tire wedge until it was squared. Tracy was standing at the head of the flat, square bow, where a heavy chain was the only thing keeping him back from the edge. There was something brewing between the men. Margaret knew that Cam and Tracy never seemed good with male companions; neither one had close friends or buddies they relied on. Cam had always been a self-assured loner. With Tracy, it was his sponsor or one of the others from group therapy who called him occasionally, but he didn't keep up with his peers at the newspaper, he didn't go to see the Red Sox or to hear any rock 'n' roll. Yet, Tracy was always invited to parties, and Cam had been, too; they were considered essential. Tracy's dark asides, Cam's romantic silences, were pleasing in a crowd. Margaret saw how she was someone who always *gave* parties. And even now, Tracy and Cam seemed to hand her the role of social director. They loitered at separate corners of the ship, waiting for her to reunite them.

Jane's place was a second-floor apartment two blocks

from the ocean. When they arrived, the afternoon sea breeze was strong, lifting the long curtains until they billowed into the front room. Gauzy panels floated level between her and Jane as they tried to embrace. They brushed the curtains away and still the wind lifted the frayed panels until they were wrapped in them, laughing.

They sat at the kitchen table. Jane opened small packets of delicatessen meats, leaving the sliced domes centered on the folded squares of brown paper. She put hard rolls in the center of the table and a bottle of olive oil with a whiskey spout. Jane brought over an armful of stubbies, seven-ounce beers. She claimed that the small bottles stayed cold all the way through. Then she served the next ones. The table filled up with empties, and Jane went to get more from the icebox. Tracy flattered Jane and made a giant sandwich of prosciutto, mortadella, and salami, adding three big dollops of oil and a dribbling of hot peppers. The meats smelled delicious, but there was an unpleasant odor that the wind stirred around. The apartment smelled of heavy heating oil and household ammonia. The oil came from a laundry basket of Jane's lover's pewter-colored overalls. "Believe it or not, they're washed but they still stink," Jane said. Then her little daughter pissed on the living room carpet.

"I'm training her, but she does this on purpose." The little girl was stark naked because of the heat. She stood in the middle of the room, spread her legs, and released a substantial stream.

"Gloria!" Jane scolded the girl, quite after the fact.

The baby smiled at her audience. She wrinkled her nose in blissful defiance.

"An imp," Tracy said. Cam kept looking the other way.

Then Jane took a plastic bottle of ammonia, gallon size, and she scrubbed the dark circle where the girl had urinated. Margaret, having had a few beers with her sandwich, went dreamy for a moment and she wondered, Why does one kind of ammonia curtail another kind of ammonia? They're different, of course, but how are they different? Where does household ammonia come from?

"Where's Chris?" Margaret asked Jane.

"Sleeping. He gets off work at seven A.M."

"Oh, God, we're making too much noise," Margaret said.

"He can sleep through anything."

"You work days and he works nights? Do you ever see him?"

"We don't even have the same days off. These are my two days. Tuesday and Wednesday. He's normal; he's got the normal weekend," Jane said.

"Not even the same weekends. That's tough."

Jane said, "Used to it." She looked at Margaret and dragged on her cigarette. "Like today. He'll wake up and go over to the VFW and that will be that."

"The VFW? I've always wanted to try a VFW," Tracy said.

"You didn't serve, did you? I don't even have to ask," Cam said.

Tracy said, "I registered. They didn't get around to asking me."

"Maybe one of your balls didn't drop?"

Jane was enjoying it, looking back and forth.

Cam said, "Don't get me wrong, I'm not one of these military nuts. I hated Korea. I hated Fort Dix. They treat you like an animal."

"Quonset huts? Aren't they kind of a nightmare? A corrugated hell, a galvanized mouse hole?" Tracy was trying to commiserate.

Cam was smiling. "The worst part was the lack of privacy, going to the shitter in a herd. They line you up in the latrine and everybody waits while you try your best."

"They watch you do it?" Margaret said.

"It was a psychological-training thing. Identity busting. They get you totally stripped down so you can work like a unit. Live, shit, and die in front of one another. As a unit. I couldn't function for days."

"I should say not," Margaret said. She didn't want to hear about this, and she peeled the labels from the empty beer bottles, letting her fingernails scratch the hollow glass.

"Then we went out on the rifle range for the first time. We spent hours out there in that Jersey steam bath, lying on our stomachs. You ever pick up an M-1? No? Firing, reloading, firing. Your shoulder takes the kickback, starts to buzz. Everything was making me sick. I went to the latrine; there were twenty of us waiting our turns. I sit on the can and I think of the M-1. It was still rocking me. I feel that M-1, *boom*, and that was all I needed. From then on, I was regular. On schedule." He smiled at Margaret, forcing her to look the other way. "I still think of guns."

"You still think of weapons in order to function?" Tracy said.

"That's what I'm saying."

Margaret gathered the beer labels and rolled them into a ball under the palm of her hand. She started to tell Jane about the affidavit Elizabeth wanted signed.

Cam said, "They want to go to science. Medical school. They never went to college, but dead they go to Harvard. It says a lot about them."

"It won't be Harvard," Margaret said, "it will be someplace nearby. Johns Hopkins, do they have a medical school? There's Temple in Philadelphia, no, that's law." Margaret stopped naming the colleges when her sister glared at her. Margaret went to a community college for two years.

"Don't tell them that they can't go to Harvard. Let them think it's Harvard," Jane said. "You always want to ruin things with facts, Margaret."

"Facts are useful," Tracy said. "Facts can be proved or disproved. You can't disprove notions; you have to have a genuine assertion before you can debunk it."

Jane said, "What is he talking about? How *do* you pick them, Margaret?"

Tracy went on, "How about this Arrow Collar Man, your dad, do you ever feel like squaring off with him?"

Jane looked at Tracy and crossed her arms.

Tracy said, "Your father. Cam's appointed himself spokesman. He might be going out there to Chicago to read him the Riot Act."

"Cam's going to do what?"

"Absolutely nothing," Cam said. "Tracy wants me to

go out to Chicago. I didn't say I was moving an inch."

Tracy asked Jane, "What's your take on it?"

"I woke up, smelled the coffee, and I don't give a fuck. Cam has always been the one. That's his funeral."

Tracy praised Jane for her "I Look after Number One" attitude. It's healthy, he said. It showed her emancipation from family aggressions.

Margaret watched her sister's face. She wasn't listening to Tracy. "You've got beautiful eyes," Margaret said, and she knew she must be drunk to say something so personal to Jane. Margaret laughed and started coughing. "No, I mean it. I'm not kidding."

Jane's eyes misted and changed shape, became elongated almonds when she grinned at Margaret. Jane didn't often give in. It was *their* laughter, Cam's and Margaret's pleasure, which drifted over her face; it took her, it transformed her features. Jane was central, in charge of that abandon, until after several stubbies. Then, Jane quieted; her lifelong distaste for family involvement surfaced, just when everyone was too drunk to get up and leave.

"So, now what?" Jane said. The table had disappeared beneath rows of bottles, which they kept shoving aside so they could lean on the table. Margaret tried to prop her chin in her hand, but her elbow slipped and several of the bottles crashed over. Margaret steered the spill with her forearm, but no one got up to get a towel and the beer pooled in the center of the table.

"Let's go down to the boardwalk. Do they still have that girl, Lady Godiva, riding that diving horse?" Cam said.

"The horse doesn't *dive* in the water. They drop it from a high platform," Jane said. "I don't know how the girl stays on."

"That's cruel," Margaret said.

"I like it," Cam said.

"What do you like?" Margaret said.

"A girl in a wet bathing suit riding bareback," he said. "I guess."

"That's a summer job for you, Margaret," Tracy said.

Jane looked at Margaret. "It's about time she took a job."

"I have a job now," Margaret said.

"Shit, I'm sorry I didn't hold my breath," Jane said.

Jane's boyfriend came into the room. Everyone exchanged hazy, exaggerated greetings. The man was sleepy, but he straightened his posture and took a beer out of Jane's hand.

"What?" Jane said. "That's my beer—"

"Had enough? Do you think? I believe," the man said. Margaret admired his short, succinct phrases.

Jane stood up and said, "You don't tell me what to do. I'm visiting. Anyway, it's my day off."

"You don't work five days and lay out for two," he told her. This was a strangely wise thing to point out, and it infuriated Jane when everyone at the table seemed to be considering it.

The little girl hugged her father's knees and he looked down to see what it was. He told Jane the girl needed some pants.

"I would have put pants on her, but my sister's here! My sister comes in here and everything stands still!"

"What?" Margaret said.

"Girl, you make me sick. It's always Margaret *this*, Margaret *that*. They think you're perfect. Richard's girl. You've got nothing to do but go visiting people? Did you come here to see what it's like to live a real life? Go back and tell them it's *just what they think*, but it's none of their business." Jane stared at Margaret, giving her a severe up-and-down, as if she had suddenly identified an intruder. "What are you doing here, anyway?"

Cam walked out and slammed the screen door. Tracy stood up, but he didn't leave.

"We came all this way to see you, Sis," Margaret said.

Jane sugared her voice and said, "*We came all this way to see you, Sis.*"

"You can't blame Margaret for everything," her boyfriend told her, but he rested his hands on Jane's shoulders, brushed the back of her neck gently with his stained fingers, letting her know he took her side. He seemed to tell her she was making a stink about someone of inconsequence, someone he'd told her to shake off.

"Do you want to sign this paper?" Margaret asked her sister.

"Fuck that. Fuck those bodies going to science."

"My feelings exactly," Margaret said. She tore the paper in half and the wind shoved the pieces ahead of her as she walked out the door. She heard Tracy say something about the sandwiches; then he came outside.

They stood at the Duster while Cam unlocked the doors to let the heat escape. Margaret looked up at her sister's apartment and saw the wind lifting the curtains.

Tracy said, "Margaret *this*, Margaret *that*. That really sums it up for Jane."

"Is it my fault?" Margaret asked.

"Richard's girl," Tracy went on. "That's it tied up in a bow." He repeated her father's name a few times trying to get the perfect resonance. "It's your stigma," he told her. "Go with it."

"Eat shit," she told Tracy, but she shrugged. She rubbed her elbow, which was sticky with a gummy residue. Her skin smelled sharp and yeasty from the spilled beer. Margaret looked up and down the street. Clapboard houses in straight sun-baked lines leading right up to the Atlantic. There was a diner or a delicatessen on every other corner, people standing around selling lemon ices and squares of cold pizza. Everywhere the familiars, humming like pins and needles in her bones. "Will you just look at this. It's the white trash of the Jersey shore," she said, but she knew it was hers, her kin, and they all deserved better.

7

C am steered into a parking lot that faced the water. Margaret went inside a restaurant and came back in her sarong-style, French-cut swimsuit, which revealed her hipbones. Tracy and Cam had undressed and Tracy was already swimming far out into the sea. She walked down the beach with her brother until they found an evocative pulse in the waves where they angled into the surf. Margaret felt drunk as soon as she went under and she couldn't rise to the surface. Cam grabbed her wrist and pulled her into shallow water. They were both too drunk to swim and they stayed together near the shore. Tracy was still swimming far out. Cam told her, "He's totally crazy." She couldn't disagree with this, and she turned on her back to float and watch the sky.

Then they waited on the beach. Having lost sight of him, Margaret was too angry to be fearful. "That fuck," she said. "He's really an asshole."

"Are you certain we don't have to get help?" Cam asked her.

"He'll need help. Just wait."

She pulled her knees up and hugged her legs. They watched the water. The wind lifted a few tags of froth, but the water was fairly calm. Tracy was gone. Farther down the beach a motorcycle was purring along. It was coming toward them. A girl was driving. She was wearing a chartreuse bandana knotted around her bosom. Sitting behind her was Tracy. Tracy hopped off the bike while the girl kept her hand on the throttle to keep the motor raging. Margaret said hello, but the girl had some wiring on her teeth that kept her jaw knitted tight, and she couldn't return the greeting. She saluted Cam and Margaret, then engaged the clutch; the wheels tore into the sandy berm and the motorcycle moved through impressive whoops and twistees as she sped away.

Cam was shaking his head, smiling. Margaret couldn't stand to watch him. Leave it to Tracy to find somebody's soft spot. He tricked them and returned with no fear of reprisal. The girl on the motorcycle *was* wonderful, both skilled and dreamy. What could Margaret say about it? Cam and Tracy were laughing about the girl. Cam was impressed. The shift worried Margaret. It was better to keep them of two minds, like a train that has a locomotive in the front and one in the back. It can change direction without a roundhouse.

Before they left the beach, Margaret walked over to a pay phone to call Elizabeth. The telephone receiver was disassembled; the coin return was laddered with gloss from a spider. She had to walk farther. At the next booth, she dialed her stepmother and told her that they were going to be late. Yes, they had a swim, they were having fun. Yes, Jane was fine. The baby was big. Margaret didn't tell Elizabeth about the affidavit. If they wanted to give themselves over to science, they would just have to do it on their own.

Elizabeth told Margaret that Darcy had reported to the police that the Duster was stolen and she wanted the thief arrested.

There was a sunset as they rode the ferry and they sat on the top deck, above the rows of cars, to watch it play itself out. The ship's engines rumbled, stilled, rumbled again as the ferry maneuvered out into the open water. Margaret told her brother what Elizabeth had said. He was staring directly at the oblong blob of sun that touched the horizon and sent a shimmering funnel across the surface toward them. Cam didn't blink.

"She's responding accordingly," Tracy said. "Tit for tat, with a little twist of revenge. It's a passion move—"

"Shut up, faggot!" Cam told him, and he walked

away, taking the ladder, hardly touching the treads. He plunged down to the bottom deck, where the Duster was parked.

When they were driving again, Margaret said, "Why don't you just telephone Darcy and tell her to call off the cops? We'll be home in less than an hour, and she'll have the Duster back."

"It's very dramatic," Tracy said.

Cam said, "She's just jerking my chain. She's a bitch to the end, that's all."

"We can get home without even seeing a cop," Tracy said.

"That's not the point," Cam said. "I don't care about seeing a cop."

Margaret suggested that they stop at the highway patrol and explain their situation before a police car pulled them over. She wondered why Elizabeth didn't explain the situation to the authorities? You know, Darcy—an emotional woman going through a divorce, that kind of thing.

Cam said, "Because Elizabeth's cold. That's why they're selling their bodies."

"They get money for their corpses?" Margaret said.

"I don't think so," Tracy said. "There's transportation costs, a fee for the refrigerator truck."

"What do you know about it?" Cam said.

"Don't you have a hair of feeling for your folks?" Tracy said.

Margaret saw it happening. She reached for the radio, but Cam brushed her hand off the knob.

"What about your own mother?" Cam said.

"I've got one." Tracy stretched his arms.

"Well?"

"We've come to terms. It's copacetic," Tracy said.

Cam couldn't let it rest. "Now Margaret, her mother's *dead*, she can't judge the situation here—"

"Tell me about it," Margaret said.

They were doing the speed limit one minute, then Cam was tightening the distance between cars. "Let's try harder," Margaret said. "Why don't we just try to get the police on our ass."

"I'm driving the car," Cam said.

Tracy said, "A little too fast."

She felt her diaphragm knit tighter, and her breath was getting too shallow. They reached ninety miles an hour. "You're doing just what *Darcy* wants."

"Sure," Cam said, "whatever you say."

Cam slowed the car and they went a few minutes at an easy speed. No one said anything. It was the new dark before the moon and stars. Everything was invisible, blotted out. A few strands of mist lifted off the fields and strayed over the road, swirled through the beams of their headlights. They were heading back through miles of vegetable farms. Margaret searched far ahead where the headlights thinned and it was a blank wall; then the beams reached through, washed over each distance. Cam must have seen what she was doing and he clicked off the headlamps. The dark plowed into the windshield.

Tracy leaned back into his seat. He cleared his throat to erase his alarm. "You're crazy," he said.

Cam cruised through the blackness for a few seconds,

then flicked his high beams on again, just in time for a hare to freeze, fluttering to the left and right, then keeping still. In that halo of chaos it couldn't escape and they felt its thud under the front wheel.

Margaret yelped and covered her face with her hands. The men were laughing and groaning. They almost seemed happy; they greeted that small death willingly.

Cam stopped the car on the side of the road. Tracy walked a few feet away from the car and urinated in the sparse weeds. Margaret could hear the stream slap the broad-bladed grasses and drill its little notch in the sand. "Might as well," Cam said, and he got out of the car to find a place. She wondered about the two men sharing this brief intimacy. What she knew of one, she could not beg from the other. Could carnal knowledge equal a brother's blind devotion? She watched the two men zip their pants. Tracy shifted his weight from one leg to the other to adjust the fit of his jeans, shoving them lower on his hips so he had room for himself. It reminded Margaret of a horse she had watched pawing the dirt in an indoor arena, his big velvety testicles shivering each time his hoof struck. The two men stood even in height and similar in physique, shoulder to shoulder in the dark before her. When they stood in front of the vehicle, she thought of a pair of exquisite drays, horses that must always be well matched in conformation and temperament.

As a child, she had never seen a man's flesh without the confusing drape of his slacks, but she had one helpful document: a catalogue from the Philadelphia Museum of Art, a book of reproductions from the celebrated Picasso show of 1958, which her parents had visited. She liked a painting called *Boy Leading a Horse*, in which a youth stood naked beside a big horse. The two walked side by side, face front. The boy's bare foot edged the sharp hoof; the velvet nostril of the horse brushed the boy's narrow hip. The painting made no concession to charm; the tones were terra-cotta and grey, with intense scumbling on the upper third of the canvas where the sky dissolved in the background. Margaret studied the painting, gauging the boy's lean figure; its proximity to the weighty beast was startling. Their intimacy seemed a great, enslaved tolerance—a patient exchange of power. The power of the flesh. The boy's genitals were like little apples; the horse's eyes were rounder, larger.

"Are you finished?" she asked. "You two have to come back in the car while I go to the bathroom. *Sit* in this car while I find a place," Margaret told them.

"She's got a toilet phobia," Tracy told Cam.

"There's no toilets out here," Cam said.

Margaret walked into the field. She couldn't see very far in front of her and the low rows of vegetables looked strange, black-leaved, like something poisonous. There weren't any shrubs or fences she could hide behind. "Look the other way or I can't get started," she told them.

She saw them turn their faces, but they were laughing. It was always the same, men thought she was making a big production. She urinated standing up, but she had to remove her panties and hold them in her hand, she had to spread her feet wide. Standing up was better than squatting. Squatting in an open field reminded her of lower beasts; aren't all beasts approached from behind during rituals of mating? Women are the only animals with vertical cunts, she was thinking. Women's cunts telescope upward and women have to be cajoled, coerced to lie down on their backs or on their bellies. They have to be instructed to kneel or straddle. Tracy often tugged her hips onto him, his weight and rhythm against her back. She didn't have to think for herself; he absorbed her as he pushed into those central inches. He liked best when he didn't have to look her in the face or reveal his pleasure to her. She allowed him that consolation.

She walked back to the car and she saw Tracy counting out something on his fingers. He was making some assertions and numbering his reasons. She felt a slight pulse high in her stomach, some kind of nausea, like when she imagined people were conspiring. When the two men huddled together like that, forgetting about her, their sudden neutrality with one another seemed too private. They seemed ready to move ahead without her.

When they were driving again, Tracy kept looking over at Cam. Margaret watched Tracy's impatience. He was pinching a crease in his jeans with his thumb and forefinger, running his fingers down the fabric, then smoothing it out with the heel of his hand.

She watched the dark. A streetlight showed an erratic cloud of June bugs, little cigar stubs circling the glare.

Cam said, "We made our decision. We pretty much decided."

"*We* did? I hate that editorial *we*. I can never tell who's talking. No one takes responsibility," she said.

"We're driving to Chicago," Cam told her.

"Hail Mary," Tracy said.

"Are you following me?" Cam asked her. "We're doing it."

"You're driving to Chicago? In this Duster?"

"With the three of us, we can drive straight through."

Margaret said, "Come on—I don't have a change of clothes. I'm dressed for the beach."

"You're fine."

"I only have these flip-flops."

Tracy said, "No, your shoes are in back."

"Those aren't mine," she said. "Those are Darcy's."

"Try 'em," Tracy said.

"I won't try them."

"We'll get something. I have a Sears card," Cam said.

"Terrific."

"She's not impressed. It's the Sears image—it could use some work," Tracy said.

"Maybe she can come down a level," Cam said.

"The Arrow Collar guy? He's not my problem," she said. Margaret pulled her fingers through her salty hair and would say no more. Tracy said that just because her mother was dead, squared away so to speak, she shouldn't shirk her family obligations.

"*We* can shut up," Margaret said.

"Your mother is—"

"Dead," Cam said.

"This is harassment," Margaret said.

"You've never owned up to it," Tracy said.

"Trace, please—" Why did she plead? She never sliced off the last syllable of his name unless she was whining.

Tracy told her that if they went to Chicago they could visit her mother's grave. It's about time. They could look it up at the town hall and find the location.

"It's not my quest—it's Cam's!" Margaret said.

Cam told Tracy to shut up. He was making it worse.

Tracy explained Teilhard de Chardin's Theoretical Axes of Happiness to Cam. He was saying, "People fall into three groups: Number one, there's *The Tired*. These are the pessimists, fearmongers like Margaret, but these are even worse than Margaret. Number two, we've got *Pleasure Seekers*, hedonists, people who mate incessantly until they're numb, people who drink without drunken relief, they tip the bottle until the last dribble is extinguished."

"He's revving up," Margaret said.

"Oh really? Number three, *The Enthusiasts*. These people are lords of the safari, soul searchers, always ready to explore life's junkyard down to the last double-chromed bat-wing window from an extinct Sunbeam convertible. Eureka! That's what we should try for. We're scavengers. Cam's our leader."

"This has nothing to do with finding car parts in a scrap heap. Cam's got a lifelong grudge."

Cam punched the radio so the news was screaming. Then it was the baseball scores, and they listened to see how the Cubs were doing. The baseball idea embroidered the issue and the men gripped it. Cam started asking about the pitching lineup. He hadn't been fol-

lowing the Cubs. Tracy was chattering. He said he once
had Harry Caray's signature on a ball, right on the
sweet spot where the stitches come together to frame
his John Hancock. Maybe they could take in a game at
Wrigley.

Margaret used to like to go to the ballparks with Cam.
In Baltimore they sold miniature Oriole pennants attached to No. 2 pencils. At Phillies' games, they purchased steaming soft pretzels—singles, or five in a paper
sack. They sold a peppermint stick inserted in half of a
lemon. She longed for the simple pleasure of that.
Those two clean flavors, contrasting cool and sour.

"Well. I might go to Chicago so you can find Lewis,
but I'm not taking any detours to cemeteries. That's out
of the question," she told Tracy.

"Don't slam any doors yet," Tracy said. "Sandra's
weedy plot could use some sprucing up. Maybe we can
get an azalea, do some transplanting."

Margaret *did* sometimes picture Sandra's grave. She had
read a magazine article about an exhumation. The article
stated that the atrophied uterus was typically the last
and final organ of the human body to decompose. The
muscular womb was tough and stringy; it condensed
into a hard knot and could be found intact years after
burial. Margaret imagined her mother's bones, the ivory
cradle of the pelvis, and centered there—a tiny amber
fossil—the shrunken pocket in which she was started
and from which she was expelled.

Tracy knew when her thoughts veered, and he

pushed her shoulder until she was settled against him. They were driving into Wilmington and argued about the Duster.

"Isn't it risky going around the city in this car?" Margaret said.

"I've got to pick up some cash at the office," Cam said.

"What cash are you talking about?"

"Who are you, Officer Krupke?" Cam said.

Tracy said, "Petty cash at the apartments?"

"Bingo."

"That's crazy," Margaret said. "I've got money at the house."

"I'm not dealing with Elizabeth at this point in time."

Cam parked the Duster in the tenants' parking lot and went into the office. Margaret got out of the car and sat on the hood, but it was too hot. Tracy saw the swimming pool and started over.

He was peeling his pants down, and then she saw his white shirt on the cement beside his jeans. He stepped down the ladder and lowered himself into the water without disturbing the surface. He disappeared. She waited beside the Duster, listening to the hood contract as the engine cooled. When she didn't hear any splashing, she wondered if maybe Tracy hit his head on something. When she walked over, he was floating on his back, pretty as you please. He looked quite evocative, his whole trunk exposed to the air, naked.

"Get out," she said. She hated standing there in the same spot where Cam had confessed his worries to her.

Tracy told her the water was perfect.

She saw the tilt of his hips, how his pelvis rose on the swell of water as he drifted supine. His body absorbed and reflected her thoughts. She wriggled out of her tank top and held it by the spaghetti straps; she was having second thoughts. Then she pushed her shorts down. She tested the water, brushing her foot back and forth. She climbed down and stayed by the gutter as he swam up behind her. She gripped the tile ledge. "Don't get my hair wet," she said.

"Jesus."

"It's too deep here," she said.

"I've got you," he said.

"I'm sinking," she said.

"No, I have you, shut up. For once, shut up."

She felt a strong jet from the filter vent, a velvety pressure against her legs. Tracy buoyed her, nipped the bony pebbles at the base of her neck, and she felt her cunt pulse and contract. He moved her the way he wanted and finding her profuse silk, he praised her.

"This is ridiculous," she said. "Why do you always do this?"

"Only when you're around," he told her.

Margaret noticed the slow pull of a searchlight over the city. Perhaps it was a new car dealership or another discount drugstore opening. The funnel turned and fell, then rolled around again. She liked its regularity; it grounded her in her weightlessness, helped to trigger her orgasm. Then Tracy held her shoulders and pushed her under. He leaned all his weight upon her and she sank. Her descent was smooth, dreamlike, and at first she didn't question which direction Tracy had steered her. When her feet touched the cement bottom, she twisted and pumped her legs, but he kept her down. She shook her head side to side. Huge bubbles escaped from her mouth, blurred pillows of air shooting upward, then two lines of tiny silver BBs. When Tracy let her rise, she was choking; the purified water burned her throat and sinuses.

Cam stepped forward to the pool's edge. How long he had been waiting, she didn't know. "Nice," he said. "People can look out their windows and see everything."

"He was trying to drown me!" She was coughing.

Cam looked directly into Margaret's eyes, avoiding Tracy altogether. He seemed more curious about her immodesty than her complaint against Tracy. Maybe Cam could have used a swim. It might have been good if they could reach some equal ground. Nudity can do that. Margaret started up the chrome ladder. Her nose was running, stinging from the chlorine.

"Wait a minute," Cam told her. He walked back to the office and came back with a towel. He handed it to Margaret.

She pulled herself out of the water and pinched the towel under her arms, leaving her back to the air. She felt her brother's eyes move over her hips. She finished with the towel and handed it to Tracy. Tracy wadded the towel and buffed his arms and legs. He didn't try to cover himself up.

"Why don't you just lead a parade," Cam said. He didn't look away as they pulled their clothes on. Cam took them into the small office. There was a vinyl sofa with some blankets folded at one end. A pillow with a dirty slip was crammed on a bookshelf.

"Is this where you're sleeping these days?" she asked him.

"That's right," Cam told her, "home sweet home."

Margaret saw his name embossed on a brass plate that was glued to a wedge of wood. This was something Darcy ordered for him. It looked stupid. "Is this where you work," Margaret asked him, "*and* sleep?"

"I'm never in here, I'm down at the new condos or running around somewhere. I don't *sit* here."

"You're not taking that money, are you?"

"It's just a loan."

"I've got some money at the house."

"We're not going back to the house," Cam said.

Margaret said, "But whose money is that?"

"It's petty cash, money for plumbers or electricians, if something went out in the middle of the night and I had to get it taken care of."

"Oh, emergency money," Tracy said. He smiled.

"That's right," Cam said. The men seemed to understand one another.

"We might have an emergency," Tracy said.

"Correct. Like Tracy here, he had a clog and got his pipes flushed, right? How much is that? A couple hundred?" He unfolded some bills and pushed the cash at Margaret.

Margaret made a face, rolled her eyes. It was an involuntary reaction; she hated to roll her eyes. Hated the way it felt.

"Look," she said, "do you even know where this guy lives when we get to Chicago?"

Cam told her the address, the apartment number, the zip code. He recited the telephone number.

"You've talked to him on the phone?"

"No. I've dialed it. He picks it up like he expects to hear from the president. Then I terminate the call. Slip it back in the cradle, nice and easy."

"You just hang up?" Margaret said.

"He answers the same every time—like he's taking reservations."

"Maybe he just has telephone manners," Margaret said.

"What are you going to say to him; what do you *want* to say?" Tracy asked.

"I don't have to say shit. I'm in a position of power." He tapped the cash against the desk so the bills were even, and he put the money in his wallet. They walked back toward the car. Margaret saw a blue light twirling toward them on the street, but it was just a tow truck. It was a tow truck pulling another tow truck. The sight was strangely compelling, as if it mirrored some aspect of their situation.

They started off without a change of clothes, without anything. Cam said he'd get toothbrushes for everyone. Margaret passed her tongue over her front teeth. She said, "A toothbrush is the least of my problems. I'm freezing. My clothes are damp."

"You're hair's wet," Tracy told her.

"Forty-eight hours, that's all," Cam told her. "We can buy something tomorrow. You can go to Marshall Field's and get Levi's."

"I can't wear jeans until I wash them a couple times," she said. "They'll be too stiff and I hate the smell of the sizing."

"What's wrong with your shorts?" Tracy said, smiling. She tried to shush him.

"Do you want some Kleenex?" Tracy said.

Cam said to Tracy, "You're some lewd son of a bitch, you know that?"

"I'm just relaxed about it, the erotic impulse. It's human," Tracy said. "I'd say you're wearing your strap a bit tight. Do you always give movie ratings to every routine situation?"

Margaret tried to imagine riding a thousand miles wedged in between the two men. It was crazy, but she didn't decline to go on their journey. If two worlds converged, making one perverse expansion, what was her responsibility? Was she central? Its magnet? The feeling was heady. The Duster hardly gripped the pavement, skating forward in airy surges. The car seemed to cruise with the globe as it plunged in rotation, rolling into the dark.

II

They were riding up the Philadelphia Pike, a narrow antique four-lane that connected Wilmington with Chester, Pennsylvania.

"I used to come up here with Richard," Margaret said. "He took me on sales trips, into Philadelphia, to U.S. Steel, to the refineries at Marcus Hook and to the

Scott paper plant. I watched them cut giant tubes of toilet paper into four-inch rolls—"

"No kidding? Toilet tissue?" Tracy said. "Welcome to the world of Freud."

"Why must you take my simple memories and dice them up into some kind of psycho salad. Will you let me alone!" Margaret said. She tried to remember the names of the drinking establishments as they passed the roadside bars, the familiar saloons displaying tipped neon cocktail glasses over their doors, one after the other. Coming home from the plants, her father had usually stopped for a drink somewhere. He might try to buy her a Shirley Temple, but the cherry repelled her.

At the White Horse Tavern, Richard argued with the bartender. Margaret loved the ornaments she saw, and Richard wanted to buy the heavy china horse heads, the handles on the taps. The bartender got the manager and the manager declined Richard's offer. Nothing could go. Not even at that price. "The decorations are fixtures, as essential as the refrigeration," the man said. Her father saw something else. He reached up to the well-stocked shelf and pulled a trinket from the neck of a brand of scotch; it was a small plastic horse on a loop of string. Richard handed this to Margaret. Margaret started to tell Cam about the souvenir, it might add a gram weight to the scales, on Richard's behalf, but Tracy could twist the detail. Tracy might say it was another example of Margaret's "equine obsession," so she kept quiet.

Cam had to stop for some gasoline and he found a twenty-four-hour Texaco place where a girl sat in a

Plexiglas booth. The girl was reading a book, underlining several sentences with a yellow outlining pen. She was going overboard with the marker, Margaret thought: what's the point if you underline every word? The girl didn't seem too interested in the Duster and Cam parked in front of the pumps. He told Tracy to go talk to the girl just in case.

Tracy was pleased by this idea, by his new partnership with Cam. He told Margaret to be cool, be like Bonnie to Cam's Clyde. "You have the hair for it," he said, "the blond hair. Just like Faye Dunaway." Margaret watched Tracy go over to the girl and start a conversation. The girl was encased in Plexiglas and Margaret couldn't hear what she answered, but Tracy was asking about White Tower hamburger stands. He was talking about the architecture of those restaurants compared to the golden-arches concept. Then the tank was filled and Cam paid the money. They drove away from the gas station and Cam pulled over to the side of the road and got out of the car. He went in back and unscrewed the tiny light bulb over the license plate. He tossed it into a vacant lot. Margaret heard the bulb pop. Cam looked satisfied and he got back into the car.

"Is this a joke?" she asked him. "I mean, if the police were looking for the Duster, wouldn't they have nabbed us by now? We were all over Wilmington, they didn't do anything about it."

"As time ticks by, they have to take us seriously," Cam said.

"Oh, you mean after so many hours, they say, that car isn't coming home?" Tracy said.

"True," Cam said, "and, by now you can be sure

Darcy's been on the horn giving them hell. By this time, it's in the hands of the troopers."

"Troopers?" Margaret said. "What in the hell are you talking about?"

Tracy said, "State troopers. It goes out over a computer network. They type it on a CRT, a description of the Duster, of us, of our wicked intentions."

"Bullshit," she said.

"Look," Tracy said, "Clyde has a lot on his mind, so be a good Bonnie."

Cam said, "What?"

"You know. Bonnie and Clyde? Don't you think Margaret looks like Faye. Faye Don'-go-away."

"That actress?" Cam said.

"Faye Don'-go-away. She's a dream. All washed-out-looking with a dark mouth. Yes. She looks almost dead, but her lips are burning. She devours somebody in an instant. Eats you up. You're in heaven."

Cam liked the description. He was smiling, watching the road, picturing something.

They reached the Pennsylvania Turnpike at around midnight. They would use the turnpike until they crossed over to Interstate 80, and that would take them the whole way. It would be good to get out of the tri-state area, Cam was saying. Margaret agreed. She was happy to lose the landscape; a familiar landscape evokes so much.

"We're tired already," she told them.

"We're fine," Cam told her.

"I've got my second wind," Tracy said.

"I bet you do," Cam said.

Margaret recognized Cam's "poor me" tone of voice. Cam almost looked like Richard used to look on one of the family's long trips. It was a mask of fatigue after driving a long way with all of them. The Scenic Route can often become a kind of hell. The winding roads, the small rise and descent from low, inconsequential hills, corresponded with the flux of Elizabeth's complaints, the children's sonorous then deafening inquiries.

Then they saw their first police car acting funny. Tracy shifted his legs and Margaret sat up straight. There had not been too many cruisers, and each had passed them without notice. This fellow was going along in tandem as he talked on his radio. The trooper adjusted his speed according to the Duster's, which gave Margaret a queasy feeling like running beside a mirror in a fun house or sliding backward and forward on ice.

"Act regular," Cam said.

"Don't look," Tracy said.

Margaret looked down at her lap.

"You're looking down, don't look down! Look natural." Cam talked with his teeth clamped.

Just as suddenly, the cruiser moved away, accelerated, and disappeared into the dark ahead of them.

"Shit, shit, shit." Margaret didn't want any more of it. The next moment she was laughing in ragged bursts.

Cam looked up at the car ceiling and rotated his head on the back of his neck, rubbing out the tension. Margaret tried to check her amusement and she pulled at her hair, pinching a clump and tugging her fingers down the strands to the end. Her hair felt strange, perhaps it was the chlorine; the strands no longer seemed to possess the ordinary properties of human hair. She pulled the rearview mirror down to study her face. Her hair looked metallic, brittle, like lamé thread. It had a strange luster as if artificially lighted by an unnameable source. "Jesus! My hair is turning green," she told Cam.

"It smells like Clorox," Tracy said.

"Can you please? I'm sort of busy here," Cam said, watching the highway. He told them not to get comfortable. The cruiser was probably up ahead checking the tag and they were going to be nabbed pronto.

"What should we do?" Margaret bit her lip to keep from laughing. She saw that Cam was serious. It was really between him and Darcy. It was something intimate; he was sparring with an absentee opponent.

Cam took the next exit off the turnpike. "Fucking mounties," he said.

"Yes," Tracy said, "they can be quite dogmatic. Inflexible. They wouldn't understand the nuances of your situation. They've never seen it face to face, Darcy's death rays. You're being persecuted for every little wrong since you got hitched, right? This is the coal in your threadbare stocking. She's dumping everything on you in one big, official zing."

Cam looked at Margaret for assistance. "Tell him to put a gag on it, will you?" Cam said.

"You tell him."

"Tell me," Tracy said.

"I'm serious. Stop analyzing my private affairs."

"Since when are they so private? Here we are, riding

in this stolen vehicle with you. I'd say we were pretty tight."

"I'd say you were a queer if I didn't see you nailing my sister."

"Did you learn the first thing about it?" Tracy said.

Margaret pulled her chin in as the two men bickered. They were talking about her. It was both vile and flattering. She hated it when her vanity took over. Then the car lurched, bounced hard, the shocks jangled. Margaret screamed. The asphalt ended and they careened off a ledge where the pavement stopped. The road stretched ahead just dust and gravel. A sign said PAVEMENT ENDS, but it wasn't properly placed. It was after the fact.

"The sign's been moved," Tracy said.

Margaret said, "That's sick." Cam turned a circle and steered around a gully to get back on the road.

Tracy said, "The perpetrator might be in the woods watching us right now." The landscape was dark, wooded. Anything was possible.

Margaret said, "If we're going to make all these mistakes, I don't want to keep going. You said we'd go straight through on the highway like normal people. I don't want to go winding all over the place like this."

"Look at that map," Cam told her. "You said you would be navigator, so navigate."

He flicked on the overhead light and she unfolded a map of the Eastern United States. She rubbed her finger over the paper. She liked the sensation; the paper was smooth, slightly furred.

"We're here, we want to go there." A bold circle

signified Chicago, a cloud of green designated the general metropolitan area. If they were going to avoid I-76, they would have to take some secondary roads, two-lane roads.

"Head-ons," Tracy said, "most of your head-on collisions happen on these country two-lanes. Then there's always deer to consider."

"Can't we just drive on the highway?" Margaret said. "It's not like we really stole this car. It's not like the time when we pinched that Dodge Monaco. This is your fucking wife's car!"

"Exactly," Cam said. "She's telling me loud and clear it's *hers*." He rubbed his shave. It was a full day's worth of growth by now. Tracy touched his own face, started scratching it. Margaret couldn't help smiling.

Cam kept adjusting his mirrors and gunning the engine desperado-style, and it reminded her of the episode with the stolen Dodge. When they were teenagers, they took a five-finger-discount on a shiny Monaco and drove it around for the afternoon before crashing it up.

It just happened to be Mother's Day.

Margaret and Cam often went driving with Cam's friend Wayne in his old Chrysler. Cam was impressed by Wayne's girl, Colleen. Her hair flashed moment-to-moment like sheet lightning. Margaret's hair was regular blond, but Colleen's was electric, white and glossy as a doll's hair. She was studious in her bleaching habits. She used a brand called Midnight Sun, like a Nordic halo, a brittle spill that shivered each time she moved her head. She separated a few strands and tugged an icy point to suck between her teeth.

They were riding in and out of the developments, screeching around the tiny cul-de-sacs. Sometimes they got out of the car to measure the length of "patch" they put down on the asphalt and to touch their fingertips against the hot smear. The radio and the hot wind off the asphalt had drugged Margaret into submission. She didn't note the exact moment when it was no longer talk and they put it into motion. Wayne was driving slowly up the street and Cam was leaning far out of the car window the way dogs ride. They were searching for a vehicle with keys left in the ignition.

The streets were deserted; they could smell the charcoal going in the backyards of the split-level houses. Acres of houses with no variance but for the decals on the mailboxes and the tiny footprints and signatures that ruined the new sidewalks. Their plan seemed highly feasible, even sensible in its way. A simple task necessitated by a complex mood resulting from a series of emotional outbursts in public places with their parents, until they reached their target consciousness.

Wayne inched up to a car, a ruby-red Monaco with a vinyl roof. Keys dangled from the steering column, caught the light, glittered. Margaret had a strange tickle in her throat, like the sharp threads of an artichoke.

Cam got out of the Chrysler and touched his toes. He stretched his arms over his head like it was seventh inning, then he got behind the wheel of the Monaco. The early cicadas were piercing the quiet in short ugly spasms that killed the whine of the flywheel as Cam started the engine. Cam rolled it away from the curb and the Chrysler followed. They left Wayne's car in Westside Terrace and tumbled into the red car. Margaret sat up in front with Cam. Wayne nestled in back with Colleen; he was already pulling her neckline down over her shoulders. Cam floored the gas pedal so that the car shivered in place for a few seconds before flying forward. He circled the block to examine the patch, a couple thick black smears, variegated like snakeskin against the new white concrete.

Cam drove them everywhere around the city. The Monaco was a rental car, the key chain said WE TRY HARDER. There wasn't anything personal in it. It was fresh, vacuumed, the vinyl seats smelled strong. It accelerated harsh but fast, it flew.

"We try harder," Cam said, accelerating to beat a light. When Cam passed a cherry top or if he recognized an unmarked cruiser, he slowed the car. He sank in his seat and bounced up and down, twisting the wheel back and forth like a hick farmer driving an old tractor. He was baiting the police, but they didn't seem to notice. His steering was becoming more and more exaggerated and frantic. Margaret began to feel weightless, anchored by a fragile string like one of those Chinese paper flowers unfurling in a glass of water. Her friends were grinding their hips together in the backseat, but Cam didn't seem disgusted. Colleen was immersed in it, her hair looked bad, it looked spent, colorless as fishing line. She held on to the boy, pulling his collar, pressing his face with little sucking kisses. Margaret thought, It's got nothing to do with me and Cam. Then the cruiser was abreast of them. The officer lifted the brim of his hat and tugged it down again. It was a tolerant warning, and he allowed them a moment to consider it before he turned on the siren and the light started circling.

"Guess what—" Margaret said.

Cam said, "I see him. I see him." Cam accelerated in a straight line up the highway. He was cutting a path right through the moving traffic, making his own get-away lane right up the middle. Cam nosed between cars and the traffic veered to the left and right to avoid them. It was a reverse wake, a terrible seam ripping upward. Margaret could hear the sirens, several of them, but they seemed distant. Suddenly the windshield went dark, like an air raid curtain, but it was just an underpass and the light came back. Margaret tried to speak. Words clattered through her like small geometric pieces, sharp, lodging in her throat and lungs.

"One hundred, one hundred five." Cam was reading the speedometer. Margaret couldn't believe he wasn't watching the road. His fear looked like a form of pleasure, a chilly, high-altitude intoxication. He kept reading the speedometer as it inched up. He looked as if he had suddenly found his purpose and accepted what it meant, its toil and labor, its rewards.

Colleen was leaning over the front seat, screaming for Cam to slow down. The intersection flashed, appeared and dissolved in an instant. They were hit once in the right front and immediately they were hit in back on the opposite side. The car whipped in a full circle, skated left, was clipped a third time, and its front axle flew off. The hood of the car curled through the windshield, glass sloshed in like a wave of rhinestone buttons. Then nothing. Stillness. Colleen fell between them. She was asleep with her eyes open. The girl whispered, but she wasn't using words; a sudsy vermilion spray surfaced on her lips. She had bitten through her tongue.

They were taken to Wilmington General; everyone needed some stitches. Colleen was in surgery, but the others were placed in jail to wait for the appropriate signatures. That summer, they had one day in family court. It was decided that Margaret would meet with a probation officer in the basement of the Wilmington courthouse for a full year, twice a week after school. Cam went straight to boot camp at the crest of a record heat wave.

8

They traveled through a breadth of woods. "Is this the dead of night, or what?" Margaret asked Cam. She couldn't stand watching the dark unless they kept talking.

"Take it easy," he told her.

"The woods have eyes," Tracy said flatly.

"I'll get us back on the highway. Once I get on, I'm not getting off. I'm not stopping. Do you want something from 7 Eleven?" Cam said.

"I don't *see* a 7 Eleven," Margaret said. "You're hallucinating."

"Don't be a bitch. I saw something." Cam pulled over to the shoulder and made a U-turn.

"That's an A&P," Margaret told him.

"Correction. A&P. Are you already starting with this shit?"

Margaret didn't like all-night supermarkets. It was always the sleepless, women with eating disorders, imperious college students, the lonely in their search, or the angry fleeing from a confrontation. Night-shift workers struggling against their biological clocks. These were the types. Then it was the three of them, sunburned, crazed-looking, twirling left and right, figuring which aisle to take.

Tracy collected some apricots and weighed them on a scale. Cam walked ahead as if he didn't know Tracy. Margaret picked up a single strawberry and pressed it into her mouth between her cheek and gum. She picked up a bag of Eight O'Clock Coffee beans and she took it through the cashier line. Tracy said she had kicked the habit last year, why was she starting up again?

"Just for the trip," she promised.

"Watch her," Tracy said. "She gets twitchy on these, real south-of-the-border. She wants to tango."

Cam pushed some sweet rolls and a carton of whole milk onto the rubber mat. "One of these days we'll get some real food," he told them, but he didn't seem all that committed to the idea. Food wasn't on his mind. Walking back to the Duster, Margaret noticed a baby had been left alone in a car. Someone had run into the store and just left the baby perched on the passenger seat. She leaned into the window. The baby was dozing, its eyes closed, the lids translucent, silky. The baby was tilting to the left, it was sliding toward the floor. Margaret wanted to arrange the infant more securely in the bucket seat. Then a fellow came toward her. "Hey, girl," he was shouting at her, "get away from there!"

"I'm not doing anything," Margaret said.

"Get your own baby." The man got into the car and drove away. She watched him pull out into the traffic; he forgot to turn on his headlights and still he kept going into the dark.

Cam was chugging the carton of milk and passing it over to Tracy. Tracy pulled the sweet rolls from the foil tray; they were coming in a doughy grid and he had to separate them. Margaret bit into her first coffee bean, then into the next. They settled down again for a bit of restful touring on the interstate. Margaret leaned back against the passenger door, sitting sideways on Tracy. Tracy was quiet, his face shaded. Something inhabited him, a dark outlook that he supervised, shrugged off with an occasional twitch, an airy lift of his chin. This was when his mask would crinkle. He might stop in the middle of a sentence to tug his head back slightly, then let it fall level again. This mannerism, despite his efforts otherwise, revealed something. That's why he kept the conversation moving. It was like watching a river, a strong current—occasionally a paper scrap floats to the surface before it's tugged deep again.

Tracy pushed Margaret off of his lap. He didn't want her weight on him.

Cam looked tired. Some people look good when they're tired. Margaret's husband used to tell her that she looked good when she was sick. If she had the flu, after two weeks of coughing, he might say she looked seductive. It was her lack of color, the hollows and shadows of prolonged weakness that appealed to him. Cam looked tired but he didn't look diminished; his fatigue seemed only to sharpen his features. His profile reminded her of something on an urn; it was angular, stern, frozen with mysterious intention. She had always loved his profile. In their early teens, Margaret and Cam shared a bunk in a small cabin on a yacht owned by the Atlas Chemical Company. Richard had been invited for a rub-elbows weekend cruise with a production supervisor of Atlas Chemical, and when Elizabeth refused to go, he took Margaret and Cam. Their cabin was narrow and tight; yet, the room had a tiny sink and a fat scallop of flowery English soap scudded back and forth in its bowl, scenting the air. Margaret shared the stiff foam mattress, letting Cam have the porthole side. A lantern enlarged Cam's silhouette against the curved wall. Even his breath rising in the cool air made a shadow, a billowy turbulence.

"You're staring at me," he had said.

The floral soap was strong; it made Margaret feel both refreshed and dizzy. She told Cam that she loved him, but she didn't know what she was trying to get across. She had some uncomfortable surges, some half-defined insights she couldn't follow to the end. She was leaning on her elbow beside Cam. She said she would do anything for him, but she might have said she would do anything *to* him. It was so sudden, a shock of hot laughter, then they weren't saying anything. Again, they laughed. Before they fell asleep they placed a row of peculiar sandbag ashtrays between them as a barrier.

Looking for a restaurant, they rolled through Niles, Ohio. A diner emitted a wet glow from its humid picture window and Margaret begged Cam to stop.

"Don't you know it's always a diner where the troopers hang out?"

"Oh, come on. You're crazy with this shit," Margaret said.

"No diners," Cam said.

Margaret insisted and Cam turned the car around and went back to the diner. There was no place to park and Cam had to leave the Duster beneath a huge yellow streetlight swirling with moths. Margaret watched the insects drawing dark coils and spirals on the Duster's shiny hood. She liked the sensation—all that movement outside of herself as she, at last, stood still.

Cam wasn't pleased with the streetlight. "Let's just hang out a sign," he told them. "It's a fucking show-room." They went into the restaurant, leaving the car to draw whatever attention it might. Margaret followed her brother with her eyes. He wasn't *trying* to act like Clyde Barrow, but he was swaggering. Maybe he was just stiff from driving. His gait was that funny mix of psychic hurt and weary indifference that comes across as a kind of self-assurance. She recognized it from her prison work.

The diner was clean but shabby, the floor glazed from years of wax buildup over the disintegrating linoleum. There were the layered scents of fried onions, burned coffee, and a sweet trace of chilled whipped topping when the refrigerator display case was opened. Margaret studied a single pie in the mirrored case; it looked old, the crust separating and falling away from the fruit filling. There were some other watery desserts, but Margaret couldn't identify them. They sat down at the counter and a woman in her fifties stopped watching the television to come over and pour them coffee. She spilled some as she served Tracy and she inverted the saucer and poured it back into his cup.

"Nice," Tracy said.

"It won't kill you," Cam told him.

"Did I say it would kill me?"

"Those little things irritate someone like you, don't they?" Cam said.

"What is it you're saying?"

"You give me a pain. You're a priss," Cam said.

Tracy said, "You don't know what you're talking about."

Margaret kept shushing them. It was getting out of hand. Cam said, "You can screw my sister underwater, can you do it standing up on solid ground?"

"What are you talking about?" Margaret was saying.

Tracy said, "Cam's got a good case of marble balls."

"God, will you—" Margaret said.

"Cam has a problem," Tracy said.

"I'm not the one with the problem, pal." Cam poured some salt on the counter, watching how it sifted.

"Classic symptoms," Tracy said. "After looking at your diary, I say it's some kind of patriarchal infatuation.

You never got your male bonding. You have a Vandal-ized Love Map."

"A Love Map?" Margaret was asking. She tried to get Tracy to explain this to her; it might derail him.

Tracy wasn't going to stop. He flicked her hand off his knee where she was pinching the flat ridge of cartilage. Tracy said, "This quest is sexual, this drive to Chicago. This is an excursion into the forbidden fron-tier. Your father rejected you and you think it's personal, it's a judgment on you as a man, not just as a child. You have a fixation, like one of those people who follow celebrities from city to city.

"How long have you been carrying around those yellowed newspaper clippings, those photographs of Lewis pretty as a bridesmaid? You've been calling him on the telephone for how many years? You think he's waiting for the phone to ring? He's not waiting. It's a romantic delusion. It's called erotomania."

Cam was stirring his coffee until it revolved, swelled over the brim of the cup. "Who's calling who queer?"

"That's my point." Tracy's eyes were black. "You tell me."

Cam stood up and nudged Tracy off his stool. They exchanged a few tight punches, inexpert uppercuts to the hollow at the breastbone, dead center at the dia-phragm. Both men connected, both felt their breath seared. They turned away, stood back, and looked at Margaret, looked at the row of silver stools as if to count them.

"Enough," Tracy said, coughing. He declined to continue. Margaret knew they were evenly matched. It could have gone on quite a while. The woman behind the counter was waiting to see what was decided.

"We came in here to eat something," Margaret told the woman, "but I guess they're too exhausted to eat. We've been driving." The woman nodded to Margaret, then she shrugged. She had no opinion. She was wiping her ashtray, the one she kept behind the counter for herself. It was an abalone shell. Margaret watched the woman dabbing at the shell; it was deep lavender, mirrory on the inside of its bowl, but along its edge there were several gorgeous dark-blue grommets. Margaret couldn't take her eyes off it.

II

Tracy said he had a cousin who lived a little south of Akron. They could have some rest and get back on the road the next day. Cam wasn't too sure of this idea, but he was rubbing his hand over his lips now and again, and Margaret knew he was tired.

"This is my cousin Franklin. He's great. He's a talk-show host on a local station. UHF. He won't mind us showing up. He's a card-carrying night owl."

Margaret said, "Does he have a shower? I'd love to take a shower."

"Of course. Everyone in my family reveres the bath."

Margaret looked at the map and measured the miles with a piece of gum cut to fit the legend. "It's not out of our way at all," she told Cam. "And look, we're going to go right past Bowling Green, that's near Tina's commune. We can stop there tomorrow."

"Look, I'm not taking some kind of family vacation," Cam said. "We'll sleep at Frank's place, that's it."

Tracy said, "It's Franklin. Two syllables. It would be good if you could remember that. Like Franklin Delano Roosevelt, never Frank Delano."

"*Frank, Franklin*," Cam said. He didn't see the difference.

Franklin answered the door in a crepe de chine bathrobe with a flamingo print. Cam looked at Margaret. When Franklin turned around, the bathrobe said BOCA RATON RESORTS and this cleared it with Cam. The flamingos were just part of a respectable hotel advertising campaign. Tracy introduced everyone and they sat around the kitchen table drinking some ginger ale from a bottle with a rubber cork. The cork was a gadget from the fifties, a rubber stopper with some kind of tension spring inside. Franklin showed Margaret how it worked. The rubber squeaked against the mouth of the bottle until Tracy asked Franklin to cut it out. Even the little glasses were from an earlier period; they were pink, green, blue aluminum tumblers with a flared lip. She liked how the tinted aluminum began to sweat, revealing secret scratches. Then Franklin brought out the Welch's jelly jars with cartoon characters on them.

"Those are the Hanna-Barbera ones, there's some Disney and Warner Brothers. I have them all."

"Where did you outfit this place, a thrift shop in the Twilight Zone?" Tracy said.

"I'm a collector. I like domestics."

Cam was looking at his ginger ale, wiggling the glass so the fizz would rise. He was smiling.

"I saw your dad last June in Bridgeport," Franklin told Tracy.

"How nice for you," Tracy said.

"No, really, he's got a good situation there with Carlene. It's a new start. Of course, she's not trying to fill someone else's shoes, but she's a nice lady. They took me to that big steakhouse, you know the one? It has a great raw bar set up on an old skiff, a Boston Whaler or something, right in the middle of the room. For atmosphere. Out here in Ohio, you miss the clams and oysters. It was a nice spot."

"Never heard of it," Tracy said.

"Littlenecks, crab claws, stuffies—"

Tracy said, "Is that right? A regular Yankee smor-go-borg."

"Next time you're down there, with your dad, tell him I told you he should take you over there."

"Sure thing," Tracy said. He wasn't looking at them. Margaret wondered how much longer until he couldn't stand it, but soon they stood up and went into the living room. There was little space to turn around. Franklin had ten-foot stacks of *TV Guides* and other periodicals. Hundreds of flattened, monotone detective journals in six or seven separate towers. Margaret liked the black-and-white illustrations: chiseled detectives, good girls in high-necked sweaters, bad girls with a little extra shading to show cleavage, gangsters in zoot suits. Margaret looked at a glass cabinet that displayed some rare *Lone Ranger* magazine covers; the illustrations were almost translucent. "God, you really do collect things," Margaret said.

Franklin tugged a *TV Guide* from one of the precarious towers. "Want to know what's on? March 10, 1959, 8 P.M.?"

"Sure."

Franklin read a few listings. There was a show about President Eisenhower's hometown and the rest were old Westerns like "Have Gun Will Travel." Tracy sang the theme song: *Paladin, Paladin, where do you roam? A soldier of fortune is the man called Pal-a-din.* The melody was familiar and it sounded quite haunting; it summoned private memory, and the men shuffled their feet. Margaret pulled the hair away from her eyes and tucked it behind her ear. For a few minutes, Franklin quizzed Margaret with the *TV Guide* until she couldn't identify the correct names of the actors on a mystery series.

"Never heard of it? Never caught the show?" Franklin said. He was smiling.

In the hallway, there was a large poster of a naked woman running across a stadium field. "That's my streaker," Franklin said.

"Your streaker?" Tracy asked him.

"One of the very first, at least the first one to be verified, documented. This was on the playing field at the University of Massachusetts. The funny thing is, I *met* this gal. I saw her come into the student union. 1971. I was just visiting, you know. Anyway, I recognized her."

"It was her? How could you tell?" Tracy was holding

his chin, studying the streaker, then he looked at his cousin Franklin.

"I recognized her right away from the poster. A real athlete. It was a thrill, you know, a kick," Franklin said.

Cam was rubbing his mouth.

Tracy said, "Are you still doing that talk show?"

"I don't do it anymore. I was on a few weeks, is all."

"They canned you?"

"Before it got out of hand and became a scandal. The pink slip."

Margaret's eyes were very wide and Tracy blinked at her. She changed her expression.

"What kind of guests did you have on the show?" Margaret asked.

"Sports celebrities, writers, actors," Franklin said.

"Really?"

"Of course they weren't all star quality. They were local."

"Oh," Margaret said, "but I guess they were interesting. I mean, grass roots individuals can be fascinating, it's your hometown scene, right?"

"Exactly, but they didn't like my approach. I had an all-girl volleyball team on the show. I had them talking, it was great. The station couldn't see the point."

"What's your line now?" Tracy asked.

Franklin said, "Plastic." He sold plastic packaging to food industry manufacturers. "Two-ton rolls," he told them. "They need a forklift with a hydraulic prong to lift them off the truck. My biggest account is for the plastic wrapping on dog-food burgers." Tracy liked the description of the forklift, that would have been fine.

"You know, Dane Burgers? That cherry-red-colored stuff that looks like chopped meat, it's loose? I sell the plastic packaging for that. I used to sell something altogether different—velveteen display boxes. You know, if you buy some earrings, they have that velveteen card? It was an interesting line. Anything looks good against velveteen. Put your potato peeler on a velveteen background and it's called a Gourmet Implement. Put any item on velvet and presto! it sells for twice the price. That's why it was a good product to handle."

He walked into the little pantry and pulled out some drawers. He came back to Margaret and gave her some tiny boxes covered in red velveteen.

"These are velvet boxes?" Margaret said.

"There's a difference between real velvet and velveteen. This stuff you're holding is actually sprayed on. It's this fuzz stuff, a plastic product; they just spray it from a gun right on to these little fuckers. Here, you can have these to keep."

She couldn't hold all the little boxes and she tugged out the hem of her shirt to catch them.

Cam was smoking a cigarette. He found the pack on the edge of a chair and Franklin gave him a light. "You smoke in *this* apartment, you've got yourself a fire," Cam told Franklin.

They decided to try to get some sleep and Franklin came back with a good selection of pillows and sheets, some flannel blankets. Margaret went away and came back. "There's no door on the bathroom."

"That's correct," Franklin said. "The door's in the basement."

"It's in the basement? Can't you go get it? Why is the bathroom door in the basement?" she asked him.

"A long story. It's an old house. It swelled. I had to plane the door, but I planed the wrong end. It's taking some time."

Margaret looked at Tracy. The bathroom was set right on the living room, there was no way she could sit on the toilet with any privacy. Cam was stretched out in an overstuffed chair in the corner, leafing through a magazine called *Corrupt*. Tracy took Franklin into the kitchen so Margaret could use the bathroom without him watching. She turned on the shower first and she kept her eyes on the doorway as she sat down, on her hands. She'd rather her hands touched the strange seat than her buttocks. Next, she pulled off her clothes and got into the shower. She didn't want to touch anything and she stood in the middle of the tub avoiding the stained vinyl curtain when it billowed toward her. There was a bar of soap dangling on a knotted cord. She had to make a decision about using the soap or leaving it where it was. She lathered herself and the wet cord slithered over her belly, her thighs. Then she heard someone come in there. "It's me," Cam said, "I'm using the toilet."

She started to hum a few notes to let him know she was indifferent, she wasn't listening to him urinate. Then she wondered if he could see her behind the shower curtain like in those Rock Hudson movies when Doris Day was always toweling off behind a dressing screen.

"That Franklin guy is weirdsville," Cam said, and he walked out. She saw how Cam was picking up some of Tracy's speech. She never heard Cam say "weirdsville." He never used that suffix. This was new, for better or for worse.

Even if this Franklin was peculiar, he was gentle and a good host. He made sure they had pillowcases and he brought them a box of FiddleFaddle in case they were hungry. Cam picked up the box of caramel corn and studied it as if he had never heard of such a thing. Then it was the three of them in the dim parlor crowded between the stacks of magazines, the cabinets of assorted Troll dolls and Buffalo Bob figurines.

"This place could spook somebody," Cam said. Again, Margaret noticed his talk: "Spook" was not a verb Cam used; it was more like Tracy to say he was "spooked." Then she saw how she was so tired, her thoughts were spinning, these random words didn't mean anything. The entire floor space, what little there was, was completely utilized. Tracy was lying one way, Cam was going in the opposite direction. Margaret was in between and she knew she should put her head down next to Tracy's, but there was a giant wood spool in the way. It was for electric cable or something. She could have moved the spool but it was covered with bric-a-brac.

"What's the matter?" Cam said.

"I'm figuring out where to sleep," she said.

"It takes a while to get her to sleep," Tracy said. "She usually sleeps with an electric clock, did you know that?"

"Get away—like a puppy?" Cam said.

Margaret said, "No, not like a fucking puppy! It's the ringing in my ears, the clock drowns out the ringing."

"It's those coffee beans," Cam said. "Caffeine makes your ears ring."

"Then she has to have her sodium pentothal injection," Tracy said.

"Are you kidding?" Cam said.

"Margaret has insomnia, so I stick her ass with 'the secret needle.' She can't sleep until I stick her." He reached over to Margaret and pinched her buttocks. "Or, I pretend to shoot her in the head with my index finger. First, I attach my silencer." Tracy closed his fist to make a gun, then he screwed something to the tip of his pointer.

"Why don't you just take a sleeping pill?" Cam said.

"Can you mind your own business," she said. When trucks went by on the street, the magazine stacks shivered. They might get buried alive, but Margaret was exhausted, and she let her head fall back on the pillow. She was lying perfectly still between the two men. The floor wasn't so bad, it was a good feeling after all the driving. She might have curled toward Tracy, but she didn't want to exclude Cam. Cam favored a hip on the hard floor, shifted his weight nearer.

Cam said, "You ever have a dream about falling? Sometimes I'm falling, I'm falling off a cliff in the Duster."

"That's the most common kind of dream," Tracy said. "If it's happening in an automobile, it's a contest between the subconscious and the superego. You know, the vehicle versus the driver. Any other passengers? No? Freud says these falling dreams are directly connected to when you were a baby and your dad pitches you in the air and catches you again. You go up in the air and you come down, plunk, but you're always caught, you land in your father's arms."

"Cam's father never threw him in the air," Margaret said.

Tracy said, "Every baby gets thrown into the air. It's a rite of passage. Cam got thrown in the air, believe me."

"It didn't happen," she said.

Her muscles loosened toward sleep. She felt both weighted and freed in an early dream and then she saw it. Across the room, it glowed, a fleshy figurine impaled on the brass finial above a lampshade—a Kewpie doll. The sun was just rising, its rosy light concentrated in the rubbery figure. The doll's queer smile looked worn, almost erased, but she could make it out—an indented line cheek to cheek. It had a submerged presence like the picture of the fetus on the chandelier. Margaret sat up.

"What is it?" Cam said.

She rested her forehead against her knees.

Tracy stood up. He saw the doll. "This is it, this little thing." He removed the doll from its perch. "It struck a nerve," he told Cam. "She's not over it yet. She's not dealing with it."

"The abortion?"

"It's taking forever, most people are over it by now."

Cam told him, "Some people don't find it so easy."

Tracy wedged the Kewpie doll behind a crowded

bookshelf. He kneeled beside Margaret. Cam touched her shoulder.

She shrugged away from them. She didn't want to be coddled. "Shit! I'm just tired. How many miles was it?" she said.

"Plenty," Tracy said.

"It was a long way," Cam said. "It's the picture on the chandelier, it stays with you."

"Your family's crazy," Tracy said.

They settled back on the covers and tried to rest. Tracy took Margaret's hand and bit her fingertips, playfully, traveling up her arm. She liked the sensation of his mouth against the surface veins on the inside of her wrist. It reminded her of a baby's suck. It made her think of nursing her baby, all babies, all over the world. It was a longing that some women carried to the grave. The multiparous nipple is a dark, ginger circle, emblem of instinct, its erectile capacity mirrors the male; milk shoots across the room. Across the sky.

Margaret had once known a girl who was born with some extra nipples. Sometimes this might happen, nipples appear along the milk line anywhere from the underarm on down to the high ledge of the hipbone. The girl was having her extra nipples surgically removed, but Margaret always thought it was a mistake to have plastic surgery. There might be something lucky about being born with this fertile sign.

Her thoughts took a possessive drift through her daughter's early years—then she saw the clinic ceiling. Margaret had her abortion at the Amelia Earhart Women's Center, a health cooperative managed by lesbians

devoted to physical fitness and volunteerism. The workers wore white smocks above Spandex exercise tights.
Margaret waited for her turn with the doctor. She sat
beneath a giant portrait of the famous flyer, who looked
more like a parking-lot attendant in grey overalls.
Margaret looked across the coffee table strewn with an
assortment of female body-building magazines and she
saw a teenaged girl from out of town. The girl had
discolored teeth and her hands were mottled. Margaret
heard the clinic nurse say the word "scabies." Margaret
studied the rash on the girl's hands. It was sad, the girl
being afflicted with scabies and then this.

When they called Margaret's name, she walked into
a room and recognized a dermatologist who routinely
visited the prison where Margaret worked.

"It's *you?*" she said to the dermatologist.

"I don't just pop pimples," he told her.

The clinic attendants steered her over to the narrow
table, and she sat face to face with the doctor, who
explained his dual role in medicine. He said he wore
"many hats."

"I guess the pimple business is slow?" she told him,
but she fell back on the rubberized pillow. She rested
her forearm over her mouth rather than over her eyes.
She waited for the doctor to remove the particle of
flesh. It happened in two or three steps, a severe
gradation of pain, then it was over. But what of its
source, that stinging complexity, the nature of "being,"
which she still could not fathom? Did that speck cling,
suture itself to her from its own desire? The doctor
continued to speak of the prison, their mutual acquain-

tances, the inmates' skin tags, prickly heat, moles, carbuncles. Was he really saying these things?

At home, she embraced Celeste, and her daughter returned the snuggling until it went on too long and she pulled free. Tracy told Margaret, "Don't think of it as someone. It's not anyone." To Margaret, these pronouns were wrenching.

That night she went drinking with Tracy but the whole Amelia Earhart softball team arrived at the same bar in bright uniforms, cheering victory slogans. Margaret recognized the woman who swabbed her vulva with Betadine, and there was the woman who, at the end of the procedure, removed the canister for inspection, searching for the purple wedge of placenta like a bit of blackened tripe.

The next day, she hoped to feel nothing, to forget it. Then, the radio announced a partial eclipse of the sun.

"Can you believe this?" she said to Tracy. She *knew* there was a connection. That afternoon, the sky greyed. It was unlike the warm half-darkness at dusk or the translucence at daybreak. Shadows evaporated, buildings were blotted dry of definition. She watched the sun until a red-brown disc, a mask of tissue, merged with the blinding circle. Did Tracy see it that way, that half-coagulated blur that moved over the sun? Why should she make him see it her way?

She closed her eyes and saw two steady torches. Then her eyes adjusted. Margaret had heard about Japanese women who were blinded by the harsh sights of Hiroshima and Nagasaki. They didn't become blind in the usual sense, they suffered no physical injury to their eyes. After the A-bomb, the subconscious lowered a grey curtain. It was a *gift*, the women said. Physicians and psychiatrists were intrigued by this phenomenon; they tried, with varying success, to coax these women to see, but they were met with refusals.

Sometimes Margaret started laughing, a tearing laughter that snagged through a web of congestion in her lungs.

"It's going to take a while," Tracy told her, but he was over it.

III

Before they left Franklin's house, Margaret telephoned her ex-husband, Phil, without mentioning to him that she was halfway to Chicago. She just wanted to talk to Celeste. Her ex-husband was in the middle of a game of Dungeons and Dragons. He refused to put Celeste on the telephone at this critical moment in the game.

"Excuse me?" Margaret said. "You can't put my daughter on the telephone because you're doing what?" Her husband had always used these commercialized fantasy worlds to evade her. During their marriage, he had arranged and catalogued increasing stacks of science fiction paperbacks at his bedside. From her pillow, she saw book covers depicting pocked moons, red-eyed snakes and reptiles, oversexed Amazon Venusians. At New Year's, he reread the Hobbit trilogy and went to the national convention. He tried to initiate Celeste; each blithe suburban ritual was concluded with a bed-time reading from one of his fantasy manuals. Phil's taste for dwarfs and dragons seemed peculiar coupled with his ongoing homeowner's odyssey.

Tracy said he understood the profile. "The American gentry live in a void. The climate is freeze-dried. Phil depends on these subterranean civilizations to fill an intellectual vacuum." Yet, Tracy couldn't find the right comment when last season Phil boasted to Margaret, saying that he had actually used his sci-fi collection to weatherproof his split-level against the New England winter. Phil had distributed his paperbacks on shelving against the north walls, floor-to-ceiling, adding a thermal resistance factor of R 11.

"I'm calling back in an hour," she told her ex-husband. "Celeste better pick up."

Then she called Elizabeth. Margaret told Elizabeth it was unavoidable. Cam was doing what he had to do. Elizabeth asked her why they were stirring things up, why didn't they leave the past the past? Why didn't they just try to accept it? Margaret cleared her throat and shifted her tone to enlist Elizabeth to her side. She said, "You know Cam—*you know Cam*, don't you?" There was silence on the other end of the line, as if Elizabeth were considering all the years since she birthed her one boy.

"Yes, I guess I know him." Elizabeth's voice sounded frail one minute, sharp the next. It was often this way.

One time, Elizabeth was leaving the house to go to a banquet and Margaret noticed that her stepmother had forgotten to smooth her makeup. There was a smear across her upper lip, a heavy stroke of beige foundation. Margaret saw the flawed makeup and wanted to take a handkerchief and dab at the smear until it was blended. She took Elizabeth by the sleeve and they looked eye to eye. There was something in Elizabeth's face, a distance that could not be overtaken, some denial of their intimacy, their connection, and Margaret could not touch up the Max Factor or cleanse that helpless defiance from Elizabeth's mouth.

Tracy was driving and Cam rested in the backseat with his feet propped, surrounded by 1950s smut magazines. "I don't want to hear Elizabeth's opinion," Cam said.

Margaret was holding one of Franklin's velveteen boxes. She clicked the lid open and closed as she talked. "She's kind of scared."

"Sure she's scared," Cam said, "she's worried I'll find out the straight dope."

"You're so certain she's guilty of something. Did you ever stop and think what it was like for her, Lewis running off like that?"

Cam said, "He jumped ship, that's all."

"Rats jump from ships."

Tracy was smiling. He said, "Nice volley, keep it up."

Margaret said, "Living with her folks all those years, the prime of her life."

"Oh, she got out of the house. She was a Dancing Queen."

"Maybe just to fill up the empty hours. She enrolled in a school and learned the fox-trot and the samba."

Cam said, "You can bet she did the samba. On her back."

"Elizabeth never fooled around. She told me."

"She's a liar."

"I'm not finished, let me tell you. One time I asked her if she had some lovers after Lewis. Negative. None? I ask her. Elizabeth says, 'I didn't make love to them, *I let them make love to me.*' I like that distinction," Margaret said.

"You're gullible," Cam said.

"No, I believed her. She didn't make love to them, she let them have a try. No one impressed her."

"You're simple, Margaret."

She was getting mad. "Do you know what Elizabeth calls you? You were just an immaculate conception!" The phrase was easy to dramatize.

Tracy said, "*Just* an immaculate conception? Only a biological miracle?"

They ignored Tracy. It was between the two of them.

"What are you saying?" Cam asked Margaret.

"An immaculate conception. You're the product of a farewell fuck. Lewis didn't even know you were coming, maybe he doesn't even know you're alive now."

"He was still with Elizabeth when I was born—"

Margaret said, "Sorry about that. She told me. She told me the truth. You were a regular, run-of-the-mill bastard."

"A leftover bun in the cold oven," Tracy said.

"You learn something every day," Cam said. She looked back at him and his face was turned. He was staring out the window.

"Didn't she ever explain anything to you?" Margaret said; she hated to let her voice soften, but Cam must be thinking how he was unwanted. Unwanted then, and now. Margaret knew a woman who openly displayed her ambiguous feelings toward her child. She was always letting the child play in dangerous areas, near open cisterns, climbing onto high diving boards, letting him roam too near his father's table saw. Margaret wondered how long it could go on. When the child was born, they said he had the cord wrapped around his neck. The tight cord made him skinny and underdeveloped as if the mother had been trying to choke him all those months he was inside her.

Tracy started singing an old Bobby Darin tune, the one about the orphan: *"They found little Annie all covered with ice!"*

Cam said, "Fuck you, Tracy."

Tracy kept singing. He had a clean, dominant tenor and he held the notes with a sullen vibrato. Cam started pitching the collectors' smut rags out the car window, one after the other, their brittle leaves tearing loose and fluttering over the interstate traffic.

9

The left front tire had a slow leak. They had to keep testing it, stopping at gas stations to give it a little air. Most of the time the air was free. Then Cam had to put a quarter in the air pump. That's when Cam decided to get the tire fixed. He said he didn't want it nickel-and-diming him. Margaret started thinking maybe Cam was stalling. They estimated eight hours and they'd be in Chicago, but Cam kept getting off the freeway. He got out of the car to scratch bugs off the front grille of the Duster.

"There's just going to be more insects," Margaret told him.

Now he was getting all the tires changed. New ones all around. They left the Duster at the Firestone Tire Center and walked a few blocks into the town. Margaret put on Darcy's shoes since she couldn't walk far in her flip-flops. Her feet were the same size as Darcy's, but the shoes were unfamiliar ballet pumps with garish leather blossoms at the toes. They went into a drug-store and Margaret found some mentholated witch hazel and some pocket handkerchiefs. The store sold sneakers and canvas pumps. She tried on the pumps; they were stiff and slipped up at the heel, so she kept wearing Darcy's. Then she went into a church thrift store and bought a skirt for herself. It was what they used to call a wraparound, three panels of fabric sewed together at an angle. The skirt swirled and flounced if she turned around sharp. The fabric was light and airy and the print was busy with Irish setters running nose-to-tail. It really was something corny, something to cheer everybody up. Franklin would have liked it. After she came out of the thrift shop, Tracy pointed to a sign up ahead. The sign said ELITE CHICKS in mint-green neon.

"It's a strip joint, I guess," Tracy said.

"Well, I don't particularly want to see strippers at this hour," Margaret said.

"Would you like to see them tonight, after dark? We could stick around." Cam was smiling.

"Ohio girls," Tracy was saying. "Interesting. Some Buckeye gals. Tell me, just exactly, what is a buckeye?"

"I'm curious," Cam said. "We could inquire while I have myself a beer."

"It's the Midwest and it's called a 'draw.' We'll ask for a couple of draws," Tracy said.

Margaret didn't care one way or another. When they reached the tavern, they stopped at the plate-glass window.

"What in the hell is this?" Tracy said.

Margaret said, "This is great."

In the storefront window they saw undulating waves of yellow pollen, a thousand hatchlings, baby chicks, balls of fluff on tiny rice feet. The big stainless-steel incubators were polished and gave off a reflection of the three of them. "This place sells chickens!" Cam said.

"They're so cute," Margaret said, leaning into the glass. "What are they for?"

The men looked at one another. Tracy said, "Easter, they must be for Easter."

"Sure, for next Easter," Cam said.

Margaret said, "I'd like to have them just like this, five in a row on a skewer!" She hated it when they condescended to her. She walked ahead of them. She could squash a baby chicken, rotate the toe of Darcy's shoe on its little beak if they wanted to make something of it.

"You wouldn't really eat chickens in a row like that." Tracy was smiling.

They went back to get the car. It had four new tires on it, steel belted, with narrow white walls. The white walls were glazed with blue soap. It was a pretty sight, Margaret thought. These tires would assure her safe return to Celeste. The sooner the better. Cam went into the office to pay for the tires. Several minutes passed and he came back out.

"They won't take my Visa. They won't take any of my cards. She's blocked them."

"What?"

"Darcy's put a hold on all my cards. She's reported the cards stolen," Cam said.

Tracy was shaking his head, but he looked impressed. He was pleased by the turn of events, he was admiring the mind of the girl behind this. All these miles and Darcy was able to swoop down, rain on their parade, right where they were standing in Ohio.

Margaret said, "Call the bank and tell them it's not stolen. They'll take the freeze off."

"Not if she says her cards are stolen, it's the same number. They'll just issue new cards and tell us we have to wait for that," Cam said. "Look at this place. It's a one-horse shit hole. Nowheresville."

There it was again, Tracy's diction invading Cam's.

"Jesus Christ," Margaret said. She wanted Cam to know she was feeling worse about it than Tracy.

"She's trying to shut me down," Cam said.

"I've got a card, you can get the tires," Tracy said.

"I don't think so," Cam said, "that's not the point here." He opened the car door and got behind the wheel; he touched the keys dangling from the steering column. He swatted them like a cat so that they jangled. "Get in," Cam told them.

Margaret got in beside Cam. Tracy came around and leaned in the passenger door until he was level with

Cam. "You aren't going to buy the tires? Is that what you're saying?" Tracy said.

"Correct," Cam said.

Tracy got into the car beside Margaret. He yanked open the glove compartment and shuffled the velveteen boxes around. Then he shut the glove compartment. He was thinking it over. "You're test-driving the tires?" Tracy said.

Cam started the engine and they drove away from the Tire Center. He followed the rules of the road, he didn't make a production out of it. Then they were back on the highway.

"Did you have to steal the tires? Stupid shit," Margaret said.

"Maybe I'll send them a check later."

"You'll be writing your checks from the nick," Margaret said.

Tracy said, "It's Darcy. Darcy made him do it. She says he's a thief, he'll rise to the occasion. He'll become a thief."

"Look," Cam said. He stopped mid-sentence and pinched his fingers high on the bridge of his nose, pressed the heel of his hand against his left eye, then his right; he finished by rubbing his temple with his fingertips. Margaret thought he must be starting a terrible headache. He wasn't thinking of her or of Tracy. He wasn't with them, he must be thinking of the Arrow Collar as he studied the road that was bringing him closer. Sometimes his shoulders suffered minor cringes. It was as if he saw something, apparitions. Margaret searched the highway; the heat waves wobbled, then subsided, wobbled again. They passed a dead dog on the shoulder; the wind from the opposite traffic was lifting the plume of its tail. It reminded Margaret of those half-alive segments, dismembered insects, their notched legs beating with only a chemical memory of life. One tiny, exhausted nerve still pulses, unaware of the fate of its whole. Margaret looked at Cam's face. When his discomfort didn't flare, it retreated into the remote ganglia. Either it's pain at rest, or pain at work. It was never an absence of pain.

Cam was pleased with the tires. He braked. He let go of the wheel to see if the Duster pulled to the left or to the right. The tires were riding smooth. Perhaps he was just stalling again, but he asked Margaret if she really wanted to visit Tina at the commune. "What's it called?" he asked her.

"Sun and Moon, I think." She kept her voice flat. "Sun and Moon Farm."

"Jesus," Cam said.

"Wait, that's perfect," Tracy said. "It says everything. Your basic celestial dichotomy. Two opposing worlds that create continuity and balance on Earth—sun and moon."

"Piss and shit," Cam said.

A big, six-foot flag was nailed between two trees at the entrance of the commune. They stopped the car and looked at the place. Margaret wondered if maybe they should just roll away before they were seen. These organic gardens and whole-grain bakeries were always tainted by an inner conflict: capitalism, or socialism, which would it be? Her sister's commune would probably be the same—flower children searching for an angle.

"That's an Italian flag," Cam said.

"No," Tracy said, "it's supposed to mean ecology, see? It says it right there on the green stripe." Tracy was right, there was something written on the flag. The words said, *Love Your Mother*.

"Nice," Cam said.

"I've heard that before," Margaret said.

"Still looks Italian. Makes me think of a pizzeria," Cam said.

They drove up the dirt road toward an old farmhouse and outbuildings. The place looked run-down, like an abandoned farm you can buy from the government for one dollar and a letter of intent. In a field near the buildings, a parachute billowed up and down, several children tugging its hem. The children ran in and out of the circle, making the silk lift, puff up, then deflate. It was supervised play of some kind, like Ring Around the Rosie using army surplus materials. "That chute's from Nam," Cam said.

"The parachute?" Margaret asked.

"Yeah, I can tell."

"But you weren't over there—in Vietnam, I mean."

"It's a Nam chute, I'm telling you."

Tracy said, "I think that's a Du Pont fiber. I'm sure it is."

Tina was bronzed. Her teeth looked white as peppermint Beechies. "I'm always out in the sun," she told them. She'd been planting trees. During the summer months, the commune was a children's ecology camp, but it was a year-round Christmas tree farm. Tina said that they had just put in two new acres of Fraser fir seedlings. It was hard work, the pine needles were sharp, stabbing, and the gluey pine tar darkened her fingers like tobacco juice. Margaret saw that Tina's hands were sore-looking.

Margaret kissed her sister and something rustled against her breast. "What's that you're wearing around your neck? Looks like some kind of origami?"

"Peace cranes," Tina said. "That's my forte. I teach peace cranes to the campers. That's my expertise, my specialty."

"Peace cranes?" Margaret asked. She looked at Tina's heavy necklace, paper origami cranes in a matted half-circle.

"There's a thousand on this necklace," Tina said, "it's my first thousand. Don't you know the story?"

Tracy said, "Yes, I know that one. About the little girl after Hiroshima, right?"

"A little girl?" Margaret asked, she didn't want to hear another gruesome story.

"She's dying from radiation poisoning, right?" Tracy said. "She makes a wish, she cuts a deal—if she folds a thousand origami cranes for world peace, maybe she'll recover."

"Is this a true story?" Cam said.

Tina said, "Absolutely." The whites of her eyes were very white, like the tiny porcelain rim around sheeps' eyes, or the overly alert ceramic eyes of dolls. Margaret studied her sister and figured it was probably the deep walnut color of her skin that accentuated the whites of her eyes. She'd seen that same dogmatic look on church rectors and overenthused athletic coaches. A single-mindedness seems to bleach the eyes as the skin weathers.

"What happens to the girl, does she fold all those cranes on time? Does she get better?" Cam said.

"Nine hundred and something," Tracy said, "then she buys it."

"Oh Christ," Cam said.

"How many of these cranes have you folded, Tina?" Margaret asked.

"Thousands and thousands. I fold hundreds a week, and I keep going."

Margaret felt a little queasy. Tina could do this to her. Tina was in her forties, still driving her VW micro bus, rust spots patched with fiberglass, its original logo altered, soldered to form a peace sign. The vehicle was a relic, something for the Museum of Natural History; Margaret could research how Tina's consciousness evolved by tracing the cellophane scabs from the decals and stickers. It all started with a single butterfly chair back in the late fifties. Margaret remembered her sister sitting cross-legged in her chair with those black canvas wings. Then she joined a group called the Peace Pilgrims. She started traveling, living out of her van. She kept several disposable toilets in neat stacks, some cottage cheese containers that she was meticulous about although she seemed to flaunt them. She sat Indian-style, no matter what the social function. Then she refused to wash her hair, she just inserted a piece of cheesecloth over the bristles of her hairbrush. "Shampoo robs the essence from hair," she said.

During a visit home, she hurt Elizabeth's feelings when she refused to eat a piece of homemade blueberry pie. Elizabeth showed her the thick slice, the rich mirrory fruit, like mercury on the plate.

"You can't eat the pie? This used to be your favorite," Elizabeth said. Tina explained, she couldn't eat anything "picked," nothing could be harvested. Fruit had to fall on its own. Fallen fruit was all she would eat.

When Tina learned to make sandals she pestered Margaret or Cam, asking if she could trace someone's foot on a piece of leather. Margaret finally agreed. She watched her sister ink a rough outline of her foot on a piece of cowhide. The pen tickled her instep as Tina drew the arch line, then she curved around her toes, leaving enough space for the thong.

Once, when Tina visited, Elizabeth washed Tina's dashiki with the family laundry and the dye ran, erasing the ancient patterns from the African cloth. Everything else was stained.

Tina was showing Cam around the farmhouse. There was a big wheel of cheese left out on the kitchen table. "Cam, have a piece," she said, shaving the cheese with a knife. "The great news is," Tina was saying, "the cranes make me financially independent."

"The cranes?"

Tina explained that she earned one-hundred-dollar stipends from the public schools. She brought her own colored paper, the glazed kind for folding origami; regular construction paper was too hairy and coarse.

Reporters wrote newspaper articles about Tina, calling her the "Origami Mommy." She kept clippings about herself, her paper empire, in a manila folder. She made Xerox copies of these newspaper articles to promote herself.

"You get paid?" Margaret said.

Tina cut a curl of cheese and handed it to her sister. "I give peace instruction, it's not just arts and crafts."

Some others joined them as they stood around the cheese. Tina pulled Cam by his sleeve. "I'd like you to meet my friends Tru and Clear."

"Excuse me?" Cam said.

"My friends," Tina said, "Tru and Clear."

Tru was in her fifties, nice-looking with strange violet eyes. They must be contact lenses, Margaret was thinking. Clear was the woman's husband. He was balding and bearded. Clear's body seemed oddly pitched, jutting forward like someone gliding off a ski jump. It was his sandals. His sandals sloped backward. "It's better for the spine. The spine is the keyboard of health," he was saying. Margaret looked down at her own shoes. Darcy's shoes.

Clear was showing Cam the collection of plastic magnets on the refrigerator. Clear had a machine that made plastic buttons and magnets, any slogan or logo you might want. Cam leaned close to the icebox to read the political buttons; his mouth was even. Margaret knew he couldn't smile without sneering. He was finding it hard to remain collected. Margaret didn't care about the buttons. Perhaps a button was the *only* way to approach a resistant individual. Somebody has to devote his life to the issues.

Tina was saying she didn't like to eat anything packaged in plastic, hence the big wheel of cheddar with a black waxy rind. Cam was eating a thin slice of the yellow cheese. Tracy poured himself a glass of cider, but it was sharp. "Is this going hard?" he asked.

"I don't think so," Tina said, and she tasted it. "You're just not used to it."

The man, Clear, was asking Cam if he and Tru could get a lift to Chicago. Cam wasn't forthcoming. He repeated Clear's question, "Can you get a lift to Chicago, is that what you're saying? A lift to Chicago? A lift to Chicago—" He was waiting for Margaret to rescue him.

Margaret said, "Sorry we can't take you with us." She pulled Cam by his elbow into the next room. "You don't have to be rude," she told him.

They were in a bedroom. It had two iron beds with faded quilts on either side, a bed stand with a Blue Willow pitcher and bowl. It was just for decoration; the pitcher was dusty, no one had been using it to wash. Cam sat down on one of the beds and rubbed his face. He looked horrible.

Cam said, "We're not staying here tonight. It gives me the creeps, these hippies. That cheese left out like a salt lick for cows."

"Tina's okay, she's making a living."

"Margaret, you're always so optimistic."

"I'm not. I'm not optimistic, are you kidding? But I don't know. Those cranes are like a cottage industry or something."

He looked half-dreaming, dead on his feet. He let himself down on the little bed and turned toward the wall. "I'm going to shut my eyes for a while," he said.

"Good," she said.

"I hope they don't mind—that guy with the sandals. This could be his bed. I don't like to think. Just closing my eyes. Just for a minute—"

Margaret went back into the kitchen. Tracy was out in the fields with Tina, they were going to plant a few Fraser fir seedlings so Tracy could have the thrill of it. Margaret wondered if Tina was trying to flirt with him. Elizabeth and Tina were quite alike along these lines, always flirting with Margaret's boyfriends. It was harmless, a test. They wanted to keep their feminine wiles greased and sleek, up to muster.

Margaret was alone in the kitchen; she watched a single fly circle the cheese. One fly was nothing. Its transparent wings, its tiny blue-green sheath looked pristine. She went back into the room where Cam was resting. He looked completely still. She felt a twinge in the small of her back as she stood over her brother. Her ribs, like the tines of a metal rake, felt sharp. It must be from driving in the Duster, sitting on that armrest; she rubbed her spine as she stood at the end of Cam's bed. She untied her new skirt, unwrapped the filmy panel, then tucked it around herself again, tying the cord tight. She looked down at Cam.

"Get in," he said.

"What?"

"Lie down, I'm so tired. Lie down here or over there, but do something. You're bothering me."

She didn't think she could wake him by fixing her skirt. She crawled into the bed next to him, the mattress sagged where her knees touched but it wasn't too bad. He turned over on his back and she put her face against his breast. He put his arm around her. The weight of his arm against her hip was familiar. Her ear was against the hard pectoral shelf, the same side where his heart was beating. She listened. A heartbeat can be lulling. It's an enslaved pulse, quite eunuched, without soul or gender. Then she heard Cam as he cleared his throat and shoved her over, turned to face her. He smoothed her throat with the palm of his hand, keeping her still. His lips touched the corner of her mouth, lifted, sank to her mouth again. She couldn't tell if she wanted her freedom or if it was his decision, but they separated. He got up and left her.

She threw her legs over the side of the bed and sat on the edge of the mattress. She let her tongue flutter over the corner of her mouth where Cam had kissed her; the taste was slightly tarry from his cigarettes. It wasn't a true kiss, his lips had brushed past her.

I don't find any problem with that, she told herself. Their blood didn't mix, no coded, glossy substance was exchanged. A kiss was an airy, transient occurrence, like the northern lights or a shower of comets. Astronomical phenomena that occur in the blinding daylight can't be seen or documented. Margaret reclined on the small bed, turned on her side, and pulled her knees up. She felt sleep coming, its fuzzy swarm over her lips, her eyes weighted by invisible thumbs. She was rotten to disturb Cam. He needed the sleep more than she did. She couldn't help herself, she was drifting. There was a bird outside, a tiny note that faded in and out of hearing until it became predictable and she stopped listening for it.

II

At five o'clock, the parents came for the campers. Tru and Clear came into the house, stopping to clean their boots on a teak crossweave. Margaret plucked apart some lettuce heads while Tina arranged a fish on a broiler pan. Tina dribbled sesame oil over the fish, counting out the drips, telling Margaret these drips cost a pretty penny. Margaret said, "Why don't you use something cheap? There's Mazola." When the fish was ready, they sat at the oval table where the cheese had earlier reigned. Margaret saw the cheese was moved to the sideboard and draped with a dish towel.

"Where's Cam?" Tina said.

Tracy looked at Margaret. "I saw him over at the Duster. I'll go see."

Tina served the fish, small flaky slices layered over brown rice. Margaret could have eaten the whole fish. The past two days had made her greedy for simple comforts—food, baths, sleep. It made her think of beasts that gorge themselves because they can smell *drought*, which then means *famine*.

"The car's gone." Tracy came back to the table and sat down.

Tina cleared her throat. She knew something and

had waited for center stage to say so. "Cam went to get Laurence!" she said.

"He did what?" Margaret said.

"He went to pick up Laurence," Tina said and she looked around the table.

"He went back to Wilmington? He left us here?" Margaret said.

Tina said, "Cam went to get his kid, Margaret. You know—"

"Why?" Margaret said.

"Life is not a riddle to be solved, it's a mystery to be lived," Tracy said.

Margaret looked at Tracy. "He can't be driving back and forth like this, he'll have a wreck. He'll fall asleep at the wheel."

Margaret avoided looking at the faces of Tru and Clear. They seemed intrigued by the turn of events— more fish for them, or perhaps they liked to watch a scene from real life unfolding in that kitchen where the flies circled over the blistered linoleum. Margaret stirred the brown rice; the food made her recoil.

"I don't know why he wants to find our father. He's a creep," Tina said. "I met him in '64. You know what he said all the time, his favorite word?"

"What was that?" Tracy said.

"He used an awful word as a superlative. Instead of saying 'swell,' or 'great', or 'splendid,' he said *brutal*. I was wearing turquoise jewelry and he said, 'I love your bracelet. *Brutal* stones, *brutal* sky-blue.' He said it about everything."

"Brutal? That's a terrific detail," Tracy said. "You

have an eye, Tina, an eye for the essence of something."

Margaret looked at Tracy. What the hell was he talking about? She wondered what might have happened between Tracy and her sister when they were supposed to be planting Fraser firs. Her sister was beaming at Tracy. Margaret said, "You mean she has an *ear*. An ear for what someone says."

"Thanks," Tina said. "I can't understand what the fuss is about. Cam should leave that guy alone, he's not worth the trouble."

"Cam's just trying to figure something out. Now he's driving to get Laurence? Darcy's not going to go for this."

Clear said, "He can't bring a kidnapped child into the camp, that could cause trouble."

"It's his own son," Tina said.

"You can't kidnap your own kid," Margaret said.

"That depends on someone's point of view. He can't stay here. When he gets back, he has to leave. This is our third year, we're gaining respectability, something like this could derail everything." Clear stared at Tina until she blinked back at him. She wasn't giving into him, but she couldn't keep her gaze steady.

"Don't worry," Tracy said, "we'll be on our way."

A car pulled into the driveway. Margaret went to the window to see if Cam had changed his mind. She pulled the curtain back, collecting the thin muslin in one hand, and she saw it was a police cruiser.

"It's the police," she said.

Tina said, "Oh, that's nothing. They come around every night. They think they might smell some marijuana or something. They're suspicious of us. They think we're growing it—"

"Getting the kids to do some cheap farm labor? Plowing the poppies? Weeding the weed?" Tracy said.

"The town's crazy. It's the Ohio jitters, it's never been the same since Kent State."

"Kent State? That was years ago," Margaret said.

"The scars are deep," Clear said.

The cruiser turned around in the driveway, stirring up a cloud of dirt, then rolled away. Margaret sat down and touched the fish with the tines of her fork, separating the flesh, but she didn't want it.

"Thank goodness they're not strict Macros or we wouldn't have the cheese. We'd starve," Tracy told Margaret as he walked her outside and down the long lines of waist-high evergreens. In the field, it was completely dark without any houses or streetlights. Where was the moon, the stars?

Margaret felt dizzy; she recognized a slow whirl of panic increasing. "I don't want to stay here in this place. It's awful, like a German fairy tale. That house, it's sort of spooky, and these lines of fir trees—"

"It's all right. It's like an HO Railroad landscape. Don't worry, baby." He put his arms around her. "You're having an anxiety attack."

They walked down the rows of trees.

"These trees will be decorated with lights, each one will have its crooked star. They'll dry out in somebody's living room. Maybe they get a loop of peace cranes to go with it, you know, instead of a string of popcorn," Tracy said.

"Those peace cranes give me the creeps," she said.

"It's harmless, like making pot holders."

She looked one way, and when she turned back, Tracy had ducked behind a thick row. "Tracy, don't hide!" she was screaming.

He came right back holding a rabbit's head by the ears. It was a fresh-killed rabbit, its neck chewed. "An owl had it," Tracy said. "It took off, didn't you see it?"

"Drop that head. Will you drop that fucking head right now!" she told him. Tracy pitched the rabbit's head high into the air.

There was a small clearing in the middle of the field where they found lawn chairs and a round table that held a beach umbrella. The campers had picnics there; Margaret saw the plastic forks lost in the grass. Tracy picked her up and pressed her down on the redwood table, knocking the wind from her voice when she tried to refuse. He found the small belt on her skirt and tugged it loose.

"Don't rip it!" she said.

He stood at the table's edge and pulled her closer. She held on to the aluminum pole as he tugged her. When he had her hips, he found the triangle of nylon and rolled it down from her. She was quiet, waiting to see what direction he was taking. He shoved his jeans away and took another hold on her. The umbrella was shaking as he rocked her, the spokes started collapsing and the canvas sank over them, but it didn't interfere.

"What's that?" she said. "I hear a baby crying."

"Nothing," he told her, "be quiet."

"I hear it."

"That owl, maybe a fox. Please," he said, and he looked up at the night as he fucked her, let his head fall back on his neck, shut his eyes against the inadequate dark. He told her she was thinking too much, she was thinking out loud.

"I really thought I heard something," she told Tracy when he was finished. He still rested against her, she could feel his heart beating. Then it slowed, receded behind a ledge of muscle. "I'm sorry," she said, "I just thought it was a baby."

"There's no babies out here. This is the middle of nowhere. We're in the plains. Plainsville."

She really thought she had heard a baby. Sometimes it was alley cats yowling, that strange wail like a human infant. For months, she had been having fantasies about finding an abandoned baby. It was in all the newspapers. Babies were lost and found in trash bins, supermarket carts, library stacks. She read a story about a jogger who found a baby. The baby's mother had noticed the jogger's predictable routine, running around a lake each morning, rain or shine. She left the infant especially for the athlete, believing exercise was a virtuous trait, when it might have been mere narcissism. A man loping for miles beside his own reflection. What kind of parent would he be?

A pedestrian was walking down the street. The pedestrian was standing on the curb at the exact moment of a head-on collision. An infant was hurled through the open window of one vehicle and landed safely in his indifferent grasp. The parents of the infant were killed in the accident. The child welfare officials were impressed by the rescue, which was merely a reflex, and they asked the pedestrian if he wished to undergo the interviews and complete the proper applications in order to adopt the baby. He told the authorities he would have to think it over. He was refusing to accept the truth. Certainly, that baby was his mysterious fate, why wouldn't he accept it? Margaret dreamed babies were hurtling willy-nilly through the congested traffic. Why wasn't she at the right place at the right time?

Margaret took Tracy's wrist, so he would face her. "We're stranded. Did you ever think of that? I have to pick up Celeste on Sunday."

"Your brother is a stupid fuck. I didn't want to say so in front of those hippies, but he's not a hundred percent," Tracy said.

"Why don't you just say it. He isn't playing with a full deck."

"He's playing. He plays solitaire."

Margaret said, "Is he coming back?"

"If he's serious about Lewis. If he needs to find that missing link."

A link is a peculiar item, she was thinking. Her father sold all kinds of links: offset links, roller links, double cleavis, weldless carbon, different sizes, round, oblong, square. They were beautiful—Blu-krome, electroplated zinc finish, shot peened finish, brushed aluminum. There were so many different kinds of chain that might become damaged, might need a replacement link. If it was a conveyor or some kind of a winch, the work stopped until Richard sent the part over. Margaret had always liked to churn her hands through the plastic drawers that held the links of chain, the silver hexagons, the bolts, the industrial diamond chips. She liked to finger these minute parts, stir and sift its heavy seed.

When they came into the house, Tina was brewing tea. The beverage smelled like wet hay as she swirled a wooden coil with honey in and out of their cups. Margaret asked her if there was a shower. Tina shook her head, no, but she looked gleeful. "It's not a shower, it's better than a shower," Tina said. "I'll show you."

Margaret followed Tina outside. Tracy went ahead and walked with Tina, they bumped shoulders as they exchanged some words. They walked to the shed where the farm equipment was kept with the toys for the day camp, the parachute crunched down in a cardboard box. Margaret saw an old-fashioned pump in the center of a muddy circle.

"A pump?"

"We usually fill the wading pool in the morning so the water can warm up during the day, and then we have a nice wash after supper. Someone forgot today, so it'll be cold. Really spicy."

Tracy said, "It sounds delicious."

Tina pumped a few gallons into a plastic bucket. "Here's the sponge," she told Margaret.

"Oh, one of these real underwater sponges. What about soap?"

"Here's my bottle of Castile—it's sandalwood, or no,

this is the peppermint. This mint soap will freeze-dry your nipples."

Margaret smiled at Tina's enthusiasm. She didn't mind undressing before her sister. She wondered if Tracy would want to bathe. As soon as she was naked, Tina lifted a ladle of water and splashed it across her back. Margaret held her breath in the cold spray, but she turned in a circle as her sister dipped the ladle into the bucket and doused her with the icy water.

"You look beautiful," Tracy told her. "Like someone from another time."

"Like Venus," Tina said as she tipped the utensil over Margaret's shoulders.

"This must be how everyone bathed for centuries. These erotic water rituals," Tracy went on. He was trying to get something going.

Margaret lathered with the Castile soap. It felt hot, the peppermint burned the corner of her eye, it stung her as it washed down her legs and swirled through the small arrow of hair. It seemed to numb her. She said so, and Tina told them that in ancient medicine, mint was an anesthetic.

"I should have had some mint when I had my appendix out," Tracy said as he pulled his jeans off and moved behind Margaret.

"Oh God, he's going to try something," Margaret told Tina. She didn't like her sister seeing this.

Tina said, "Some people just invite rape. It's a *fait accompli.*"

Margaret looked at her. "You believe that? You're crazy."

Tina was working the pump handle until the bucket was refilled; then she went back to scooping the water and sifting it over them. "The Egyptians used mint in their embalming, mint and anise," her sister said. "Comfrey, fennel, costmary, lavender, coriander—" Tina stopped naming herbs when Tracy took Margaret's soapy wrist, pulling her hand to him.

"Shit, Tracy!" Margaret said.

"Give me a hippie hand-job," he whispered.

"Out of the question," she told him.

He was smiling. A smile in the dark looks strange, disembodied; you can't be sure what it means because the eyes aren't lighted. Tracy knelt down and scooped his hand over the bronze floor of mud then slapped the clay against her belly, smoothing it down. Margaret started to walk away, but he held on to her. She stood there. He pushed a handful of mud against her cunt, rubbing it into the slit. Margaret felt the velvety grains of earth, gritty but pleasing as he touched her, sculpting notches around her labia. The clay began to tighten over her belly and along the inside of her thighs. Tracy kept dabbing it on until she felt weighted, heavy with pulses. She dipped at the knees when it rocked over her and she saw her sister's teeth, luminous flashes. Tracy patted the mud against Margaret's thighs and over her buttocks, then he stood up. He fitted himself behind her, tugged her hand until she took him. His brief, omniscient shuddering was sudden and afterward he leaned into her. He rested his forehead against the shallow plane between her shoulder blades; she felt his eyelashes swipe her vertebrae.

Margaret pushed herself away from Tracy. The clay coated her legs and belly, glimmered with a metallic swirl and she thought of the starlet in *Goldfinger*. Wasn't that girl painted head to foot until she suffocated? Hollywood made it look glamorous. She grabbed the sponge from the bucket and she began washing the whorls of mud from her belly and thighs; her muscles rippled, her breasts bounced in tight shivers under her vigorous scrubbing. Her sun poisoning looked raw, pink as cigarette burns above her knees. She had to jerk the handle on the pump to wash herself better, and she straddled the stream, the clay rinsed white in the flow. Her cunt was stinging from the mud's abrasion or it was the icy water, knifing her until a new wave ascended, but she turned away from it. She threw the sponge down and picked up her clothes. "You go too far sometimes, Tracy," she told him.

"They charge a lot of money for this mud treatment in Vichy and those other spas," he said. He was telling Tina they might have a new angle if the Christmas trees were blighted. Margaret couldn't bring herself to walk away into the darkness and she waited for him as he washed himself. When he was finished, he grabbed her elbow and led her away from the muddy circle. Margaret could hear the pump screeching as her sister worked the handle, the water slicing a bevel in the mud.

III

The next day, Margaret played with the day camp children. She braided the girls' hair and tied yarn at the ends. The children were pleased to have someone new. They showed Margaret small bottles of insects, spiders and dragonflies asphyxiated by wads of cotton soaked in alcohol. She tried to identify different leaves and scabs of bark displayed in a windowcase.

After lunch they took the nylon parachute out to the field and invented new games. They stretched the parachute like a satin sheet for one of those round honeymoon mattresses. They ran into the middle and the weightless fabric billowed with air, then they ran backward, pulling it taut until everyone's arms were tired of tugging it between them. She jerked the chute, looping her fingers through its big grommets, which sliced into the tender insides of her knuckles. She avoided Tracy most of the day, letting him brood about his actions the night before. Then Tracy confessed to her.

"I was losing control. I thought you could help me. You know, I used you as a safety net," Tracy said.

"I don't buy that," she said. Then, if she thought of Cam, a cold feather brushed down her spine. Cam, too, was suddenly unreliable. Cam had turned her over, touched his lips to hers. His kiss didn't give to her or take from her. Anything. She didn't know its meaning. He had run off and left them.

Margaret sat on the sagging planks of the front porch as Tina showed her how to fold her first peace crane. Margaret tried to pinch and tuck the tiny squares of paper according to her sister's instructions, but her attempts always failed. Margaret's birds never looked like birds. They looked like crinkled napkins. Tina told her it takes a lot of practice. Margaret tried to imagine practicing such a thing for a long enough time. The thought discouraged her. Tina's fingers were sore from Fraser fir seedlings and still she used them to crease hundreds of these glossy sheets of paper. Couldn't Tina be doing something more worthwhile? There were premature infants at the hospitals who needed cuddling; they needed stimulation twenty-four hours a day just to keep them breathing and not enough nurses to do it. Those babies were left squalling until a volunteer came in. Couldn't Tina do that? Tina told Margaret she shouldn't be so upset just because she watched Tracy fuck her. "Sex is a visual high," Tina said.

Margaret looked at Tina working deftly, intently, with the papers. She could probably roll a good cigarette, Margaret was thinking. She tried to imagine other uses for Tina's gift. Sometimes, the apparent insanity in her family alarmed Margaret. She wasn't related by blood to her sisters or to Cam, but perhaps this malaise was airborne. Perhaps it permeated the environment of her childhood and was absorbed through audile or visual receivers. Despite the fact that not even a drop of her blood matched anyone's, they all might have shared, enriched one another's dementia.

Tracy spent the afternoon tinkering with a go-cart

motor for the children. It wasn't coming along. "It's tight as a ten-year-old," Tracy complained. What kind of standard was that! Margaret saw a blue cloud of smoke; then she heard a shrill complaint of metal ringing in the air. The smoke billowed upward, the children covered their mouths with the hems of their T-shirts. When the motor died some of the children moved off in clusters to sit in front of the rabbit hutch, and others walked down the rows of Christmas trees, tugging green nuggets off the tops.

In the morning, Tina was cutting leather shoelaces from a length of calfskin. They were sitting on the front porch drinking cups of tea. Tina drew an Exacto knife from one end of the hide to the other, making tiny lines in the floorboards underneath. Cam drove up the driveway; a wake of rosy dirt lifted behind the Duster. Margaret jumped down from the porch and ran up to Cam's window. Laurence was sitting in the backseat with a new toy, a plastic wheel of recorded barnyard noises. "The coyote says—*yawa, yawa, yawa.*"

"It's been driving me crazy," Cam said. He reached out of the car and grabbed Margaret's wrist. He kissed her fingertips in apology or hunger, she couldn't tell which.

She was at a loss and she turned to her nephew. "Laurence," she said. "Laurence, you're here!"

The boy pulled the cord on the toy and the recording chirped his reply. His forefinger was red where it was hooked through the plastic ring.

"You didn't drive straight through, did you?"

"No, we're fresh. Are you ready to go?"

"In a blink, I can't wait to get out of here. It's like Charles Addams meets Arlo Guthrie around here."

"What?" He wasn't listening. He looked out the windshield at Tracy walking up from the shed. Tracy waved and Cam's chin wobbled upward a degree and down again. It was halfhearted, Margaret was thinking.

Margaret said, "This time, let me drive. I haven't driven yet, I could use the change."

"Go get lover boy, and we're gonesville."

"What did you say?" she asked him. She wanted to see if he would say that word for her.

"Get Tracy. Hurry up. These tires are cooling down."

Margaret was driving when Tina said good-bye to them. Tina slapped the Duster with a new shoelace, whipping the passenger door with the bright peel of leather. "Good-bye, my dears. Give Lewis the cranes!"

"I'm not hand-delivering any of those cranes," Cam told Margaret.

"Why not?"

"What kind of an impression would it make?"

"It's not so bad, this peace stuff. It's not going to kill anybody to have these paper cranes," Margaret said.

"Looks like I arrived just in time. Your brain is a little soaked already." Cam looped the necklace of paper cranes over the rearview mirror the way someone might hook a pair of foam dice. "I can't be confused with this. These scraps!"

Margaret took her turn driving; she chewed her coffee beans and they intensified her reflexes. Her hands started to sweat a little and she drove with Cam's handkerchief on the steering wheel, switching it back and forth from her left hand to her right. She drove until they were out of Bowling Green and back on Interstate 80. Then it was Tracy driving. Margaret asked Cam about Darcy. It was just like they figured, Darcy didn't know what was happening. Cam explained how he jimmied the sliding glass door, went into Laurence's room, and took a drawer from his little bureau with all his clothes in it. He took the drawer outside first, then he came back and took Laurence.

"You took the whole drawer?" Tracy asked. "Now, we can add B & E, Petty Larceny, and Child Abduction to our original and pristine Grand Theft Auto—"

"Tracy's right, this is going to look bad in court," Margaret told Cam.

"It's too late now," Cam said. "I'm tired of all of it."

Cam slept in the backseat. Laurence was driving a Matchbox car over Cam, steering it up his thigh and over the plane of his hip, continuing up his arm until he reached his father's chin, then he went backward. Laurence was purring loudly to show the car's acceleration over rough terrain where Cam's knee was bent. Margaret kept shushing him. Next, he was standing up behind the seat, looping his arms around Margaret's neck, fingering her hair. "Whisper, so you won't wake your father," she told him.

Tracy said, "Nothing's going to bother Cam. If that awful barnyard toy didn't wake him up, nothing will. He's seeking refuge in Duster dreams."

"You should have your seat belt on," Margaret told the boy.

"But my dad is lying on it."

"Oh, well, don't wake him up yet."

"Where are we going?" Laurence asked her.

"Going steady," she said, and she pulled him over the front seat and into her lap to tickle him. The boy started to annoy Tracy, and Margaret helped him into the backseat, where, soon, he fell asleep.

Tracy was showing that he was tired or nervous, letting the car sweep left or right, changing lanes too often. They approached one urban area, then another. Margaret tried to talk to him, but he snapped at her. Margaret picked up a big plastic milk jug filled with tap water. The container was heavy and she steadied it in her palm as she tipped it to her lips. When she started to drink, Tracy shoved the bottle, collapsing it against her face. The mouth of the jug cut her lip. The water sloshed down her breast and still Tracy crushed it against her. She shoved his arm away and the bottle rolled off her lap, wetting the seat.

Then Cam was awake while Laurence continued to sleep. Margaret sucked her bottom lip; the cut wasn't serious, a loose shaving of skin she could smooth with her tongue. She started screaming. She tried to describe the incident to Cam, but he was arguing with Tracy about driving the Duster. Cam said he wanted to get behind the wheel, but Tracy didn't answer.

"I mean it, I want to drive," Cam said.

"If we stop, you can drive," Tracy said. "I'm not stopping."

"Whose car is it?" Cam said.

"It's Darcy's car," Tracy said.

Margaret was laughing. The laughter didn't start in

her lungs, it rolled over her in icy waves. She was helpless. Cam tried to get her to stop, but Margaret kept going.

Then Margaret thought that maybe Laurence missed his mother and her name might stir him up. They shouldn't mention Darcy's name. She missed her own daughter.

When they stopped for gasoline, Cam took the keys and waited for Tracy to shift out of his seat. Margaret went to the pay phone to call Celeste. She was forced to call collect, she had to say "from Margaret" when the operator asked who was placing the call. The phone rang several times, but there wasn't any answer. "Let it ring," she told the operator. The operator was quiet as the ringing continued a while longer. Margaret watched the cars going past on the freeway, then she looked down at the ground. An ant was dragging a butterfly. She watched the small red ant pull the giant Monarch to a mound of fine dirt, like sifted flower, the entrance of an anthill. The ant backed down the hole and started to tug the larger insect in after him. The wings, of course, were too big to fit. A little orange dust fell from the wings each time the ant jerked it. Was it only a smear of pollen, or was it the substance of the wing itself? "There's no answer, miss," the operator told her, and Margaret agreed that there was no one home at that number. She hung up the telephone. She looked down at the anthill once more to see that the butterfly, the ant, were gone.

10

t's so green," Margaret said, looking at the sky.

"It's unnatural," Cam said.

Tracy told them, "No, it's natural, it's *too* natural if you ask me."

The horizon was dark, roiling with odd hues. Once and again, at shorter intervals, serrated lightning ripped a bright fissure through the storm canvas, and the six-lane highway was illuminated with a sheet of blinding flash powder.

"We can't just drive right into this thing."

"It's a tornado," Margaret said, "I've heard that the sky gets really green when there's a tornado. I knew something like this would happen—"

"Sssh. Don't wake the kid, there's no reason," Tracy said from the backseat with Laurence. Then he was leaning over the front seat, his face level with Margaret's so he could study the storm. He was interested in seeing how Cam would navigate.

The windshield started to tick with hail. Then the hail came down harder, like pea gravel. The wipers couldn't brush it off fast enough. Cam was driving in the far left lane when suddenly he couldn't see out the windshield. The windows were sudsed with the force of the rain, it was as if someone had thrown a bed sheet over the car. The windows went white. It rained milk. Cam pumped his brakes and they heard the traffic, its sudden pulse, screeching in behind them. All the cars were halted in an odd arrangement on the freeway, like monopoly pieces, as the storm rocked over them.

"It's a cyclone," Margaret said.

"Just be quiet," Cam said.

The wind was tugging the Duster until it wobbled on its shocks. Water was leaking in over the rocker panels. Then the rain slowed. The cab was steamed up and Cam rubbed a handkerchief over the windshield. They saw some heavy branches on the road; a section of guy wire was left in loose coils in a middle lane. A license plate flipped across the asphalt like a square wheel rolling away on its corners.

"It really was something," Cam said, "a big mother-fucker."

Margaret saw the green horizon on the other side of her now, as the storm moved off.

"They go from the Southwest to the Northeast," Tracy said.

"How do they know what they're doing?" Margaret said. Then she remembered the science column in the newspaper: "Why do cyclones swirl in one direction across the U.S. and in another direction south of the equator?" The cars were starting to roll again. Margaret looked over at a station wagon. A woman was holding a baby up to the window; the baby's face was contorted, red. It was wailing.

It was the rush hour when they came into the city. The traffic was stopped and it gave them time to look at the skyline, follow the Sears Tower until its point dissolved. Tracy was leafing through an old Holiday Inn directory. Cam said that a Holiday Inn was too expensive.

"I don't want to go to one of those really cheap motels with paper bath mats. If we have Laurence, it has to be decent," Margaret told Cam.

"I'll have to use your card," Cam told her.

Tracy said, "Does it matter? We're coming in here so you can go soul-to-soul with the Arrow Collar, not so we can take a sauna."

"A pool would be nice for Laurence," Margaret said.

"You want a pool? There's the whole lake."

"I don't see any lake," she said.

"It's over that way," Tracy said.

Margaret looked over the hoods of the cars, trying

to find any sign of Lake Michigan. Then she saw a billboard with a familiar face. It was Merv Griffin's face. "Look at that!" she said.

"Merv Griffin?" Cam asked.

"He's coming to that dinner theater," she said. She was smiling.

"We're not going to hear Merv at any dinner theater," Cam said.

Tracy said, "God, Merv. I haven't seen too much of him lately."

Margaret told him, "He's a big producer. He makes shows for syndication. They say he has a business sense."

"He can make millions, but he's still a three-dollar bill," Tracy said.

"He's of that persuasion, that's sure," Cam said.

"What do you mean?" Margaret asked.

"He's like the stamp that has the airplane flying upside down," Cam said.

Margaret was laughing. "You mean he's gay? I think he's probably just like Tracy. You can't spend years with Arthur Treacher and Viva, people like that, and maintain any kind of innocence."

"That's what we're saying," Cam said.

"I'm not arguing," she said. "I knew his marriage was bad when he said his wife wore vanilla extract behind her ears instead of Chanel."

"Is that right?" Tracy said, "His wife used vanilla for cologne? She smelled like cookies—"

"I still like Merv," she said, her voice firm.

"Dinner theater is out!" Cam told her.

"He had some famous songs, you know standard numbers," she said.

"Are you still at it?"

"We have to eat somewhere," she said.

Margaret read the grid on the city map and found the block where Lewis's apartment should be. After making some wrong turns, they asked directions. Then they found the right area and patrolled the neighborhood in the Duster. It was pretty bad, there was trash lofting over the sidewalks, the cars were double-parked where some action was happening and Cam had to wait. Yet, some of the buildings had green canvas awnings, a few of the storefronts showed pretty marquees.

"Looks druggy around here," Tracy said.

"Who is that?" Cam said. They saw an older man walking down the sidewalk with three French poodles in a triple harness. The dogs were grey at the muzzle. "He looks kind of dapper."

"A dandy," Margaret said. "His dogs are ready for social security."

"That's not him," Cam said.

Then they found the building, THE GREGORY HOTEL written in red and white tile above the front entrance. A dirty square of Astroturf covered the sidewalk before the big glass doors. One door had strapping tape following a crack.

"It's not world-class," Cam said.

"No, but it's charming, it's Art Deco," Tracy said. There were two waist-high urns, one at either side of the entrance. The urns showed some salmon-colored geraniums. Cam told them they should find a motel near the Gregory, he'd be in and out in no time. They could relax, watch Johnny Carson. They'd drive back to Wilmington the next day.

"Sounds good," Tracy said. "Maybe we'll go find that cemetery tomorrow."

Margaret said her head was aching, they almost got sucked up in a twister, and Tracy better shut up about visiting any graves. Tracy said that it wasn't a real twister. "You have cancer of the imagination," he told Margaret.

"It was a funnel cloud," Cam said, taking Margaret's side of it.

A funnel cloud. Did a funnel cloud pour its contents, those wet sheets, the water white as muslin? Or did it siphon the world upward? This was a question for the science column. Whatever the answer, it was just another detail she found strangely telling. It was true, wasn't it? The past few days were crazy, revolving. The world was spinning, the horizon bulging, expanding beyond human perception. How was she supposed to keep free of these spirals? Sometimes she hyperventilated, she felt her heart palpitating, the palpitations increasing for moments at a time, then diminishing—until she couldn't verify if her heart was beating at all.

"I can't feel my heart beating," she said to Tracy.

Tracy said, "You aren't supposed to feel your own heart beating. It's when you notice it pumping that something is wrong. You're confusing a symptom with a strength."

She told him, "It doesn't have anything to do with the heart, anyway. Does it? Let's be straight. It's the mind. It's the mind playing tricks on the body. That's what I hate!"

.   .   .

They rented two rooms that connected if they unlocked a set of doors. The rooms were identical, with heavy maroon drapes and carpeting. Cam showed Margaret the setup and she told him what she thought of it. "It's a fucking mortuary," she said, but she had her shoes off already and he knew she wasn't going to make him find another place. The hotel was cleaning up after some conventioneers, but their rooms were ready and Margaret walked through the first one right into the other, deciding which side she liked better. Laurence turned on the television and found "The Muppets." Thank God for these Muppets, Margaret thought. She watched the show for a moment, attracted to the cloth puppets, their felt eyes and pilled cheeks.

"What's that sound?" Tracy said.

"It's that marble fountain out in the hall," Margaret told him. "It's noisy."

"Like something's frying. That spattering."

They went to see the fountain with Laurence. It was a tall display of miniature Greek statuary and descending trays, shaped like grape leaves, made of marbleized plastic. The water fell, level by level, to a scalloped trough on the floor, and circulated back. Tight, bouncing drops sounded like a paradiddle on a snare drum. It mimicked, then directed everyone's tension. "Shit, it makes a racket." Tracy said. "Smell the chlorine?"

Margaret gave Laurence a penny, but he missed the fountain and the penny rolled down the hall along the dirty baseboard. There goes one wish, she thought. "No, don't get that one, the floor's too dusty," she told the boy. She gave him a new penny.

Tracy rested on one of the double beds. He looked at the ceiling. Margaret thought of Tracy crushing the water jug against her face. She remembered Tina listing the herbs for Tracy; Margaret could still hear her sister's clean enunciation. These incidents had frightened her, but she hated it when Tracy ignored her. No matter what happened, his silence was what unnerved her. He made it clear that she was banished from his kingdom, his wordless reign. His silence seemed to manipulate every dust mote, every swirl of sunlight until she couldn't stand it. Margaret went over to the bed and climbed onto Tracy, full length. Her toes pushed off the insteps of his feet and she balanced herself, the small hill of her pelvis, against him. She kissed his mouth, ready to accept the rich greeting she expected, his breath accelerating, but he rolled her off of him.

Cam walked in from the other bedroom. His eyes were narrowed, as if he had been walking into some floodlights.

"It's set," he said. "We're going over there. We're all going over there for some kind of dinner."

"You called the Arrow Collar? You actually spoke to him right now? You don't waste a second," Tracy said.

"Dinner?" Margaret asked him. "That's bizarre. Dinner after all these years? Not me. I can't go over there."

Cam said, "I told him I was his son who he had never met. I said, Lewis Goddard? This is your son, Cameron. He didn't know what I was talking about."

"He drew a blank?" Tracy said.

"Dead at the end of the line. Then I gave him her name."

"My name?" Margaret said.

Cam looked at her. "No. Elizabeth. I said that name."

"Did he know who you were talking about?"

"Absolutely."

Cam was showering in one of the bathrooms and Tracy went down to find the *Chicago Tribune* and the *Sun-Times*. Margaret put Laurence in the bathtub on the other side from Cam, and she gave him her plastic hairbrush with the hollow handle and one of her flip-flops so he could float them in the water. Then she went and sat down on one of the beds. She called the hotel operator and placed a call, but her daughter still wasn't home. Perhaps they were riding the cabin cruiser or they'd driven to the harbor to see the new Baltimore Aquarium. She asked for another number in Wilmington. She was calling Elizabeth, but it was Darcy who answered the phone. Margaret recognized her sister-in-law's voice, and the shock of it kept her words back for a moment; then she said, "Darcy, this is Margaret."

"Where in the hell is my son?" Darcy said.

"He's fine. That's why I called. To tell Elizabeth not to worry."

"My son has been kidnapped, do you realize that? Do you know you're an accomplice? An accessory?"

Margaret said, "Shit, am I Patty Hearst? Am I? I'm his aunt, for Christ's sake! It's this thing with Cam's father, you know, it's finally getting going—"

"Cam is breaking the law, he's stole my child and took him across state lines, you tell him that. Tell him he's across state lines."

"Look, we're driving back soon."

"He's out of Delaware, and that's his big mistake, that's a federal mistake." Darcy kept telling Margaret about these state lines as if the offense, the violation, was against these boundaries and had little to do with the unity of their family.

Darcy went on, "You aren't here to pick up your daughter. What kind of person are you?"

"Celeste doesn't come back until Sunday," Margaret said. "What day is it?"

Darcy told Margaret that Phil was delivering Celeste that afternoon. "Elizabeth doesn't know what to do with her until you get back. Phil is pretty burned up to hear you drove to Chicago. He agrees that it's irresponsible. He says it's just another example."

Margaret wanted to ask Darcy why Celeste was coming home early, but she didn't continue. She was afraid to ask. Maybe her daughter couldn't wait the weekend, she was disconsolate. Perhaps she'd had some kind of an accident, some stitches or something. A wave of helplessness rocked Margaret onto her feet and she jerked the phone from the table and pressed it hard against her waist. She thought of the distance between herself and her daughter, a thousand miles like a sea of glue.

"It's ironic, it's ironic in the most fucked-up way," Darcy was saying. "You're out there with my kid and I'm here with yours."

"Is Celeste there?" Margaret asked. "Let me talk to her. Put her on."

"She's not here, not *yet*," Darcy said. "I'm telling you. She'll be here any minute. Looking for her mother. Believe-you-me—"

The conversation became strange, undulating. Margaret lost the thread of its meaning, and she felt a threat, an ominous tenor in the other woman's words. Just who was kidnapping who, Margaret started thinking.

"Darcy? Are you listening to me? Let's say we switch kids for a day. I'll take care of Laurence, and you promise to watch Celeste. Even-Steven." Margaret waited for Darcy to answer. "I'll bring Laurence home safe as soon as I can. You explain it to Celeste. Tell her something a kid can understand."

"Isn't she used to this insane stuff after living with you and that weird reporter?" Darcy said.

She heard Cam coming through the other room. "Don't worry," she whispered to Darcy, "Laurence is okay; he's taking a bath right here." Then Cam was standing there. He jerked the telephone out of her hands and slammed it down on the bed table. He picked the receiver up. Darcy was still on, Margaret could hear her voice, an insectlike murmur that stopped and started. Cam said something to his wife, he was giving her his condolences; he was acid. Then he crashed the receiver down once more.

"Stupid shit," he said. He pushed Margaret down on the bed. "They can trace that. Did you have to do that?"

"You can't just steal your kid and forget that his mother exists—"

"First, let me tell you something. A man doesn't steal his own child."

"Yes, he can. It's against the law. Legally, I mean, somebody steals his kid if he's not supposed to have him."

"I'm not supposed to have my own kid? Since when did you decide this?"

Margaret looked down at her feet, she pushed one foot forward, then the other until her toe snagged on the shag carpeting. "I just mean—"

Cam turned up and back before the window, walking like someone who's burned his hand or slammed his fingers in a drawer. He said, "Who's asking you to pony express our plans to her? I'm the one to tell her if I'm coming home."

"Aren't we going back tomorrow? We're not staying here, are we? I have to get Celeste—" She looked at her brother. They stared at one another. They both felt the same surge—they saw how their tactics regarding their offspring were turning a corner, becoming twisted. Cam's mouth turned up on one side. It wasn't a smile she recognized, she had never seen a smile like this. It looked ingenious and desperate all at once, like a soldier who is wearing grey suddenly recognizes his brother is wearing the blue. They could shoot one another, for what?

Laurence was calling to them. She went into the bathroom and lifted the boy from the water. She wrapped him in a towel and carried him to the chair where she had his fresh clothes. Cam tugged a jersey over Laurence's head; the boy's ears immediately blazed red.

Tracy came back with three newspapers. "I'll stay here and read these while you go visit your old man," Tracy said.

"No, we're all going. We're going chain gang," Cam said.

"I don't think we should go, we'll distract you from your work," Tracy said.

"No," Cam said. "I want backups."

"Well, all right. You talked me into it," Tracy told him. They were grinning back and forth.

Cam took a bottle of bourbon from a paper bag and twisted the seal. He picked up the glass tumbler from the motel desk and flicked off its paper crown. "Do you want any of this?" he asked Tracy, but he didn't include Margaret.

"I'll take some," Tracy said.

Cam poured two glasses of bourbon. He said, "What is it exactly, in your mind, Tracy, that I'm supposed to do now that I'm here?"

Margaret started laughing; her laughter lifted and dipped, was punctuated by rich growls low in her diaphragm, but the men weren't smiling.

"You know what you have to do, man," Tracy said.

"What is that?" Cam said.

"Just go introduce yourself. Go face to face. No thumbs. Identify that mystery guest. Name that tune."

"What's the point of it, though?"

"That's what I've been saying all along," Margaret said. She walked over and poured bourbon for herself. "I could have told you that two days ago!" she said.

Cam and Tracy didn't acknowledge her. They were involved in a peculiar exchange. It was like pilot and copilot going through a checklist, making sure the needles rested at the appropriate angles on all the gauges. Then it was resolved. The four of them would go over there to the Gregory Hotel. Cam would have his little entourage since he said he needed somebody to flank him. "I need backups," he said.

"We're behind you. Your slaves to the end," Tracy said, and he draped the newspaper he was holding over his sleeve and rolled the neck of the bottle against his arm as he poured another drink for Cam.

"Jesus, you missed your calling," Cam said.

"What about you? Sweetheart, you could have hustled. You're perfect for the Oldest Profession," Tracy told him.

II

The street was smoky from chimney stacks spewing flecked clouds from basement incinerators. The soot filtered down on them as they stood outside the Gregory Hotel. Margaret had bathed and nicked her leg shaving, a row of garnets bloomed in a vertical line along her ankle. Cam gave her a new handkerchief. He had to tear its cellophane. She dabbed at her leg and folded the handkerchief so Cam could put it back in his pocket again. She had combed Laurence's hair, parting it on one side and wetting the comb to make the strands stay in place.

"He looks like Alfalfa," Cam said.

"Alfalfa wore his part in the middle," Tracy said.

Their attention to Laurence continued as they took an elevator up to the sixth floor. They encouraged the boy to watch the lacy arrow rise and Laurence counted the floors. Tracy commented on the elevator; it was Art Deco.

"Art Deco, art schmecko," Cam said, "it's a scummy flophouse." Margaret studied the romantic lines of paneling inlaid with strips of mirror. The ribbons of mirror were tarnished with metallic lichens. They lifted slowly in the unusual stall, as if ascending into another time, but Cam wasn't sure of its checkpoints. Cam showed the strain of it. Margaret didn't like riding the elevator, and she thought she could smell something burning. Like the electrical insulation was smoldering. Then the doors opened.

Looking for the right apartment number, they found the door was left open. Tracy knocked against the molding and waited. "Hello," Tracy called into the apartment. Cam didn't wait and walked past Tracy and Margaret. They followed him inside. The rooms were painted deep umber, the rich color accentuated by the candelabra flickering on the sideboard in the living room. More candles on the dining table swelled and shivered with their arrival. Margaret noticed a familiar end table with lion's head brass pulls. It was a perfect match to a table in Elizabeth's sewing room; it must have been a pair split apart. The room had lamps with frosted glass shades, pink as sherbet, and these, added to the candlelight, gave a cabaret effect to the cramped apartment. Margaret found these cluttered rooms instantly appealing. Her head felt light as if she had

already drunk too much of something, but the sensation
came from the plumped upholstery, the tight satin pleats
of the seat cushions. These satin pleats gave her unwholesome shivers.

The walls showed the familiar drawings of Lewis by
Leyendecker. Several of the Arrow Collar ads were
matted and framed. Some of these were the original
Leyendecker paintings and sketches. Margaret liked the
Sanforized-shrunk ads, and one for Pepperell rayon
coat linings that showed Lewis being dressed by an
Oriental servant. Another picture had Lewis tugging
his cuff high on his ankle to reveal glossy Bostonian
wing tips. Finding these pictures all together, tracking
them in one whirling glance, wall to wall, was stunning.
Lewis had been more handsome than she'd ever imagined. Some of the angles in the photos showed similar-
ities to Cam, and she found herself looking back and
forth between the advertisements and her brother.

"Are we vain, or what?" Tracy whispered to her.

"Be quiet," she told him.

Lewis entered the room. He held his face high,
allowing his sculpted jaw full prominence. His shoulders
were still broad and level even as his physique appeared
perhaps a bit slight. It was just a hint of his age; his
bones might be hollowing. His face was startling, and
Margaret forgot her surroundings and moved past the
beautiful sconces that decorated the wall, although she
had wanted to study them. Lewis lived up to his legend.
Margaret had seen certain people—usually an actor or
a singer—who possessed this same trait, the blessing or
burden of looking always larger than life. Lewis pulled

his left arm backward in an elegant motion, inviting them inside the living room, although they were well past the threshold already.

Lewis stood squared with Cam. There was no question that Cam was his progeny. Cam introduced everyone, but he didn't offer his own name or greeting. Lewis complimented Laurence, calling him "a little Freddie Bartholomew."

Cam squinted for a moment; Margaret saw he probably didn't know the reference to the child actor. Cam would have known about Mickey Rooney, but then, of course, Laurence *didn't look* like Mickey Rooney.

"Of course, you must be Cameron," Lewis said after long enough.

Cam nodded. Cam's smile was immediate, warm, but he checked it. His mouth fell even.

"Cameron Goddard," Lewis said, "Goddard, we share that coat of arms."

Cam looked at his father. His eyes followed the man's face from the high forehead, along the smooth terrace of cheekbone, and down the jaw to the well-defined mouth, Cam's mouth. Margaret saw how Cam avoided looking directly at Lewis's eyes.

"This is an unusual moment, but probably for the best. It was probably unavoidable," Lewis said.

Cam was trying very hard to concentrate, to understand if his father's comment was warm or defensive.

"I thought it was time," Cam said.

"We might have been ships passing in the night," Lewis said.

Again, Cam showed some uncertainty about Lewis's

meaning. Margaret saw how he suffered. What a thing to say to your own son, "Ships passing in the night." Margaret recognized a peculiar sensation, the drilling at the base of the spine as if riveted to this one moment in a previous lifetime. Some people called it *déjà vu*; scientists say it's chemically induced, the brain repeats its own thought. It happens in a fraction of a second and someone senses a distant connection, a dream or vision. She felt that bitter tingle.

Laurence was sleepy and Margaret suggested they feed him something soon. Lewis carved an edge of lasagna from an aluminum foil tray of pasta. The lasagna was from the restaurant on the corner. He'd ordered the whole meal—pasta, garlic bread, salads in Styrofoam bowls—and he'd told the restaurant to deliver it to the apartment.

"I thought the child would like lasagna. Spaghetti is sometimes cold by the time it comes," Lewis told her.

"How nice of you to think of these things," Margaret said. Laurence ate his dinner and Margaret put him to sleep on an overstuffed chaise longue; its feather upholstery encircled the boy in lovely billows. "It just makes you want to go to sleep," she told the boy.

When she came back to the dining table, the men were sitting down. Lewis was telling Tracy a chronology of his modeling career, pointing to different drawings and clippings on the walls. "This was my first *Collier's*, and that one, that was a full page in the *Times*. Women wrote letters, a half ton of them, a literal half ton of letters, asking who I was. Dinner invitations, marriage proposals, threats of suicide, real estate opportunities, a half ton of them."

Tracy was skeptical. "Did they actually weigh these letters at the post office?"

"They can tell the weight of something by figuring the volume alone. A sack of mail is a certain volume, then they figure the weight. So many sacks of mail, love letters you might say, equals so much volume from which they figure the weight. One half ton from a full page in the *Times*. A record, really," Lewis said.

"Why didn't you go into films?" Tracy said.

"Oh, you mean Hollywood? That was Fred March and Brian Donlevy."

"Fredric March was an Arrow Collar man?" Margaret was impressed.

"Several went into films with some success. I like to think there was a distinction between the two professions."

"Didn't you want to be a film star?"

"I liked the modeling. Posing for Leyendecker was a dramatic test in itself. He was demanding."

"This painter, Leyendecker, wasn't he a lavender colleague of Norman Rockwell?" Tracy said.

"No, Rockwell came after; Leyendecker was first," Lewis said. "Very different types. I wouldn't say exactly lavender for Leyendecker; he deserves a better word, something more particular. His sensitivities were, let's say, acute. He was often attracted to someone's bee-stung lips. He had a reputation with that. But I was his subject for work, not his amusement. Critics said that Leyendecker could never paint women with any sympathy. As for Rockwell, he painted children."

Tracy leaned on the table; he said he had an interest in this, he had come to believe the artist's studio was much like a casting couch. Was that the case? His curiosity was piqued. "You're saying Leyendecker was single-minded and painted the male animal expressly; he couldn't paint women?"

Cam said, "This isn't Twenty Questions, is it, Tracy? Can you back off?"

Lewis smiled at Tracy and lifted his shoulders as if to say he might have answered his questions or he might not. The matter was derailed. Margaret scratched at a petal of wax on the table cloth. Lewis poured wine from a double-sized bottle. She imagined the four of them drinking the whole amount; that would be several glasses each, and she knew Cam couldn't survive it after drinking three drinks at the motel. She decided to slice the big square of lasagna so they could eat something along with drinking the wine.

"Did you leave my mother before I was born?" Cam asked Lewis.

"Let's jump right in," Tracy told Cam.

Lewis said, "Oh, that's all right. I expect there's many things to clear up. You weren't born. Actually. She kicked me out long before that. I was surprised to hear about you. It was a shock, really."

"I see."

"We're not denying the truth, though," Lewis said.

"We're not?" Cam said.

"No, it adds up. I mean it wasn't impossible; it was just a matter of luck." Lewis lifted his glass and cupped its bowl without drinking.

"What kind of luck?" Cam said.

"Luck. Just luck, the roll of the dice—you tell me? I don't have any claim to it."

Cam said, "This reminds me. Did you send me that five-pound chocolate Easter egg in 1960?"

"Excuse me?" Lewis said.

"I was fifteen. Someone sent me a gigantic, solid chocolate Easter egg with a pair of dice inside."

Margaret said, "I remember that. I was jealous. Solid chocolate with two gleaming dice inside."

"I don't know anything about a chocolate egg," Lewis said.

Cam said, "I thought you might have sent it to me. No one knew where it came from. You're so *into* this idea of luck, I thought maybe it was you. That's okay. Excuse me. Strike one."

Tracy said, "Luck is an interesting concept for some. Random chance is an impressive thing, isn't it? I like throwing the cubes. African golf. Does it fascinate you, I mean, as much as it does me? Did you roll a number and decide to invite us here, to dinner?"

Lewis shook his head. "I had time to think. Bette rang me yesterday. I knew you were coming."

"You mean Elizabeth? Elizabeth called here? She couldn't keep out of this?" Cam shoved himself back from the table, but he decided against standing up.

Margaret noticed that Lewis had called Elizabeth by her French pet name, one syllable, "Bette."

"She wanted me to have a chance to escape," Lewis said. "She's afraid of what might happen. The two of us together like this; we could unite in an opinion. All of us here, we could have a quorum."

Cam drank the wine and smiled. He looked at Tracy to see if Tracy understood what this meant to him. Lewis showed the same sarcastic tolerance of Elizabeth as he himself felt. But Cam's expression changed quickly; he was reevaluating each notch of feeling as it came to him.

"So tell me what's new with your mother?" Lewis said.

"She sold her body to science," Cam told Lewis.

"To science?" Lewis asked.

"I tell the truth," Cam said.

"My God. I can't think of Bette in a laboratory. Imagine the experiments even I didn't try," Lewis said.

The men laughed. Their laughter accelerated, dipped and rose again. It was the joke's vile resonance that prolonged their laughter. It was terrible to watch Cam. His waves of comprehension, his shifting expressions reminded her of films using fast-forward, time-lapse photography. A nature film shows a seed germinate, then the little green shoot struggles upward through the baked clay, next the bud forms, swells taut until the blossom explodes.

Margaret asked Lewis, "Did you ever know my mother? My mother, Sandra Rice?"

"Sandra? Sandra. The name itself rings a buzzer. The name in itself is delightful, endearing, but I don't believe I had the pleasure."

Margaret said, "Of course you knew her. She was Richard's first wife, Elizabeth's acquaintance. My mother. You must have met her."

"I probably did know her. Rest assured I didn't really *know* her."

"You didn't have the pleasure?" Cam said. The men chuckled in three distinct notes, blending into a rude chord.

Margaret didn't like this.

"Sandra was the one who died in Granville Sanatorium. Now do you picture her?"

Lewis looked hard at Margaret. "Of course, my dear. I was avoiding the subject. It was terrible, you know, they *snuffed* her. A feather pillow to end her misery. It was ghastly. Out of pity we can do devil's work and call it charity."

Margaret was standing up. She couldn't find her voice and whispered, "Pillow? What pillow? Are you saying what I think you're saying?"

"Mercy killing, no kidding?" Tracy said.

"Sit down, honey," Lewis told her.

"She had cancer. This pillow idea—are you mad?" Margaret said.

"Just a metaphor, my dear," Lewis told Margaret. "I didn't mean she was actually asphyxiated. Your father running around with Elizabeth must have killed her off a lot faster. You know, Sandra was a poor invalid unable to do her duty. Then, here comes Elizabeth with her love calisthenics, her feats of exceptional endurance."

"Elizabeth?" Tracy asked. "She was athletic in the sack?"

Margaret looked at Cam to see if he was going to put up with this. Cam was scraping a knife over the faded gold rim on a china saucer; it was coming away like a piece of old cellophane. He didn't have an opinion.

Lewis apologized to Margaret once more. He told

her she shouldn't cling to morbid thoughts. He reached across the table and took her hand. He forced Margaret to meet his eyes. She tried not to return his look, even as she studied his onyx pupils; his eyes looked hard as glass, as if she couldn't scratch them with a pin. She tugged her fingers, but he wouldn't release her hand. He started to recite some lines of poetry—

> Margaret, are you grieving
> Over Goldengrove unleaving?
> It is the blight man was born for,
> It is Margaret you mourn for.

Lewis seemed pleased with the little stanza, its immensity. He pulled it off. The other men were impressed. It was an eye-opener for Tracy. Verse might be a new angle for him. Margaret tried to look at Cam, but Lewis kept her; she was tethered by his gaze. She felt her spine curl and tighten, an imperceptible response, yet Lewis seemed to know it. Margaret licked her finger and touched it to the red ellipses along her nicked ankle. "Do you have Band-Aids?" she asked Lewis. Her voice was flat.

There were some first-aid supplies in the bathroom cabinet. She went in there, glad to be out of hearing. In the narrow bathroom there was a skylight window. The skylight could be propped open by pushing a lever. When Margaret pushed the lever to open the window, a good ration of soot studded with the shiny husks of flies fell down upon her. She saw the veil of insects and black granules in her hair and was repulsed; she had to grip the sink and take her breath carefully. In a few moments Tracy came in to find her. She was trying to wash the floor with a triangle of sponge. "Cam will kill me if he sees this mess."

"What is that all over you?" Tracy said.

"It's filth from out of nowhere! Crap from the stratosphere."

"It's hard going for Cam," Tracy said.

"Cam had to come out here to see it was true," Margaret said. Lewis was coldhearted. He displayed such a chilly amorality, or maybe he was just crazy. How long could Cam hold up in front of them? Margaret thought of a sword swallower. A sword sinks in inch by inch, past the vocal cords, into the gullet. When is it deep enough to impress an audience? Deep enough to meet one's own test of strength? Tracy would remind her that the blade collapses; it's a simple trick.

When they returned to the table, it was empty. They found Cam and Lewis in the bedroom. Lewis pulled a shirt from a drawer, an old-fashioned shirt without a collar. The shirt was yellowed but Margaret could see it was finely tailored, its front bib still crisp, the pleats sharp, each tuck an even line. "We're the same size," Lewis said, "and I have so many. I thought I could give Cameron—Cam, something as a memento of our extraordinary meeting tonight."

Lewis's bedroom was dark and narrow. The wardrobe looked frightening, like a locker in a mausoleum. He jerked some clothes loose from tight layers on the shelves; he struggled with overburdened drawers. He said he had often kept the shirts that he modeled; they were a bonus. It was the suits he had to return. They wouldn't have suits altered for the models; the suits were pinned and tucked with tape, and then he had to return them. He tried to walk away in overcoats; sometimes it worked out.

Cam didn't seem comfortable with the idea of a shirt. These shirts were thirty or forty years old! The room smelled of the pressed linens and Pima cottons; it was an ancient scorched smell coupled with a trace of liniment. There was something ugly about the transaction. Cam didn't want to wear his father's clothes. Lewis sensed this, and he went to the wardrobe and pulled a jacket from a wooden hanger.

"Cashmere," he told Cam.

Everyone reached to touch the sleeve. The fabric was soft, like the short velvety hide of a hamster.

"Very nice," Tracy said.

"Try it," Lewis told him.

"I'd like to," Tracy said.

The jacket looked good on Tracy, the lapels too wide, but the overall effect was pleasing. Lewis said the jacket had been made for him in London. It was a gift years ago, and look how it had held up.

"Do you want it?" Lewis asked Cam.

"No, I don't want the jacket."

"I understand," Lewis said.

Again, they went back to the table. The food was cold. Margaret tried to stab a cherry tomato in her salad, but the plastic bowl wobbled each time she poked the tiny sphere. Cam kept drinking the wine, but Tracy declined a refill.

Lewis was telling Cam, yes, he had loved his mother, Elizabeth. He thought so anyway. He *would* have loved her, but he wasn't the Master of Love. Love was a dictator, he told them. He explained how he suffered if he saw an attractive woman. "Just the turn of an ankle, the flare of the calf can be like a hot poker to the eye! I wasn't responsible for utter reflex," Lewis said. He told them he suffered for months, for years at a time.

"A leg man," Tracy said. "What about you, Cam?"

"Tracy, shut up," Margaret said. As the men talked, Margaret studied the photographs. It was less a gallery documenting someone's vanity than a tribute to youth itself. All the pictures were more than thirty years old; there was nothing that documented that Lewis continued to exist after a certain decade. Margaret noticed that not all the images were professional. There were some small snapshots, society clippings, but it all stopped at the same time, somewhere in the mid-forties. Then she saw it. The little catboat with Elizabeth. Margaret got up from the table and went over to the sideboard. The candelabra flickered, increasing the yellow tones of the photographs. "This is Elizabeth on Lake Michigan, am I right?"

"That's correct, I liked that one," Lewis said. "I kept it as a record. You'll notice that she's not alone up there; there are several ladies."

Margaret looked at the faces of the women in different snapshots. They were all pretty, but Elizabeth was the most appealing. Not one of them added up to Elizabeth's perfection. Elizabeth reigned. She would love to know that, Margaret thought.

"She has her own copy of this snapshot, I saw it," Margaret told him, but she suddenly felt she might have betrayed her stepmother to tell him that.

Then Cam shouted to her just as she, herself, saw it. Her hair caught fire, the flame lifted over her head, pulling the blond strands upward. The burning hair condensed, crackled at her ear. Cam was beside her, tugging the rope of flame and slapping her cheek until the fire was out. She screamed and Laurence woke up. They went into the kitchen, and Cam shoved her head under the tap. He rinsed her hair, separating the blackened debris from the rest. She hadn't lost too much hair, but her cheek was sore and they couldn't tell if she was burned or if it was red where Cam had slapped her to put the fire out.

"You don't stand over candles with shoulder-length hair," Tracy was scolding her.

"As if I need this."

"You're okay. It will grow back."

"It stinks," she said. She recognized the smell of charred protein from the time she watched a farmer poke a branding iron against a steer's flank. It was the same when a farrier placed a red-hot horseshoe against a hoof to measure it; the smell is everlasting.

Her hair was frizzy, curled at the temple. "We'll trim it," Tracy said. They stood in the bright kitchenette, relieved to be out of the dark parlor. Cam was looking at a stack of mail on the kitchen counter. Government checks of some kind. Social Security checks, disability, and various military pension checks. There were almost twenty envelopes.

"They've passed on," Lewis told Cam.

"These checks passed?" Cam asked, trying to follow what Lewis was saying.

"These folks are deceased. They didn't have offspring, no one waiting in the wings. It's a small existence really."

"You mean you can cash these checks?" Cam was grinning.

"For a fee. I can have them cashed for a fee, let's put it that way."

"You're telling me, you cash these dead people's checks?"

"If not me, someone else."

Margaret said, "I heard of that. It's a racket, but it's a federal thing, you know. You better be careful. We have people in the joint who stole mail trucks, that's U.S. government. They get sent up immediately, no lengthy evaluations. They go to those federal prisons. It happens fast. They send them up without a lot of pre-trial."

Cam was still grinning. "You mean to tell me you're a crook as well as a queer shit?"

Lewis shrugged, but he didn't lose his elegant posture; he was the same, he didn't stiffen. He wasn't someone to flinch. Margaret believed he might have felt disappointed in his own carelessness. He'd permitted his son to discover a detail that could have been easily concealed. He could have put those checks somewhere out of sight. He wasn't thrown off balance by what had happened in the last several minutes, not by her hair catching fire, nor by their discovery of these checks. Lewis was asking them if they wanted some Rémy-Martin.

"Absolutely," Cam said. He tapped the envelopes against the counter's edge, evening their corners, leaving them in a neat stack.

"Sure," Tracy said, accepting the glass of brandy from Lewis. "A little nightcap for old times' sake. *To our ghosts from the past.*" Tracy lifted his glass. He swallowed the brandy, keeping his face level. Margaret didn't like the toast, but she admired the way Tracy drank his brandy. Another man might toss his head back or make a grimace. Tracy held his glass steady for another golden dribble of the Rémy-Martin.

"So you're doing quite well for yourself," Cam said to Lewis.

"It's hit-and-miss. I have to deal with scourge, but I have a few loyal compatriots."

"Fellow crooks," Cam said.

"You're coming through loud and clear, son. I don't blame you. One day you'll reach my age and the first part falls away like a rotten log. Then make your accusations," Lewis said.

Cam told him he wasn't accusing him. "I'm just a bystander," Cam said. "Your stump can fall off for all I know."

It was beginning to degenerate. The light was scratchy on the walls, the candles sputtered. Laurence was sitting on Margaret's lap after waking when Margaret's hair caught fire. "We should take him back to the motel," she said. She saw the excuse was welcomed by all. They stood up to leave. The cashmere jacket was on a chair, and she brushed it with her hip as she passed. The coat slipped onto the floor. Tracy picked the jacket up and patted it admiringly before putting it over the chair. The ancient garment disturbed Margaret, its decay steamed and pressed, shaped and brushed.

They took the elevator down to the street. "Hello. Good-bye. That's it," Cam was saying. He must have had too much to drink. He kept repeating variations of the same words. "Hel-law. Good-bye. Thaz sit." Tracy had his arm hooked around Cam's neck and he knocked his hip into Cam. Cam pushed him off.

The motel's long, carpeted hall caught the soles of their shoes. Margaret watched them stumble like a three-legged beast. Laurence was preoccupied, eating an ice cream sandwich from a freezer case they saw out on the sidewalk, and he followed a few paces back. Margaret had to take the key from Cam to unlock the door. Inside, Cam went right over to the bourbon and lifted it high, eye level, as he poured his drink. He was filling a Dixie cup, since the glasses were dirtied with cigarette butts. It was ridiculous. Then she saw it was a way to come back. Like dogs after a long swim—they walk onto dry land and shake themselves. They shudder, their hide twirls loose with water, their hair stands out straight like a wheel of fur, ridding one environment for the other.

She helped Laurence brush his teeth. "Open," she said, "like a dinosaur."

"A crocodile," Laurence said, "you mean like a crocodile." She saw how it starts early, the dogmatic search for the specifics, the insistence on correct details. She could hear Tracy's voice, Cam's laughter. She couldn't make out the words; they sounded like sudsy rivers running into one another, a crosscurrent, alternating force and submission.

When she finished brushing the boy's teeth, she started to brush her own teeth. Tracy came into the bathroom. He grabbed the toothbrush from her hand and tried to insert it into her mouth; he tried to brush her teeth.

"Stop it," she told him when he poked her, scraping the bristles against her lip. Then he held her jaw with one hand and pressed his weight against her so she was pinned against the sink. He maneuvered the toothbrush in and out of her mouth; he brushed her teeth. She saw herself in the mirror, the small web of burned hair at her temple. She was laughing, but he was hurting her. She started choking on the minty foam. Still, Tracy circled the brush over her teeth. Cam was at the bathroom door, but he wasn't going to help her out. Then Tracy was finished and he stepped backward. She kicked him in the shin; her toes cracked, but he didn't flinch. She was furious; she looked into the mirror to check the abrasion on her lip.

"Look, leave me and the baby alone. You're a couple of swills." She took Laurence into the other room and put him in bed. She adjusted the air-conditioning unit so it wasn't blowing too hard. Laurence rolled over and she rubbed his back; she recited "The Three Little Kittens," which she knew by heart. They lost their mittens, they found their mittens, they soiled them, they washed them.

Margaret went back on the other side with Cam and Tracy; she ignored them, walked across the room and pulled on the TV button. The knob came off in her hand, and she had to find the way it was threaded before she could put it back. The picture flashed on, spiraled up and down for a moment, then cleared. It was an old movie. "Hey, look at this," she told them. It was Fredric March in *Death Takes a Holiday*. She was asking Tracy if he liked the coincidence, two Arrow Collar Men in one night. She was pleased, this was something she could enjoy, but she couldn't raise the volume without replacing the little knob that had fallen off in her hand.

She was holding the knob up to her eye when the light was switched off. She couldn't see in the half dark of the room. Tracy took the knob from her hand and said, "We don't need this button." This didn't surprise her, she saw it coming, but then she heard Tracy say, "Do we need this button, Cam?"

"What's this?" she whispered.

Cam said, "We don't need the TV." She felt his breath on her shoulder. She could smell the sweet, caramel odor of the brandy.

She said, "Look, I don't have a problem with this, just don't rush it."

Cam lit a cigarette and sat down on the edge of the bed. The match flared beneath his face: his dark eyes looked twice as shadowed; the mid-line crease of his lower lip was exaggerated. He must be having his second thoughts. Then Tracy was steering her over. She didn't resist. He positioned her before her brother and tugged

her blouse down to expose her breasts. She was illuminated by an external glow, rosy lumens of refracted city
light coming in the window. Tracy was showing Cam
something, but this didn't alarm her. He was telling
Cam a litany of erotic phrasings, his voice steady,
convincing. He kept referring back to her, as if she
were a case in point, but she didn't try to follow, she
didn't gather the words until Tracy said, "Look."

Cam lifted his face, his eyes narrowed in modesty or
in restraint of appetite. He smiled, giving calm acknowledgment to her, then he looked down again. Tracy
stood behind her, his front teeth sinking against the
plane of her shoulder; he wasn't going to wait much
longer. Cam picked up Margaret's hand and squeezed
it. He dropped it again. She weaved slightly before her
brother, Tracy in back of her. Still, Cam didn't invite
her.

As she moved onto the bed with Tracy, she searched
her brother's face, but he didn't return her look. He sat
hunched over on one corner of the mattress, his back
to them. Tracy was fucking her, reciting directives when
he surged and shifted. If her breathing increased or
halted in effort or with pleasure, could Cam tell? For
moments, she didn't think of Cam. Tracy knew everything. He went ahead until her pink spur was jittering,
then he paused. She felt the pillow weighted beside her,
Cam's face turned to her. His mouth moved down her
throat to the narrow well at her sternum. Margaret lost
her sense of location. She touched Cam, moved her
palm down the tight plateau of his belly, but he rolled
away from her.

"What's wrong, what's wrong with this? It's lovely," she told him; she refined her diction to hide her impatience. She could have just screamed for it. Tracy murmured in agreement. He said something flattering to Cam.

"It could change us. It's changing us, Margaret," Cam said.

"Right here," Margaret whispered. She tugged her brother's wrist and opened his fingers.

Tracy moved away. He turned on his side and leaned on his elbow. He was reciting the Serenity Prayer: "God grant me the serenity to accept the things I cannot change . . . courage to change the things I can . . . and the wisdom to know the difference.

"Change is a constant. The past is fluid, it merges. History is never static, events shift in meaning—"

"Shut up," Cam told him.

Cam rolled onto Margaret, stretching her arms over her head. He smoothed his palms down the insides of her wrists, went lightly over the creases of her elbows and swirled his fingertips in the hollows of her armpits. He traced her breasts with weightless, unfrightened scrawls. He wrote over her, wordless crosshatches and dreamy numerals. His lips tightened around her nipple and she shuddered, grinding her hips deeper into the mattress. She guided his cock, centering its heavy tip, letting it sink through the silky hymenal curtain. He was steadied there and she thought about the Horror of God, how painful love is without representation. Then Cam was deep, his cock different from Tracy's; perhaps in circumference, larger. He was fucking her and she wasn't feeling it in one place; it was everywhere. She felt the door of the soul ripped free from its house, an airy whiteness like sheets snapping. Her muscles triggered, twisting like knotted linens, sea-sweetened ropes. He tugged her hips and froze, then moved farther in, kept going. Cam watched her; if she closed her eyes, he exhaled his breath, a cool jet to arrest her, keep their gaze even. He stopped moving and she felt his release, an internal wing-beat, a whirring. Then her own tight hitches of sensation.

He was almost too shy to withdraw from her. He rolled his forehead against her throat and dragged himself away without looking back. Then Cam was standing up. She heard some coins fall from his pockets as he picked up his jeans from the floor. They were Tracy's. He dropped them in an even fold, and reached for his own clothes.

Margaret reached into her paper sack and took a fresh coffee bean. She had only nine beans left, eighteen if she nipped each obelisk. The bus window turned back her reflection; her blond hair fell in ashy spirals against her face. Laurence was in the next seat, prying the tiny ashtray from its recessed notch in the armrest. The sun was coming up, its harsh red condensed, trapped in the lines and droplets on the glass. Outside, the Pennsylvania landscape scrolled by. She hugged Laurence, but he squirmed. She tried to explain why they had left his father in Chicago, but he could not believe her fluttering eyes, her eyebrows too highly arched in false crescents. It was awful to see his alarm, his button-sized Adam's apple rising and falling. Before taking the bus, she had tried to buy him some fruit; she stopped at a market that displayed a misted cluster of grapes in the window, but the grapes were plastic, studded with artificial dew-drops. She bought him a cellophane package of six miniature white doughnuts. Laurence sat down in his seat and arranged the doughnuts on his knees, ordering them in two lines of three, then he began eating the sugar off the first one.

During the night she was unable to rest. The low skimming sound of the bus tires wasn't soothing to her, as it might have been to some. She slipped into dreams once or twice, but the dreams were unpleasant; the dreams awakened her. She dreamed of the ant towing the Monarch under the earth. Too often, she fingered the frizzy patch where her hair was burned and she sniffed her fingers for the scorched scent. She took some relief in having crossed three state lines during the darkness of night, and she figured it would be less than a half day's drive to reach Wilmington. She watched for the tiny luminous flecks of the mile markers that spar-kled on posts and guardrails. She was pleased to be returning with Laurence, although she wasn't sure she should hand him over to Darcy. Mostly, she longed for her reunion with Celeste. Yet the thought of greeting her daughter made her uneasy. Recent unwholesome events churned through her. She would have to transform herself, shedding another skin. It was always like this: During the day, she must wear a mother's face; then at night, it was the cold mask of Venus above a constant searing below her waist. It wasn't to scale.

Early that morning, when the bus stopped in Toledo, she had tried to call her daughter. Elizabeth answered the phone and told her the child was in bed. It was the middle of the night. Margaret demanded she go wake the girl up, but Elizabeth talked her out of it. There wasn't anything else to say without having to explain everything, and her words started to catch when she told her stepmother that, yes, she was on her way home, but without Cam, without even Tracy. Margaret thought of Celeste in Elizabeth's house with all its expensive bric-a-brac. What if her daughter bumped into a shelf and the Canton china shattered, a splash of porcelain sharks' teeth? Margaret tried to see the past few days from an official point of view, that of a judge or a state trooper: the long drive in the Duster, the stolen tires, Laurence transported across the state border. These illegalities didn't plague her. She was disturbed by images of Sandra's tombstone; Tina dipping a ladle into the icy water; Jane's gauzy curtains filled with the sea wind; Cam, his erection bumping against her hip as he lifted her arms over her head the way men open the wings of their hunting trophies, caressing beautiful flight feathers serrated from tiny shot pellets.

The night at the motel, she had hardly slept. After that airy, supernatural moment with Cam, Tracy was fascinated and wanted her again. Then he dozed. Margaret tiptoed to Laurence, covering him with the blanket. She picked up his hands, gently sucked the fingertips, then rubbed them dry. Cam was up, he walked in and out of the rooms, sometimes going down the hallway to the outdoor stairwell to smoke where the air was cool. She told him to lie down, but he refused. He was unable to get off his feet, to lie supine in his state of shame. Each time she started to fall asleep, she was awakened by Cam. Cam clearing his throat, Cam shifting in the vinyl armchair, Cam hiking up and down in the hallway outside their rooms. Then she heard the incessant circulation of water in the plastic fountain parallel to their door. The drops fell hard and separate, tier to tier. It was impossible to ignore it.

Soon Tracy was up, getting after Cam. He told him he was wasting his time worrying about his momentary plunge into *Margaret Heaven.* "It's downhill, after that," Tracy said. Cam shouldn't lose sleep over it. They shouldn't all have to lose sleep.

Cam said he was sick of Tracy's opinion. He called Tracy a "mind eater," and this was interesting to Margaret, it was a clumsy epithet, but it seemed to fit.

"Mind eater!" Cam said.

Tracy said, "You sound pretty disappointed in yourself. If you couldn't enjoy fucking your sister, don't blame me. You're what we call a *blamer.* You're naïve, a sexual initiate. You could have had both worlds. Do you know what I'm saying? Both worlds."

"Both worlds?" Cam said.

"Love and sex. Love and sex, don't you see? It's a combo some people strive for," Tracy said.

"I don't know what you're talking about," Cam told him.

Margaret listened to this. She thought she knew what

Tracy was driving at, but if she did, she was making a big admission to herself. Tracy was saying he didn't have that ability, elementary to some, but he had never attained it. Tracy was saying Cam could have been lucky with Margaret, body and soul.

"God, that dripping water!" Margaret said.

Tracy went out in the hall to see about the fountain. He didn't stop to put his pants on; he just strolled out in the hallway and leaned in between the network of plastic trays searching for a water connection. Margaret waited at the door of the room. Tracy crouched over the pipes, his skin shivered over his backbone, his ribs flared open and collapsed tight as he reached in and out of the fountain.

Then Cam came out there. "What do you mean, I'm a sexual initiate? Because I don't always stick my dick in just anyone? Because I don't belong to Sex Anonymous?"

Tracy said, "You have to know your poison before you can decline to drink it. You haven't signed the dotted line. You're Sex Unidentified. Casanova in the Bermuda Triangle. You're a love letter without a cancellation mark—you don't know what you want. You're drifting."

Margaret closed the door, shut it until the brass tongue clicked in the lock. She didn't want to hear anymore. Tracy was using his purple journalese to bait Cam. He was flirting with him. Perhaps it was just more of Tracy's curiosity, but maybe it was appetite. Maybe it all came down to that. She went to check on Laurence and stayed on the other side with the boy when she heard the men coming back. She heard their voices rising and the words broken off, torn by physical blows. They were striking one another. Then it was quiet.

She climbed in bed next to Laurence. He rolled to her, it was natural. When the men appeared at the foot of her bed, they looked unsteady, similarly crazed, depleted, their knees jellied from surges of adrenaline. Was it really *two* of them? Did she suffer that exhaustion that brings delirium, an episode of double vision? She straightened herself on the pillow and tried to focus her eyes. She looked at Cam, then she looked at Tracy. How many days without sleep until a man loses it all? His normal height looks decreased; he slumps, stumbles, loses his elegance. Even if they wanted plain mothering, she wasn't inclined to offer it. She wanted to invest the remaining night in the little boy. She peeled the sheet back from her shoulder and showed them Laurence, his arms and legs drawn tight in a sphere of warmth beside her.

In the morning, Margaret heard the maids running a vacuum in the next room. It was later than she thought, past one o'clock in the afternoon. She jumped out of the bed, fearing for Laurence, but he was in front of the television, on his stomach with his legs crossed in the air.

"You must be starving," she said to him.

"Daddy got me McDonald's," Laurence said. Then she saw the cheeseburger in three separate discs on the rug.

"Did you eat any of this?"

Laurence told her he ate the French fries. She pushed through the door into the adjoining room. Tracy was in one of the beds, a phone book splashed over his knees.

"I'm looking for Sandra's address," he told her.

"Sandra's address? Sandra's address is a cemetery somewhere."

"I know, I'm trying to find out," Tracy snapped at her.

She looked at him. He had smudges under his eyes. She asked him if those were some black eyes, and he told her, no, he was just tired. She sat next to him on the bed and smoothed her thumb beneath his bruised eye, across the tight cheekbone, swollen from sleeplessness or injury. His two-day-old whiskers were golden and spiky. He didn't respond to her touch. She let her hand drop. "This is really fucking crazy," she said.

He slapped the phone book shut.

"All of this, not just Sandra's address. I mean this whole business," Margaret said.

"We can forget Sandra, it's Saturday. The courthouse at Downers' Grove is closed, we can't get hold of any records. You don't know the name of the church?"

"I don't even know what denomination it was."

"You're lying," he said.

"What's the point? What's the point in lying or telling the truth." She liked saying it.

"We could visit Resurrection Cemetery; that's the largest in the U.S. Then, there's Mount Carmel, where Al Capone is buried. What do you think?" Tracy said.

"You're getting a big kick out of this, aren't you?"

Cam came out of the shower, dressed and shaved. She looked him square in the eye. They tried to speak at once. They didn't go any further. The truce, the apology was sealed.

Tracy said, "Versailles, we're not."

Margaret told Tracy he should get dressed and shaved, they didn't have all day.

"He's got some time. I'm going over to see Lewis first," Cam said, "I forgot something."

"You forgot something?" Margaret said. "What did you forget? That old cashmere jacket?"

"Maybe that," Cam said.

"I don't like it," she told him. "Now I see, you're duding yourself up for something. What's in your imagination now?"

He was brushing his hair in front of the mirror, smoothing a short tuft of sideburn against his temple and tugging it in place. "We'll be on the road later," he said.

Margaret told Cam that, if they waited too long, the police might come and get Laurence.

"If they really wanted to come get Laurence, they would have nabbed him in a second. We're riding around in the only Duster with Delaware plates, it's got hot tires, we park it right on the street. They aren't playing with us. Darcy's full of shit."

"You changed your tune to suit the band," she told him.

He looked over at her, waiting to see if she was going to elaborate on the figure of speech she was trying. He told her, "I'm just going over there, that's all." He pulled the heel of his shoe over the back of his foot and ground his shoe on. He told her to be ready in about an hour or so. Tracy should get the car tanked up, they'd be on schedule.

With Cam gone, Tracy wanted to drive Margaret and Laurence over to the lake. They cruised in the Duster, sightseeing, but they were heading in the wrong direction. Margaret asked Tracy about this, and he shrugged his shoulders. She saw he might be taking her toward Downers' Grove. "I'm not searching through any cemeteries," she said. "I don't give a shit who's buried where." She edged over in her seat and slammed her left foot on the brake. The car jerked twice as it stopped; Laurence crashed against the dash and started crying.

Tracy was angry and hit Margaret hard on the crest of her thigh. The ligament burned with immediate pain, and she bent in half. "Don't ever do that," Tracy was yelling. Laurence was hysterical and Tracy pulled to the curb. Laurence's face was cloaked by a sheer red curtain. Margaret wiped the blood with the heel of her hand; it was just a little cut above his eye, but the blood continued to spill each time she took the pressure off it.

"I'm sorry, honey," she told the boy. "Why did you unbuckle your seat belt?"

Tracy said, "You're asking him! Ask yourself why you did such a crazy thing."

They found an Osco drugstore and the pharmacist gave Tracy an iodine wipe to wash the cut. The woman looked at the injury and told them it might need a stitch, but maybe a butterfly bandage was enough.

"Hey, a butterfly bandage—" Margaret told Laurence, trying to distract him. The pharmacist pinched the boy's forehead together and applied the adhesive strip.

They had checked out of their motel rooms, and they had to wait in the Duster until Cam came back. An hour passed. They went to the Howard Johnson's down the street and bought scoops of ice cream in stainless steel parfait cups. Laurence tapped his spoon against the metal dish until Tracy lost his temper. They went back to the sidewalk where they had parked the Duster. Nobody wanted to get in the car. "Why aren't there any park benches in cities anymore?" Tracy said.

"I don't see any park. There's no park to begin with," Margaret told him.

"You're a bitch, you know that?" Tracy said.

After a while, Tracy decided that they should go over to the Gregory Hotel; what if Cam was drinking more of that brandy?

Margaret studied the ornate dial on the elevator, watching the needle arc to the right as the compartment rose heavily, jolting at each floor. The arrow wobbled frantically like the gauge on an old-fashioned scale. She thought of the compartment's weight, she pictured the rotted cable as it jerked them higher.

"This is not groovy," Tracy said, when Cam met them at the door of Lewis's apartment. Cam was holding a gun. Margaret looked past Cam and saw Lewis sitting, knees together, in a straight chair in the center of the crowded parlor, his hands in his lap. "You're reaching a new plateau," Tracy told him.

"Is that a gun?" Margaret stood at the threshold between the front hall and the parlor. Cam was fingering the pistol; its small barrel was the size of a pill box. She pushed Laurence behind her, reaching back to press the boy's face against her buttocks so he wouldn't see his father holding a pistol. "It that a real weapon?"

"Looks like some kind of snubby with a sissy rod. Silencer," Tracy said. "This is a different chapter to the story. Well, why not?"

"I'm deciding what to do about this old scum bag," Cam said. He seemed pleased to have Tracy there. He was more than willing to describe his motivation, his tactics, make his projections. "I can turn him in to the police for fraud, or I could cash his checks right here. Bing." Cam touched the nose of the gun to Lewis's ear. "Bing," Cam said again.

"The word is 'bang,' " Tracy said.

"Who asked you?" Cam said.

Lewis said, "It's probably just a cap gun."

"You wish," Cam said, and he stamped his foot beside the old man's chair.

Lewis jumped at the noise, the vibration, but he was smiling. It was an unusual smile, an inaudible but telling phenomenon, almost like Buster Keaton's, the tolerant, world-weary grin of silent-film stars.

Cam smoked a cigarette, but he didn't light another one or offer his own to his father. He had not yet reached that stage of intimacy that sometimes occurs between people at opposite levels of power. Cam's shirt was riding up, and she glimpsed the formal row of knobs on his spine. "I don't remember anything about a gun," she told him.

"Don't be crisp, Margaret," Cam said, imitating Richard.

"I have a question," she said. "Is that thing real?"

Tracy touched Cam's elbow, but Cam whipped away from him. Tracy followed a step behind and they prowled in a half circle. Tracy said, "Look, let's just get out of here nice and easy."

"Don't give me that *Easy Does It* stuff," Cam said, "I'm not a member of that club."

Someone holding a gun was almost as bad as someone shooting it. Why didn't Cam go home and point a gun at their mother? Margaret imagined Elizabeth sitting on the sun porch in Wilmington, reading a new *McCall's*. A perfect lens explodes in the windowpane above the high auburn crest of her permanent.

Tracy inched closer to Cam. He looked at the ceiling. Then Tracy grabbed Cam by the wrist and took the gun. Tracy lifted the gun up to his eye and handed it back to Cam.

"What are you doing? Don't let him have it back!" Margaret said.

"It's a starter's pistol," Tracy said.

"A starter's pistol? Like for a hundred-yard dash? A race? You're just *saying* it's a starter pistol to shut me up," Margaret said.

"You're losing sight of the issue," Tracy told her. "It's a noise tool, pretty nice. Let's leave it at that."

"Is that thing loaded or what?"

"Why don't you practice a wait-and-see attitude? You always want to have things *now, now, now.* Sometimes the truth has to trickle out," Tracy told her.

Cam was enjoying their quarrel. "Go ahead, all you want. The fact of the matter is, it has nothing to do with you," he told them.

Lewis sat forward in his chair and crossed his legs, tucking his toe behind his ankle. He was dressed in a worn silk jacket, the cloth polished at the cuffs and elbows, the lapels yellowed, rippled from too many trips to the cleaners. His pumps looked Italian, but one sole was peeling away from the upper leather. He looked a great deal older than the night before. He was bony; his face looked translucent in the daylight, milk-blue and shimmery like an opal. He looked like a romance-novel invalid—what was the use of scaring him?

"Elizabeth will delight in this story," Margaret said. "She'll say, 'Like father like son.' "

"It's undeniable," the old man said.

"What's that?" Cam said.

"My blood courses through your veins," Lewis said.

"It stinks," Cam told him.

Margaret steered Laurence to the small kitchen. There was a box of safety matches on the small gas stove; one match was removed from the box and placed on top. She opened the icebox and pulled a carton of juice onto the counter. She poured a glass for Laurence, but he shook his head. There were six or seven refrigerator magnets, small black discs, and Laurence asked for these. Margaret plucked the magnets off the enamel door. She had to remove a few slips of paper; one piece said *Eggs*. It was funny to think of a bachelor writing this word *eggs* and attaching it with a magnet to the appliance. She thought about the word itself. Eggs. It lost all its domestic meaning. She heard Cam talking in the next room. He was telling Lewis that there should be consequences when a father abandoned his children.

"What consequences?" Tracy was trying to block a linear progression.

"Shut up," Cam said.

"If you threaten someone, you should be more concrete," Tracy scolded.

"A consequence isn't a threat, it's an end result. I'm saying, an action causes a reaction. A drought, several years of drought, makes a desert. My life is a desert," Cam said.

Margaret leaned around the kitchen door. Tracy sat down heavily in an overstuffed chair; his mouth dropped open a quarter inch. Cam didn't speak in metaphors very often. They wanted to see.

His explication was flat, squarely detailed, unembellished; his voice was even, dipping low when he said something self-deprecating. He reminded Margaret of someone coming back from a lethal war skirmish, the shell-shocked noncom standing before a conference table of hardened officers. The only survivor, someone asked to give an itinerary of the confrontation, counting losses and injuries on both sides.

"Did you think I would just dry up and blow away?" Cam asked Lewis.

"Maybe you let it slip your mind? Maybe you forgot?

Well, I started wondering about you—even when I was small. One question, the *same* question.

"The glass is half empty or it's half full, you know that saying? You know the one? Okay—

"Let me tell you. Full means all the way to the top. Full means nothing's missing. There's no such thing as *half* full. You don't have to be a genius to see that.

"I'm not saying I'm a genius, but I've been doing some thinking. I've been crystallizing my thoughts—"

Margaret's mouth was dry. The room was hot. She couldn't listen to Cam. His story was not entirely free of blame, but more often it followed the shape of a confession.

Cam told his father, "You see, because I'm unclaimed, I don't trust anyone. The backlash being, no one gives a shit about me.

"My wife wants me arrested.

"My own sister can't see any difference between me and the next guy. Or maybe she'll just fuck anything that can keep still long enough—"

"Don't blame me for that!" Margaret said. "We made a mistake; we tripped up."

"*You* tripped, at *my* feet. Aren't you forgetting?"

She was rising and sinking on her heels; tears burned the outside corner of her eyes.

"I don't blame you, Margaret," Cam said. "It's Mr. Marathon over there"—he shoved the gun toward Tracy—"he's making a whore out of you."

Tracy said, "That word's archaic. Let's see, we have the word 'nympho.' That's a little stale. Shit, what *is* the word we're looking for?"

"Whatever you want," Cam said.

Tracy said, "Did you ever think Margaret could evoke her own sexual chaos? Maybe it's her blueprint. Sometimes it's *her*, she's cracking a kind of whip. It has nothing to do with us."

Cam stopped him. "Shut up. You have a mouth, you know that? Save it. I don't want to duel with you, Twinkletoes."

Margaret heard this word, "Twinkletoes," and she looked at Tracy. He wasn't happy with Cam's remark, but she allowed herself a full chord of laughter. She didn't think twice about it.

Lewis stood up from his seat, "A gala event, sorry I must go now." Cam gripped his shoulder and pressed it down, leaned his weight against his father, but the old man struggled to stay on his feet.

"I'm not through," Cam said.

Lewis said, "Yes, but I'm finished. I've had enough. We meet once in a lifetime, and this is what you come up with."

Cam looked at Lewis and shook his head. "No, you don't. The shoe's on the *other* foot, not the foot you're talking about. I'm the one who gives the thumbs-up or the thumbs-down."

What shoe was on which foot, thumbs up or thumbs down? Margaret tried to follow. Margaret heard Laurence scraping the dark magnets across the surface of the refrigerator. She listened to some Spanish coming from the kitchen window where a fire escape ascended. There must be people sitting out, she thought. Infants were crying across the alley; their wails intensified before breaking off. Laurence had slipped out of the kitchen to show the magnets to his father. He was standing in front of his father, his palm flat. Cam saw his son. "What happened to his head?"

"Nothing," Margaret said. Why should she explain it to a madman? She had waited as long as she could, until the scene was too warped and razory, as if the events she watched were painted on sheet metal and circulated like a mechanical mural. Again, Cam poked the air with his gun or scratched his shave with its muzzle. Margaret watched Lewis. She saw a look of surrender surface upon his refined features. Then, a moment of warmth drifted across his lips, registered in his eyes, made his horror uneven. It was this complexity, this turn of mind, which made her frightened. If the old man was just going to sit there smiling at this craziness, she was helpless to do anything.

She pulled Laurence by his shirt collar. She was leaving, but the dead bolt was sticking. She forced it, cranking its thick tongue, and the door fell open. She took the child's wrist and tugged him down the landings. It rained when they walked to the bus station. A dusty vapor that never touched the street, but she could see it collecting in her nephew's hair as she shoved him across the intersections. Then it rained hard.

II

She heard a siren increasing in the next lane, one blaring note. It wasn't a siren after all; it was the flat, monaural pitch of a car horn. She looked out the bus window and saw a vehicle ripping past. She thought she saw the Duster—its compact blue form, the sweptback roof. She recognized her flip-flops where she had left them on the rear deck. The car moved off ahead, then it drifted back and rode alongside the bus. She saw Tracy leaning out the window, signaling to her. No, he was rotating his wrist in circles to catch the attention of the bus driver.

Laurence saw the Duster and squealed, three arcing bursts. He ran back to the end of the bus and wriggled between two riders to look out the back. The people allowed him to stay there so he could wave at his father. She thought of Cam driving behind the bus, and a smile needled her lips. She thought of the phrase, "I'm your back door." It was truck-driving lingo Cam had explained to her. Then the Duster plowed past her window once more, braking to ride level with her. The bus slowed or accelerated, trying to shake loose the other vehicle, but whatever the bus driver decided, Cam mimicked in the Duster. Some passengers were laughing and shouting. The bus resumed its normal speed, braked suddenly, then pulled out into the fast lane. She saw the Duster falling behind on the right as they went past.

The bus accelerated, exceeding the normal speed. Margaret smelled the strong diesel fumes increasing.

The Duster was in tandem again. Cam leaned on the horn, swerved in tight zags shoulder to shoulder with the bus. Margaret stood up to look at the man holding the wheel. He kept his head perfectly straight, ignoring the ruckus outside his window. Cam weaved in front of the bus and slowed the Duster abruptly. The bus pulled around him, Margaret felt the gears shifting; the grit on the rubber tread over the aisle bounced with the strain of the transmission. Cam repeated the maneuver. People on the bus were getting more uncomfortable; some men called out suggestions. Finally, Margaret walked up to the driver. She had to grab the backs of the seats to keep her balance and everyone looked at her with suspicion.

"Can you stop this and let me off?" she said to the driver.

"Do you know the driver of that car?" the man asked her.

"Will you pull this thing over? There's going to be an accident."

"Is that a hunch or are you making threats?"

"I'm telling you, I know that man out there. I'm his sister. He's kind of upset. I guess you noticed? Just let me and the boy off."

"You're his sister, you say?"

"I thought that's what I said," she told him.

He studied her. "It's against regulations to stop at an unauthorized spot unless there's a breakdown or something unavoidable such as that," the bus driver said.

"Look, stop jerking me around. Are you going to stop this bus?" she said.

"Is this a police matter? Pittsburgh is next, are you saying you need to get off before Pittsburgh?"

"Look out!" Margaret told him. The driver wasn't watching the road. The Duster was directly out in front, hardly crawling. The driver jerked the huge steering wheel, throwing his weight into it as he paddled it counterclockwise. The bus scraped the left rear fender of the Duster; Margaret heard the metal squawk and snap free. Then, as the driver jerked the wheel to regain control, she was thrown down the little stairwell. Her weight triggered the hydraulic lever and the door brushed open. She might have fallen to the blacktop, she saw it slipping past, its strokes of white paint threading together. She grabbed the railing and climbed the steps slowly. "Pull over, you fucking asshole! I almost fell out!"

The driver steered off the highway and glided to a stop. She took Laurence by his wrist and they jumped to the asphalt shoulder. The driver came after them to look at the front of the bus. A flow of sky-blue paint marred the thick chrome body, but it wasn't serious. Cam was a half mile up ahead when he noticed the bus on the side of the highway. He had to drive the Duster in reverse down the shoulder to get to where she was standing. She pinched Laurence's shoulders, keeping him centered before her as they watched the rear of the car approaching. Then she saw something crazy— that pale, exquisite face. It was Lewis staring out the back window.

The three men got out of the Duster. The bus driver walked over and told them he didn't want any trouble. He had to make sure it was Margaret's choice to leave the bus; it wasn't an authorized spot. Margaret told the driver she was exercising her free will. The bus driver started to say something to Cam, but he decided against any involvement and he started back to his bus.

"Wait, sir!" Lewis called after the driver. "I'm coming with you. I'm taking the girl's place."

"Your dad's making his move," Tracy said.

Cam grabbed Lewis by his hand. Lewis jerked his hand away, shaking his fingers, kissing the backs of his knuckles, as if Cam's touch had scalded. He pleaded with Cam. He held his face in his hands, clutched his cheeks. It was a theatrical gesture, it reminded Margaret of the actor, Robert Merrill, in *Man of La Mancha*. "I won't go any farther," Lewis said.

"You're this far already."

"I have no interest in seeing her!"

"That was the bargain," Cam told him.

"I don't make bargains with hoodlums," Lewis said, and he trotted after the bus driver. Tracy followed him to the bus, but Cam called after Tracy, "Let him go, he's a worthless shit."

Margaret looked over at the bus; Lewis had one foot on the first step. He was showing something to the bus driver, an ID or some proof of his finances. The wind was lifting the lapels of his silk jacket and he kept smoothing them. He looked ridiculous, harmless.

"You tried to kidnap your old man?" Margaret had to raise her voice above the lanes of traffic.

"What about you? You took Laurence without my permission."

"I'm his aunt. I've been his goddamn nanny through all of this." She saw how the world shifted. She smiled, it wasn't the world exactly, it was them. People's claims to other people. Her loyalty was put to the test, it was altered or reworked, she didn't know. Her own daughter was waiting for her, knocking around without benefit of her own mother. Margaret had Laurence. She tried to align herself with these innocents rather than take her place beside Tracy and Cam.

Cam stared at her face, but she looked down at the blue gravel on the side of the highway. She kicked a frayed strip of rubber to the left and rolled it back with her toe. There were several of these black ribbons, sections of a truck's exploded re-tread. She avoided looking at Cam and she eyed the highway debris—little twists of chrome, colored glass, a greyed bandana.

Cam said that the Duster was pretty conspicuous out there on the side of the interstate. They drove all this way, front and back, without a tangle with police, they should get moving. They looked over at the bus. The driver was behind the wheel looking down at his side mirror, the turn signal pulsing. The bus was pulling away.

"My God," Margaret said. "Tracy—"

"He can't be serious," Cam told her.

"That fuck!" Margaret said. Then she saw Tracy. He ran forward from the rear seats. He jumped from the bus steps, falling to his hands, his palms digging two skids through the gravel.

The bus turned into the traffic, rolled passed them. Lewis looked through the window, he was laughing. She saw his head thrown back, his hands clasped beneath his chin. It was a display of utter pleasure, relief. A devil exhausted, freed.

III

Margaret watched Tracy pick the pebbles off his raw hands. Some black grit was embedded and would have to work its way out. They sat in the car and Cam edged back into the traffic. Cam wiped his hand down his face, brushing his lips with the back of his fist like someone coming through cobwebs, a constellation of spidery tethers. Margaret watched him scratch his hair, smooth the back of his neck until he squared his shoulders; he was clear of it.

Tracy discussed Lewis's plan to turn around in Pittsburgh and catch the next bus back to Chicago. Tracy was saying they should try the bus station and corner the old man again. Lewis might change his mind. Cam said Lewis could tour the world, drop off the end, he didn't care. Cam said, "If you want more action, join another circus. There's Ringling Brothers."

Margaret pulled open the glove box and found the gun Cam had been waving around at the apartment. She laughed. "Did you really force him to come in the Duster with this starter's pistol?"

"Careful," Cam said, "give it to me."

"What?" Margaret said.

"I said, right here." He held out his hand.

"Isn't this an imitation? Tracy said it was for track and field. This is real?"

"It's got a full chamber. Loaded," Cam said.

"Real confetti. It's heavy, isn't it?" Tracy was grinning.

"My goodness," she said. She didn't believe them. She turned the gun over in her hands and pulled it up to her face. She saw a tiny insignia, a crown, and the word *Webley*. "Webley. What's this mean, Webley? A gun?" she asked.

"Jesus," Tracy said, "will you get her to put that down."

"I'm telling you Margaret—" Cam was saying, but it was too late. Margaret hurled the gun out the car window and watched it sail over the guardrail and sink into the brush. It looked like a rise of corn behind that.

Cam braked and pulled hard onto the shoulder. He slammed into reverse, ripping over the gravel. "You can't leave a gun in that field, you stupid shit."

"Is it registered?" Tracy asked Cam.

"That's not the point," Cam said. "I don't want to leave it out here."

They got out of the car beside the cornfield, but the gun could have landed anywhere. Laurence got out of the car and was pushing his tiny sports car along the silver guardrail.

"Well. Don't stand there. Start looking," Margaret said. She had no desire to hunt for the gun, but she didn't want to wait there in the middle of nowhere.

They crossed the fence and started into the matted brush by the highway. Laurence came along, tugging Margaret's skirt. Gluey squares, undefinable seeds collected on their clothes; a golden burr like a tiny buzz saw cut into her skin. Cam turned into the corn rows and disappeared. Margaret walked in the other direction until she saw something in the brush, a platinum crescent, the gun in its cradle of nettles. She decided not to announce her discovery. Why not leave the gun where it was? But Tracy was watching her. She reached down for the pistol. "Finders, keepers," she said. Tracy gripped her wrist until she felt her blood knocking in her fingertips, and she released the pistol. He shifted the gun from one hand to the other, then he pointed the gun at Margaret.

She stumbled backward into the dense briar, which snagged her legs. Tracy put the nose of the gun to her forehead. Lifted it off once, and centered it again. "Listen to me, I want you to suck me."

"What?"

"You heard me, Margaret."

"You're kidding."

Tracy said, "Don't argue. Just do it." He kept the gun steady. Without its pressure, its icy nozzle against her forehead, she might have become weightless, she might have ascended past fear and lofted into a stupor. She didn't faint after all. She entered several levels of awareness, but in each different phase she still could not act. He was pushing his jeans down with his free hand. "I've always wanted to do this."

Margaret was breathing in short, convulsive sips, but

her lungs could not expel any air. Her tears lowered a glycerin curtain, and she couldn't see Tracy's face.

"I'm not going to kill you, Margaret—just pretend. Make believe," Tracy whispered to her. His voice caught, deepened, as his erotic pulse congested his lungs. He swayed, lifting his weight off one leg, then the other. He couldn't keep from shuddering, and she knew it was a serious matter. He leaned his elbow hard against the top of her shoulder until she sank down to her knees. He turned the muzzle back and forth in gentle swipes across her face. Then he tucked it behind her ear.

"Yes. That's right. You know, Margaret. You know." She did what he wanted. She smelled the strange odor of the gun, its bitter graphite and cold shell. She struggled to stand up. Tracy told her, "Don't fool around, Margaret. It's got your U.S. Daily Requirement of Iron. Ready to twirl." He laughed, pleased with his talk, but she started again and he tugged her hair in one hand, nudged the gun with the other.

Cam had already started into the cornfield, and who knows what happened to Laurence. The cornstalks were dense, like bamboo thicket, rising in a wall eight feet high. A child could become lost in these acres. She wanted to find him, but Tracy took his time. She rolled her tongue, fluttered it, she let him sink deep into her throat to hurry him along. He was close; she tasted the first surge, salty and ferrous. She heard his shaky stuttering, and when he shivered against her, his knees dipping, she pushed him off-balance, stood up and ran.

She plunged into the cornstalks and moved down a row. The papery tassels closed over her head until she couldn't see in the dark. The dried stalks rustled behind her, rattled in metallic clusters as she burst in one direction, then another. Then it was Cam. He had Laurence in his arms. Together, they made a wide circle around Tracy, who was whistling for Margaret in long, piercing notes. Cam placed Margaret in the car and she held on to the boy. "He has the gun," Margaret told him.

"He could have killed you. He was shooting a wad and could've brushed the trigger."

"You saw us?"

"You're lucky. That gun could have fired."

"Shit. You saw what happened?" If Cam had watched them, it was proof. She didn't want to have any proof.

Cam went to get his gun from Tracy. The gun didn't matter anymore. Cam didn't want the gun now, it was repelling. Cam looked interested in something final. An ending. He couldn't drive away without cutting it off with Tracy. Men have ways of making things official, Margaret was thinking. She couldn't see from where she was sitting and she got out of the car and climbed onto the roof of the Duster. Tracy was standing where Margaret had left him, his jeans pulled up but still unbuttoned. Cam moved up to Tracy until they were face-to-face. She couldn't hear what they said.

Tracy handed the gun to Cam. Cam aimed the pistol and the gun went off. A tight snap reverberating high in the air. Then its echo, immediate, but softer, waffling over the field. They all wanted to hear it. Again, Cam shot into the dirt. The sedge exploded in tight clods, mottled scruffs fanned in a loose broadcast, a red chevron. Field birds lifted and funneled together. Cam walked back to the car.

Tracy came after him, but he wouldn't let Tracy near her.

"You're hitching, pal."

"Give me a chance," Tracy was talking beside Margaret's window. "Tell Cam it's all part of the picture. Tell him the whole story. Our story, Margaret. We're doomed. Maybe all three of us, and tiny Laurence. The whole tribe. You can't single one person out, Margaret—" He was shouting as Cam drove the car away. Margaret fought the glare in the side mirror and watched a mile, two miles, until Tracy condensed into a burning speck. Her breath came and went in severe notches. Minutes later she thought she saw Tracy on the shoulder, thumbing, but it was nothing. Tracy had disappeared. The hot western light sliced into the Duster. She moved over on the seat, into the shade with Cam. The sun turned its serrated wheel.

IV

It was late afternoon when they came into Wilmington. Margaret saw the stacks at the chemical plants, still pumping, a lattice of artificial cloud ascending over the Delaware. When they came down the street and turned into the driveway, they saw an ambulance parked behind the garage, its interior lighted, showing the movement of people.

"What's this?" Cam said, "somebody's in trouble—"

"Is it Celeste?" Margaret said, but Celeste was standing on the blacktop, bouncing a superball. Margaret pushed out of the Duster. Celeste ran to Margaret and tucked her face against Margaret's waist. The girl climbed onto the insteps of Margaret's feet and they waltzed a few steps right and left, tugging themselves off balance. The ambulance doors opened out, and Margaret saw Elizabeth sitting on the edge of a gurney, her back to them. Cam asked the paramedic what was happening. The paramedic said, "Oh, she's getting her blood pressure done."

"Her blood pressure?" Margaret said. "Is she all right?"

"She gets it taken every week. If we're in the neighborhood, we stop by to do her," the man said.

"Community service," the other paramedic said. "We keep a list of the heart patients. She can come right down to the fire department, say, if she's out shopping at the Merchandise Mart. We can do her out at the station anytime." He tore loose the Velcro patch and unwrapped Elizabeth's arm. He told Elizabeth it was good, 120 over 80, she'd outlive everyone.

Cam was resting against the hood of the Duster. Then he pushed himself up and rubbed the sting away from his elbows; the hood was shimmering. The ambulance had frightened Cam. He studied his mother, who had not yet turned around to greet them. She wasn't in any kind of hurry. Nothing could pull her away from her health check. Then the fellow was taking her pulse. He

extended her arm and propped her elbow. When the
man was finished, he patted Elizabeth's knee, looked at
her, and patted her knee again. The paramedic was
speaking to Elizabeth in a low voice no one could follow.
Again, the man patted the back of her hand. When
Elizabeth turned to face her son, she was shivering. Her
tears glazed her face powder in narrow lines, like glass
shatters. She pressed her knuckles against her mouth,
keeping back a spill of words. She stepped down from
the ambulance and caught Cam by his shirt. She jerked
his shirt tail loose from his jeans and tried to reel him
closer. "Do you feel better now? Are you happy?" she
said.

Cam looked over his mother's shoulder at a stand of
trees, Norway maples, burning red in the sunlight. He
followed the power lines sagging through the upper
limbs. He blinked at his mother's face, then returned
to the trees in the distance. Elizabeth inhaled, held her
chest expanded, her sobs extinguished. She told him
she was sorry, she was sorry he went out to Chicago.
"For nothing." She was kneading his shirt in her hands;
she wedged herself into the narrow straddle of his
legs. She wanted to hear the conclusion, Cam's verdict,
but she couldn't bring herself to beg for it.

Cam freed himself, regained his posture, took his
mother's elbows and steered her backward a few steps.
He shoved her gently, the way someone releases a model
sailboat on the water. He turned and walked into the
house.

Celeste found the little velvet boxes strewn around
the Duster. These she collected, placing one inside the
other, the lids snapping shut. Margaret told her, yes,

she could keep the mysterious gradation of boxes, but she hoped the girl would forget to take them back to Providence.

Richard was working in the yard and Margaret walked over to him. "I have to get the next train," she told him. He smeared potting mix on his trousers, patting his left pocket, then his right, until he heard his car keys jangle. He had been digging an even shelf along the terrace. Small mounds of grass clippings steamed along the flagstone sidewalk; a basket of weeds stirred, as if still searching. The black earth was neatly etched with fresh seed. He said he was planting autumn flowers, specimens that can hold on late, far into November.

"I wish I could dig up that yucca and take it back to Providence."

"Impossible," he said. "It's naturalized; it's got some big roots. It would have to be sectioned."

"Oh, is that right?" she told him. She didn't really want to know the procedure for something that she had mentioned for its larger meaning. "Besides, I live in an apartment, you know."

When Margaret went into the house, Cam took her aside. He told her, if she wanted to, they could go once again to Ocean City. He would try to reach that fellow and make an official appointment to test the Donzi. His face looked electric, newly chiseled with fresh concerns. His eyes were black, dilated, the pale gold of the iris dissolved except for a tiny flashing band. He pleaded with her. "We need a small vacation," he told her, "we deserve it. A little cruise is the thing," he was telling her.

"I have to go home," she said.

He looked puzzled. He looked as if he didn't believe she existed outside of their forty-eight-hour triangle. "I guess it doesn't matter. It had nothing to do with you in the first place," he said.

She didn't want to be dismissed like this. Didn't he see that she felt awful abandoning her post? Wasn't she the navigator, folding the map into a manageable square? Didn't she light Cam's cigarettes, taking the first drag, the tiny pink lines of her lipstick smearing the filter? Didn't she punch the radio, finding all the chartbusters? Now it was over? She still felt the vibration of the Duster and a high ringing in her ears like the imperceptible seismic shuddering that makes an entire anthill pick up and go elsewhere to start over. Whatever it was, she insisted to Cam that her participation in his search must have had an effect on the outcome.

She embraced Cam. The hug's brief force seemed simultaneously felt and delivered. She rubbed her eyes, rotated the hooded spheres beneath her fingertips. She was suddenly weighted with the knowledge that all of experience must be memorized. She would always have to recall the truth and also what the truth summoned, what the truth seeded in her imagination. There's just no end to it. All of childhood, *imperishable*, and now this. The truth, the existing truth as it must be recognized, and years from now, rebirthed, reinvented.

She sat against the edge of the drop-leaf table made of glossy wormwood. She fingered the gullies, the tiny mars and spirals that gave the wood its value, its beauty. She wanted to ask Elizabeth if it really was *worms*, if worms designed these golden planes.

There was the doorbell. Margaret went to the front

hall and tugged the heavy door. It was a woman in a breathtaking Kelly-green suit. Her hair was dark auburn and fell in several loose crests. It was beautiful, like Elizabeth's hair had once been, and Elizabeth took notice of it. The woman was the social worker Cam had mentioned. She wanted to speak with Cam, and Margaret went to get him. Cam walked the woman out to the front lawn and they stood on the flagstone path. She was explaining something to Cam, and he listened, his head cocked in hopeful submission. The woman was trying to help him keep his son, and Margaret thought the woman looked strong, efficient, like she might be able to do it. Then Margaret wondered if maybe this person was using Cam's difficult case to further her career. Margaret wondered about this woman. Her suit the color of the healthy turf.

When the social worker departed, Cam stood alone on the flagstone sidewalk. He waited for her car to drive away and he lifted his arm, keeping it high; then he let it drop back. Next, it was Darcy pulling up in Cam's Bronco. She edged onto the lawn's velvet shoulder, but Richard was around in back and couldn't tell her to roll it back onto the road. She walked into the house, calling the name of her boy. Laurence ran into the room, leaped up, falling against her. Margaret noticed that Darcy did not bend her knees, she did not meet her boy's wild greeting. She stooped just slightly, her kisses hardly fell upon the boy's hair. Darcy was dressed up; her skirt was pale pink pleats that belled at the knee like an inverted flower. She had her hair in a tight spiral with a tortoiseshell clasp. Her lips were edged with cinnamon liner, her eyes accented in ascending hues of smoky coral. Cam went forward and Darcy lifted herself up on the ball of one foot to reach his lips. The kiss was a public gesture, neither stiff nor friendly. Darcy was making a claim without promising any further contract.

Margaret was filthy, the hair at her temple burned into a scruff; the rest was knotted from riding with the Duster's windows wide open. The two women nodded at one another in an agreement to remain uncompromised by conversation. They didn't share small talk. After a moment, Darcy asked, "Are you wearing my shoes?" She knew perfectly well they belonged to her. Margaret tugged the pumps away from her feet, but she didn't hand them to Darcy, she arranged them on the piano, and Darcy collected them.

"The Duster has new tires," Cam said.

"New tires? Why?"

"They're radials," Cam told her.

"That's bizarre." Darcy was frowning. "Why the new tires?"

"A second thing, it's going to need some body work. I'll take care of it, don't worry. We backed into something," Cam said.

"I didn't think you could go anywhere and not smash something. Well, as long as you pay for it." Darcy was taking Laurence out the door, she was taking him home. She didn't even notice the cut on his forehead. Then they saw Darcy was taking the Duster. She left Cam's Ford sinking into the sod and she walked behind the house to get the other car.

"Have you got anything left in the Duster?" Cam asked Margaret.

"No, I have everything."

Cam said, "You have those little boxes?"

"Celeste has those." They might have been thinking of Tracy's cousin Franklin, or the storefront with ELITE CHICKS. It might have been something different for the two of them, but together they enriched their private memory in one synchronic, scary sensation.

The wall phone jangled in the kitchen and Margaret went in and lifted the receiver. She recognized Tracy's tenor. He was singing. He was singing some Bob Dylan lyrics:

"Down along the cove, I saw my true love coming my way . . ."

"You need help," she told him. She turned the receiver upside down as she spoke into the mouthpiece. She tried to tell him one or two of her thoughts, but the Dylan song was still coming from the inverted speaker.

"Do what you have to do," she told him. "Go right ahead. Sing. We're not together. We can't *live* together."

Elizabeth was standing in the kitchen doorway. "Who is that? Is that Lewis?" she said. Her color drifted, whitened. She walked out of the kitchen, taking careful steps as if she were crossing a glass bridge. Margaret hung up the telephone and went into the living room. Cam was leaning forward on the piano bench, ripping loose bits of cat hair from the carpet.

"The beat goes on," Cam said.

"I think he cracked up. Tracy has lost it. He might

need some money to get back to Providence. He might be stuck out there without any cash," she said. "I didn't inquire."

"Sometimes it's better not to find out," Cam said. "Isn't that right?"

Margaret said Cam was right.

Elizabeth came into the room. She was wearing some lounge pajamas, something crazy. Her shoulders were bare and gleaming with dots of baby oil she hadn't worked in. The gown was translucent and gauzy, it wrapped around her torso and flared at her ankles. The fabric was draped in taut folds, flecked with silver threads. She looked like the angel of a burn victim. "What are you wearing? What the hell is that?" Margaret said.

Cam touched his fingertips to his temples, he rubbed the bridge of his nose; he couldn't look at his mother without massaging his face.

"Well, is he going to show up here?" Elizabeth said.

"Who?"

"Cam's attention span is that of a flea," she told Margaret. "I'm talking about Lewis, of course. Is Lewis going to grace us with his presence?"

"Your Better Half took the bus back to Chicago," Cam told her.

"Lewis took the bus?" Elizabeth said. She looked pleased that Lewis wasn't going to show up. "Lewis got on a bus? Really? He used to jet around, he did everything top shelf."

"Circumstances change."

"He's down and out?"

Cam declined to answer.

"He doesn't have to rehash this with me? Wasn't that the whole point? He gets off scot-free—" Elizabeth moved to the picture window and stared at Richard smoothing the flecked marl at the edge of the terrace.

"You tell *me*," Cam said, "what did he get away with? Oh, I wanted to thank you, thanks for removing that picture from the chandelier."

"That picture?" Elizabeth looked confused.

"That embryo," Cam said.

"Just an innocent victim," Elizabeth told Cam.

"Who's innocent?" he asked her.

"We are. Each one of us, innocent. To begin with."

Margaret was disappointed. She was following what Elizabeth said; it sounded as if she was on the verge of soothing them, she was their mother. Then Elizabeth turned back; she had made a qualification; she told them, "Innocent. *To begin with.*" What could they say for themselves now? She had been sure Elizabeth was trying to evoke a sense of hope, but it wasn't to be. It was like those days when they coasted downhill. They leaned forward on the vinyl car seat, they were refreshed by the new possibility. With help from the law of averages, it might turn out in their favor, they might glide all the way to the end. In that bright plunge, Margaret's bangs lifted off her forehead, but then the vehicle stalled, her hair washed back over her eyes.

Elizabeth was laughing. She told Cam he was acting foolish. He was making a production. How did she deserve such a moody child? How did he get like that?

"Just born with it," he told her.

"That's what I mean. Why, though? It rubs off on people. Why make me suffer?"

Cam said, "Don't ask me. The child is father to the man?"

"That's stupid—that's just an old saying." She prowled back and forth on the carpet; her peculiar attire was beginning to unravel. One veil drifted behind her, catching on a chair. She tugged it free and fingered the folds at her waist, then smoothed them flat with the heel of her hand. She said, "That's just it, I'm asking you a question. Who's torturing who? Can either of you tell me that?"

Cam stood up; his foot snagged one leg of the piano bench and it toppled over. Yellowed songbooks and brittle leaves of sheet music fanned across the carpet. Everyone's eyes searched for the bold print of the song titles, the familiar tunes, any of the old favorites. There was nothing. Margaret saw the parallel lines of the staffs, the dark, singular whole notes or ones in wild clusters.

Richard came into the room and told Cam that while he was away there had been a problem over at the apartments. The Edgemoor plant had released corrosive ash and the vapor had blistered the paint on the cars in the tenant parking lot. Du Pont was looking into it, but Cam had to take statements and get the vehicle ID numbers from the dash plates for a written report.

Margaret said her good-byes to her parents and she went with Cam to the apartments. From there, he would drive her and Celeste to the train. Cam tried to tell her what to do about Tracy. She asked him to whisper because of Celeste. Cam instructed her, "Put all of

Tracy's belongings in boxes and put the boxes out on the sidewalk. Go down to the police and fill out a written complaint. They'll put somebody on it. Don't open the door without the chain."

At the apartment complex, they looked at the damage to the cars, tiny veins and nickel-sized webs where the paint had crackled. The corrosive discharge from the chimney stacks had been checked, the vapor had cleared. There was nothing to worry about, but Cam thought he should test the water in the pool to see if the pH was altered. Cam took water samples and measured chemicals from his kit. The water was fine. Celeste wanted to swim and Margaret decided she would like it, too.

It was the three of them. The twilight made the water murky, and Cam switched on the underwater floodlights at either end of the pool. The submerged beams swelled in a golden crisscross as Celeste nosed back and forth on a Styro paddleboard. The water was silky; its surface tension seemed peculiar. Cam said that it was ironic, but there might have been softening agents in the industrial fallout. Margaret swam laps for a few minutes and halted at one end. She studied the skyline. Stars collected like froth, sudsing the horizon. The night was clean. Cam called to her from the opposite side. He was going to swim the whole length underwater and touch the floodlight. One breath. He sank below the gutterline and pushed off the tile. He followed the glassy funnel, glided toward Margaret. He drifted to the finish, into its phosphoric lens.

ABOUT THE AUTHOR

Maria Flook has published two collections of
poetry. She teaches writing and lives in Truro,
Massachusetts.